SLEEPLESS

SCARLETT KOL

ISBN: (ebook) 978-1-7752260-7-9
Print: 978-1-7752260-6-2
First Edition: 2021

Cover Art by Atlantis Book Design

Author Photo by Regina Wamba

Published by Vicious Pixie Press

To those who are good friends and to those who are lucky enough to have them.

"Fair is foul, and foul is fair."

- William Shakespeare,
Macbeth

ONE

O ne thousand five hundred and sixty-one, one thousand five hundred and sixty-two, one thousand five hundred and sixty-three ...

Urghhhh!

Pressing my pillow over my face, I muttered more unintelligible sounds. The images of the day cycled through my consciousness, as brilliant and lively as when I tried to go to bed three hours ago. Bright flashes of faces and colors twirled on an anxiety-fueled carousel. Each one another box on my never-ending list of things to worry about. Why couldn't my brain shut off for even five minutes and let me panic about them tomorrow? Long enough to maybe, possibly, close my eyes and get a moment's rest.

Please. Give me one night.

As I chucked my pillow to the floor, I stared up at the tiny peaks of the popcorn stucco ceiling. The only thing more frustrating than not being able to sleep was lying awake thinking about how terribly school would drag if I didn't get any rest. I rolled my head toward my nightstand and tapped my phone screen. Already a quarter after one. Looked like another zombie day for me tomorrow. The third one this week.

I closed my eyes and tried to recollect the relaxation techniques from that lame yoga class Lane dragged me to last summer. The instructor spent the entire session sitting on a chair, bellowing instructions while she scrolled on her cell phone. But I vaguely remembered her saying something about thinking about your breathing. Be one with your breath? Whatever it was, I'd try anything. I inhaled deep until my lungs burned and my chest swelled like an over-inflated balloon.

Exhale.

Air flowed out of my body, and a calm tingle prickled through my limbs. My fingers stretched out from my clenched fists and sank into the mattress. Maybe this wouldn't be so bad.

My covers rose as I breathed in again, and my brain waded in the stream of lightheaded dizziness that followed.

Exhale.

My heart slowed its banging against my ribs. Maybe that class wasn't a waste of time after all. Lane might need to take control of my life more often.

Inhale.

Maybe I could convince Dad to sign up for yoga? Get him to relax a bit too.

Exhale.

But that meant he'd have to stop drinking long enough to make it through the full hour.

Inhale.

He'd probably just laugh it off or go into one of his self-depre-cating rants that I didn't want to listen to. And it wasn't my respon-sibility to take care of him. Wasn't he supposed to be the adult? I needed to deal with my own problems. Not like he'd ever notice anyway.

Exhale. The scholarship panel. Inhale. The state volleyball finals. Exhale. Josh and all his frustrating plans. Inhale. Exhale. Inhale. Exhale.

Ahhhh!

I threw the covers off my body and dangled my feet over the edge of the bed, my head gripped tight in my hands. What was wrong with me? I couldn't even relax properly. Tears welled in the corners of my eyes, but I pushed them down. A familiar heaviness crept into my chest and tugged at the hollow deep inside. If I could only talk to Mom, she'd know exactly what to do. She always did. I shouldn't still miss her, but I couldn't stop.

A knotted ball built in my throat as I struggled to push the painful memories from my brain, the smell of her rose-scented shampoo still flooding my senses and refusing to let go. I swallowed and pressed my fingertips into my scalp until it all subsided. A roaring wave receding back into the ocean after crashing on the shores of my near-delirious mind.

I peeked between my fingers into the darkness. A slit of blue moonlight cut across the floor, silent and still. It seemed to stare up at me. Like it didn't understand why I was sitting there so sad. A strange companion, but at least I wasn't the only one awake. I could always rely on the moon.

Pushing myself off the bed, I sank my toes into the scratchy carpet and followed the line of light to the window. The cool night air fell off the glass as I pulled back the bulky plum-colored curtain. Goosebumps spread across my bare arms, and I hugged them to my chest.

The moon hung close tonight. Big and full. It cast a glow over the tops of the evergreens, then splintered into shards through the mass of thick branches before it touched the ground. Pieces of light dotted the grass like fallen stars plucked from the sky and discarded—some stranger's wishes never coming true.

My shoulders dropped as the tension in my muscles flowed out onto the floor, and my eyes started to droop as I gazed out into the night. I sighed, and my warm breath made a foggy circle on the windowpane. I drew a smiling face with my finger, but it didn't cheer me up. If I ever got through all this stuff on my brain, I needed to take an entire day off just to sleep. Maybe if I could get to Thanksgiving, everything would be okay.

One month. I could handle that.

As if agreeing with my plan, my mouth fell open into a wide yawn. *Finally*. I started pulling the curtain back into place, but my hand stopped midway. Orange light flashed just beyond the backyard gate. I wiped away the smiley face and leaned closer to the window, but the light disappeared. *I must be tired.* Now I'd started seeing things. I blinked and tugged at the curtain again. Another flicker flashed in the distance. I rubbed my eyes with the back of my hand.

The flicker came again. An orange flare blazing out in the dark —bigger and brighter than before. It stayed this time, growing more intense as I stared at it. *Dammit. It's a brush fire.*

I grabbed a sweatshirt and my phone then bolted out of my bedroom. It was probably those middle school wannabe deviants from up the street. They were always egging houses and knocking over mailboxes, or lurking on the sidewalk pretending to be little juvie hall villains. Last time one of them lit a fire in the backwoods, it almost took out the entire neighborhood.

From the hall closet, I pulled out the fire extinguisher, then slid through the patio door and across the back lawn. A cool fall breeze zapped the last of my growing drowsiness and shocked me awake. *Great. These little punks better run.* Through the slats of the fence, the fire seemed to disappear, but it still danced amber and tangerine against the treetops. I struggled to dial 911 on my phone as I yanked open the back gate and rushed into the woods, fire extinguisher balanced in my other hand, ready to strike.

"Hello," said a chipper voice at the end of the line.

"Hi, I'd like to report—"

"You've reached the Lethe, Illinois emergency dispatch center. If this is an emergency, please stay on the line and an operator will be with you shortly. If not, please hang up and call our non-emergency service number during the hours of eight to five, Monday to Friday."

The line clicked, and a too-loud piano cover of "Für Elise" assaulted my eardrum. My head jerked, and the phone nearly slid down my shoulder, but I, thankfully, kept it from falling in the dark. Only twelve thousand people even lived in this town. How could there be enough emergencies that all lines were full?

I stumbled on the uneven ground but managed not to trip. I'd played back here enough times to follow the pathways led only by the dim light of my cell phone, but not being able to see my feet still presented a challenge.

The piano lulled, then burst into another song as I neared a clearing by the creek. I skidded to a stop. Flames flickered in the wind all around. Fat red and gold candles ran against the edges of the tree line in a perfect circle. *What the hell?*

I crept closer. More candles burned in the middle of the space. I stepped over the fiery line and knelt near a basket of marigolds. Picture frames of what looked like tarot cards sat among misshapen gourds and pinecones. Was this someone's idea of a joke? I slipped my fingers across the red blanket under the collection of random trash. Soft and silky. Too luxurious to be sitting on a forest floor. Stolen goods, maybe? But why all the candles?

A chill crept up my back, and I rose to my feet. I pulled the phone away from my ear and hung up.

"I don't know who's out here, but I've already called the cops, and they are on their way."

No response, only the whisper of the water flowing against the rocks in the creek.

"I mean it. Don't mess with me. You've got about one minute to get out of here before they show up."

Still silence.

I bent over and blew out the center candles. If they fell over, this whole place would go up in an inferno. I followed around the circumference of the circle, quenching the wicks one after the other. The creepy tarot cards watched me in their cheap gold frames. I couldn't see them in the dark, but the weight of stares sat heavy between my shoulders. I shivered and shook my head. It had to be the freakish cards.

As each flame died, it plunged me deeper into the darkness but also brought me closer to getting back to my bed so I could stare at the ceiling for a few more hours before school. I turned the last corner of the circle. The wind blew harder against my skin. Cold. Wintry.

Leaves rustled from the bushes behind me. I spun around.

"You'd better get the hell out of here. The cops will be here any second," I yelled into the emptiness as I pulled my phone out of my hoodie.

The bushes kept rustling.

"I'm serious." I tried to dial the emergency line again but struggled against my trembling fingers.

Voices echoed off the trees, and the hurried crunch of footsteps headed away from the clearing. My eyes narrowed as if squinting would help my sight against the dark, but only inky shadows raced up the creek bed toward the street. I backed up, my finger still positioned on the send button. Looked like I'd scared them off. Whoever they were.

My legs quivered, ready to run, but my brain screamed to not leave the candles burning. A disaster waiting to happen that would be all my fault if I walked, or ran, away. Besides, it was probably some stupid kids. It had to be. Although my racing pulse tried to convince me otherwise. But what were they doing?

The wind whistled again, and the remaining flames shimmied in an eerie rhythm. Inhale. It's only the wind. Exhale.

I leaned over to blow out another candle and froze.

A bright green light wavered ahead of me in the dark. Too green for a flashlight, too bright for a cell phone, and headed my direction.

Standing stick straight, I grasped the fire extinguisher tighter.

"Who's there? I'm not afraid of you," I called out, my legs shaking in contradiction.

The light stopped. It rose higher then plummeted to the ground, taking my stare with it. Finally, it hovered for a few seconds before speeding right at me.

I backed up, tripping over the candles, and dropped my phone. The light zoomed closer. Faster. Brighter. My ankles burned from the flames at my feet. My heart smashed against my chest. The light kept coming.

"Get away from me!" I pulled the pin from the fire extinguisher, then pressed the lever, aiming at the radiant beam. White smoke billowed around me. The light intensified. I dropped the canister and ran. The flare swooped past and came at me from the other direction. I screamed. It expanded in a feverish glow, blazing, until it collapsed and rammed at my stomach.

I fell to my knees, gasping and choking for air. Trees and moonlight swayed back and forth as the world moved in and out of focus. I lurched forward, my hands in the dirt. The flames from the remaining candles rose like hazy pyres into the sky. Taller. Frenzied.

My head slammed into the ground, and the musty smell of damp leaves seeped into my nose. An explosion of sharp copper stained my tongue. Then everything fell away, except for a bright green light fading into the black.

Two

P *lease stop.*
   With eyes closed, I fumbled to find my phone and silence the alarm's infernal buzzing. *A* calm stillness fell over my room, and my muscles relaxed, sinking my body deeper into the mattress. Much better. How could it possibly be morning already? I struggled to open my left eye, and a blaze of sun pierced my retina. With an irritated groan, I pulled a pillow over my head. *What time did I finally fall asleep last night?* I thought harder, but nothing materialized. How did I even get to bed at all?

After tossing the pillow aside, I sat against the headboard and curled my knees up to my chest. Not better. My head ached at the base of my brain, and any movement aggravated the pain more. I closed my eyes. Fire flickered in my memory. Candles. A strange green light. I ripped my eyes open again, my breath coming hard. *Just a dream, Berkley. Just a weird, screwed-up dream.*

My legs shook as I stood and staggered over to the mirror on my closet door. I yanked up my T-shirt, exposing the stomach of my reflection. No marks or bruises. I sucked in a breath then ran my fingertips across my abdomen and down the faint squiggly birthmark to the left of my belly button. Nothing out of the ordinary. I poked my index finger harder into my skin, but other than the sharp sting of my fingernail digging into my flesh, nothing hurt. I dropped the shirt hem and grabbed my forehead. Something hit me last night. Socked me right in the gut. I swore it. The pain flashed through my mind. So real, so vivid. It knocked the breath from my lungs. I couldn't have really imagined something so realistic. Could

I? My arms quivered as I hugged them close to my chest. I shook my head—trying to rattle my memories or dreams or whatever into place—but regretted it instantly as my headache pulsed at the back of my skull. Maybe I'd never know.

Steam filled the bathroom as I took my time in the shower, letting the scalding water soothe my aching brain. Time slipped away in the haze of my unfocused thoughts until my skin burned scarlet and I reluctantly turned off the taps. After sliding into my favorite jeans, I tiptoed down the stairs. Bright and cheerful sun streamed into the kitchen from the patio door. I recoiled and threw my hand over my eyes, hissing and wincing like a newborn vampire in a low-budget horror flick. I should march back upstairs and disappear under my duvet until tomorrow, when I could make another attempt at functioning as a human being, but missing class meant skipping the biology test third period and tanking my GPA. But today, I really wished I didn't care.

In the cupboard above the sink, I sifted through the cough syrup and antacids until I spotted the red-and-white bottle of Tylenol. I tapped the last pill into my palm and swallowed it dry. It tasted like chalk and scraped down the sides of my throat, but I needed it working as fast as possible. Just the thought of relief eased the tense muscles in my shoulders.

I chucked the empty container in the trash, and a pinging sound rang from the bin. I pulled off the rotating lid of the can and cringed at the glass bottle lying among the remnants of last night's spaghetti. No wonder Dad wasn't awake yet. Whiskey benders always hit him the worst.

The kitchen blurred. I floated around in a daze, making toast and pouring juice on autopilot, too distracted by the headache to focus too intently on anything else. After flopping down into a chair at the table, I squinted and gazed out the patio door. The branches of the oak trees bent in the breeze over the top of the high wooden fence. I rubbed my stomach again, still expecting to feel something, but only rough cotton slid under my fingertips.

I sipped from my cup. Icy-cold orange juice flowed down my throat, but did nothing to quench my thirst. I chugged harder, my gulps audible as I savored every drop. Unfortunately, the thirst persisted. I refilled the glass and drained it again, then wiped the back of my hand across my mouth, out of breath. My stomach rumbled. I devoured both slices of toast and even picked at the crumbs on my plate. Since when did dry bread taste so fantastic? I slumped in my chair, still far from full. Volleyball practice had been intense lately. Maybe it had finally caught up to me?

A faint knock drifted in from the front hall, and I hurried to the door. Josh stood on the step with a beaming smile and freshly styled hair. Tall and broad and well slept.

"Ready to go?" he asked as he leaned down and kissed me on the cheek.

Closing my eyes, I breathed him in. The crook of his neck smelled clean, like fresh laundry and bars of soap. I sank into the scent and let it try to scrub away my lousy mood.

"Not quite," I mumbled. "It's been a rough morning."

"Yeah, you look like you've been through hell."

I snapped out of my Josh intoxication and jerked my head back. "Thanks."

"Just saying." He shrugged and twined his index finger around my pinkie, swinging my arm forward. A lazy, sympathetic smile curled across his lips. "Is it your dad again?"

I pulled the door closed behind me. "No, he's still sleeping."

"Well, can you hurry, please? Coach wants to talk to me and Brett before class today, and I don't want to be late."

He glanced over his shoulder toward the street, his jaw clenched and cut ridges in his cheeks. Five days until the big game in Rockford and already the pressure bled into his expression. An elastic band pulled tight enough to break. A different kind of discomfort rose from the bottom of my stomach.

"Maybe you should just go then." I cast my eyes down and

followed the deep crack in the concrete step. "I have a few things to do before I leave."

Turning his head to the side, he sank low to catch my duplicitous gaze. "But what was it you wanted to say? You said it was important."

"Never mind. It can wait. No big deal."

He tugged my hand closer and slipped his fingers between mine. "Are you sure? I still have a little time. You made it sound like a big deal on the phone last night."

I shook my head. "Just go, I'll catch up with you later."

He narrowed his stare and scanned my face, each piercing smoky-blue glance burning hot against my skin. I couldn't do this now. I wasn't ready. My rough draft of the speech I needed to give had bounced around my brain for weeks already. A few more days wouldn't hurt anything. Besides, what kind of awful person dropped something like this on someone when they were already struggling with other things? It wasn't fair.

"All right, I guess. But you know you can tell me anything, right?"

"Of course." Except this. This would hurt.

He yanked my arm forward, and I fell against his chest, the zipper of his football jacket scratching against my cheek. He wrapped his arms around my shoulders and squeezed. "I hope your morning gets better. See you later."

"Yeah, later."

He released me and bolted down the driveway in a few quick strides. He opened the door to the Charger and stared back at me with an uneasy smile. Did he already know? He disappeared inside, and I jumped at the hollow slam of the door. Upsetting him before a big game would be a colossal mistake. The school would never forgive me. Besides, my tired mind couldn't handle any sort of intelligent conversation with anyone right now. Especially one this delicate.

I fell back against the door and watched Josh's taillights disappear down the street, regretting that I hadn't left with him. Let him hold my hand on the drive and give me that smile. His charming, dangerous smile that made everything else fall away. The one I'd lost myself in too many times over the last two years we'd been together. A superpower far more impressive than his record-breaking passing yards stats.

Cars drove by and kicked up the leaves on the side of the road. My scattered brain drifted from Josh and wandered back to the mystery of last night. The green light had shone so bright. Too real to be imagined. Right? And the candles. A perfect circle like that couldn't have appeared out of nowhere. I rubbed my face with my palm. *Forget about it, Berkley. You'll drive yourself insane.* Why couldn't I let it go? Except I never let anything go.

I ducked through the garage and cut out across the dew-soaked backyard. Closing my eyes, I took a deep breath and tugged the back gate open. The thick of trees behind the fence whispered in the morning breeze. Beckoning, or maybe calling out a warning. Although my knees shook, I marched forward. The warm sun beat down on my skin, but my goosebumps covered my flesh as if ice water ran through my veins. I needed to see the clearing. Prove to myself that these crazy visions were all in my head. Or at least I hoped so.

I'd run through these backwoods so many times before, but now they seemed different. Wrong. I cowered at every little noise; the birds chirping overhead, a squirrel jumping between branches, or even the cracking of twigs beneath my own feet.

The trees thinned. I shook out my arms and summoned my last ounce of courage and jogged forward. It wasn't far now.

The red and gold treetops above me shimmered in the sunlight as a soft breeze drifted off the creek and fluttered the falling leaves as they rained down. The leaves already on the ground swirled around my ankles and glided across the earthy floor. A picturesque autumn morning. The kind you'd see in a calendar or on a postcard. Unfortunately, it did little to untie the knot of dread in my chest.

Dusky sun rays glowed in the clearing, illuminating ... absolutely nothing. *What the hell?* My shoulders dropped. The entire area looked undisturbed as if I'd discovered it for the first time. Completely wild and untouched.

I crouched and picked up a handful of leaves, crushing them in my fist. Dry as paper. Brittle as potato chips. The candles should've left wax drippings, but not a drop appeared on the brown flecks in my hand. I ran my fingers along the ground. Nothing. There should be burnt leaves too, but it would be impossible to tell with them already decomposing to a dead black. I blinked. I guess I did imagine it all.

Falling backward onto the ground, I scanned the space. Weird. It all seemed so real. Tangible. But if my visions had happened, that would definitely be worse. I rested my elbows on my knees and rubbed my temples, letting my breath slowly drain out of me. Enough. It was really just a dream.

I pushed up to my feet and brushed my hands across my butt for any debris that might have caught on my jeans, then headed back toward the path. A rustling sound echoed to my left. I stopped walking and scanned the bushes beside me. The branches shuddered. Slowly, I stepped away and my fists clenched. The sun disappeared behind a cloud, draping the woods in shadow. The bushes cracked again. My body tensed. Wound tight and ready to run, or fight, or who knew what. The sound intensified. Closer now. I froze. A small gray bunny leaped out from the leaves and bounded up the path. I shrieked. It sat up on its hind legs and wiggled its whiskered nose at me before running off toward the creek.

My heartbeat thumped in my ears, and I buckled over, grabbing my thighs and trying to slow my exaggerated breathing. A dream. Nothing more. And now I had proof. Just bizarre delirium from lack of sleep.

I hurried back to my yard and gasped as I latched the gate, locking my nightmares on the other side of the fence. My pulse slowed, and I walked toward the house.

Through the patio door, Dad sat motionless at the kitchen table, still in his bathrobe and plaid pajama pants. As I approached, he startled in his chair.

He sprang from the table and slid open the door. "Shouldn't you be at school?"

"I was just leaving. I needed to check something first." The words spilled out fast. Too fast.

He raised an eyebrow, and his lips clenched into a tight line. "I hope you locked the gate. I don't want anyone breaking in here when we aren't home."

"Yes, I locked the gate." I glanced back over my shoulder as a double-check. Looked shut tight. "Don't you have to get to work?"

Dad crossed his arms, and his stare hardened. "That's none of your business. Besides, I'm not feeling very well today."

Right. Or any other day this past week.

"Plus, I've got a splitting headache. Have you seen the Tylenol anywhere?"

"We're out. I had the last one."

Grabbing the back of his head, he cursed under his breath. "And you didn't think to get more?"

I jumped. My nerves still raw from the bunny encounter. "I just took it this morning. I will pick some up for you after school."

"That doesn't do much for me right now, does it?"

"I'm sorry." I stepped back and stared down at the yellowing grass beneath my sneakers.

He sighed. "It's fine. My head is just killing me."

He ventured out barefoot onto the cold concrete patio, his shadow looming closer. I looked up, and his face softened. A pained smile broke across his lips. "I'm sorry. I shouldn't have snapped at you."

He pulled me into a hug, and I gagged on the musky scent of sweat and stale booze.

"Now, get out of here. Don't want you to be late for class."

I let go and left through the garage. Who needs nightmares when you have real life to contend with?

THREE

I sat at my desk with my forehead resting on my crossed arms. People arrived and buzzed around me. However, I didn't bother to look. My headache finally let up about fifteen minutes before, but I wasn't about to give up my last few moments of rest. I needed the world to stop being so cloudy if I had any hope of making it until the final bell.

"Morning, Berkley," a familiar voice said.

A breeze ruffled my hair as Ethan walked past me to his desk. A whiff of cinnamon toast. My stomach grumbled. *Seriously? How could I be hungry again?* Very slowly, I raised my head and turned around.

"Hey," I replied with such little enthusiasm, it almost sounded like slurring.

"Rough night?"

"Is it that obvious? I must look like a train wreck."

He laughed and pulled off his ball cap, his hair flopping messily into his eyes. My fingers twitched, wanting to push it off his face, but he ran his hand through it before my brain could coax my hands to move.

"You look fine, you're just not quite your upbeat, high-strung self this morning."

"Was that supposed to be a compliment?" I narrowed my eyes to little slits. My head throbbed again, so I stopped.

"Take it however you want." He pulled out a notebook and pen from his bag and arranged them in a neat row on his desk. "By the way, Lane was looking for you."

"I was running behind and decided to come straight to class for a few minutes of peace."

"Are you really feeling that bad?" he asked, the smile fading from his lips as he tilted forward.

"I'll be fine. Had a terrible sleep, messed-up dreams and all."

"Yeah, been there."

"Then I get here and find this on my desk." I swung the battered copy of *Macbeth* in front of his face. "Really?"

His forehead crinkled as he backed away from the book in my unsteady hand. "What's wrong with *Macbeth*? I think it's one of the better plays."

"Define better?"

"Well, it's pretty dark." He shrugged and thumbed through his own copy in front of him, the hint of a satisfied grin whispering across his lips as he scanned the lines of stodgy old English. "And it's got cool stuff like witches."

Frowning, I slumped against the desk. "If you find that stuff cool, I guess. Sounds lame to me. I mean, witches? C'mon. So fake."

"Wow." He laughed and leaned in his chair, his arm bent casually over the back. "You truly are a killjoy this morning, aren't you?"

"Sorry, I'll return to my nap."

I tossed the book onto my desk and stretched out again. Ethan's deep voice chuckled behind me. I smirked into the bend of my elbow as his stare rested softly on the back of my head.

All too soon, the clack of Mrs. Franklin's heels echoed into the classroom, followed by the sharp click of the door closing. I winced. *Just great.*

"Everyone, I'm excited to announce that today we will start our study of Shakespeare's *Macbeth*," she said, clapping her hands. Each strike pierced the base of my skull.

Perfect. Welcome to hell.

···•˙ (•˙•···

THE HEAT of the midday sun beamed on my dark-haired head and soothed some ache in my brain. Throughout my morning classes, the pain fog thickened until I could only keep one eye open at a time. A unique challenge when trying to write a biology test. Luckily, science made sense to me—one of the few things in my world that did lately—and multiple-choice didn't require a lot of writing.

The rough wooden picnic table scratched at my arms, but I'd trade the open air for squinting under stifling fluorescent lights any day. I might just stay out here until school ended.

"Berk," a voice called from the opposite end of the schoolyard.

I propped my elbows on the table, chin in my hands, and stared into the distance. Lane's short curls bobbed up and down as she bounded across the grass toward me. Her neon-green scarf drifted in the breeze, as if the embroidered owl near the edge was flying beside her. Her rainbow-striped fingerless gloves complemented the look, giving her a cozy, yet totally clashing vibe. She pulled it off better than yesterday's cheetah and zebra print poncho, though. Sometimes I wished for her courage to wear whatever I felt like, other times I was ridiculously grateful for my more conservative, if not bland, sense of style.

The table shook as she dropped herself in the seat across from me. The muscles in my back flinched.

"Hey," she said. "I was looking for you this morning."

"I know. Ethan told me."

"Where were you anyway?" She pulled a container of baby carrots out of her plaid and camouflage school bag, then held them out to me.

I recoiled and waved my hand in front of my face. "I can't. Just thinking about food makes me want to throw up."

"That sounds sucky." She snapped a carrot in her teeth. The crunch thundered louder than normal.

"Yeah, especially since I'm completely starving." My stomach gurgled loudly in agreement. "Except I didn't sleep very well last night, and now I have a ridiculous headache."

"I might have something that could help." She put down the carrots and rummaged through her bag again. "Tylenol. Advil. Aleve. Motrin. Package of M&M's. Pick your poison."

"Do I want to ask why you have a pharmacy in your backpack?"

"Probably not." She gave me a crooked smile and chucked a bottle of Advil at me.

I missed the catch, and it fell to the ground, rolling just out of my reach. *Figures.*

"I'm okay, I already took a Tylenol this morning." I got up, my legs shaking, and retrieved the bottle, hoping I wouldn't fall flat on my face in the process.

"And that seems to have gotten you far. Take one. Maybe it'll be enough to make you feel better. Besides, I need you in fighting shape by four."

I pressed down on the bottle and struggled to release the child-lock lid. The medicine rattled around inside, taunting me as I turned the top around and around again. Lane shook her head and tossed her open palm in the air. I surrendered the Advil, and she easily popped the top, then handed me a green gel cap.

I swallowed it down with a mouthful of water from my bottle. "Why?"

"I was hoping we could go for a run after school. Trying to stay in tiptop shape for volleyball finals this weekend. Or have you forgotten about the biggest thing happening in our lives right now?"

Must be nice. If only volleyball was the most important thing going on. I'd be giddy like Lane too. "Well, that explains the carrots."

"I eat healthy." She rolled her eyes and looked away. "Sometimes. What are you working on?"

"Math stuff." Technically, it was true, but if I could concentrate for longer than five seconds, I'd probably be more productive.

"Keener." Another noisy crunch.

I cringed. "I had the craziest dream last night."

"Really? Was it the one where you were naked at the circus again?" She snickered, then started peeling the wrapper of a Kit Kat bar.

"I thought you were eating healthy?"

"I did. Didn't you just see the carrots?"

With a heavy sigh, I looked back down at my notes, all the happy equations staring up at me and begging to be solved. But not today. I pictured the green light and the strange circle of flames. Maybe telling the story out loud would prove how ridiculous it all seemed? Or maybe I'd never hear the end of it? Lane had been my best friend since second grade, but she had no problem ridiculing me until we were sixty if the right ammunition came along. Besides, I'd already decided it was just a stupid dream.

Lane snapped her fingers, and I blinked. Black shadows appeared in my vision from staring blankly at the sun.

"So, about that run later?"

I let out a long dramatic sigh and dropped my chin down onto my textbook. "I don't know. If I feel better, sure. If not, I'll have to pass, I think."

"It's okay if you're still a little sore. Might give me a chance at beating you this time."

"Thanks. Take advantage of my suffering."

"Of course. That's what friends are for." She winked and popped an entire Kit Kat stick in her mouth.

Four

I gripped the coarse bark of the tree trunk as I kicked my right leg back and grabbed my ankle. The stretch hurt, but with that euphoric kind of pain. Re-energizing the flow in my muscles and waking them up again. I pulled tighter, exhaling loudly as the stretch deepened and burned through my thigh. Sometime between Physics and Calculus, my headache evaporated, leaving just my cloudy brain and tired body to drag around the rest of the day. It would've been enough to bail on Lane's offer of a run, but maybe if I got some exercise it might knock me out later.

My stomach gurgled. Hungry again? Seriously? I'd already gorged myself on pasta after school. Two full bowls of ravioli and my mouth still watered for more. Maybe I was getting sick or something? But didn't you eat less when you felt ill?

My phone vibrated in my pocket. Josh. I sighed.

Josh: *Didn't see you at the end of the day. Everything okay?*
Me: *Yep. All good.*
Josh: *Want me to come over?*

I hovered my finger over the screen. My shoulders drooped, aching to rest my head against his chest and let the rest of the world float away. To breathe him in and feel okay for even five minutes. But that wasn't fair to him. I couldn't let myself fall under that spell. My stomach churned, the hunger for something else bleeding into my soul.

Me: *Thanks, but I'm out with Lane. Maybe later this week?*

A pause. Three little dots pulsed in the corner of my screen.

Josh: *Are you sure you're okay?*
Me: *Yep. All good.*

As I hit the send button, the air thickened, and I struggled to swallow. I didn't want to lie to him. I never did. He'd been my first kiss in freshman year. The shy, goofy guy who picked me daisies and left them in my locker with a post-it note heart. And even after he grew out of the awkward phase and became the quarterback king of Henstridge High, he'd always been the same with me. Except with everything going on over the last few months, I knew I'd changed, and I just wished I could find a way to get my old self back.

I switched the phone off and slid it back into my pocket, then flipped directions and stretched out my left leg. In the haze of pending twilight, Lane skipped up the sidewalk toward me.

"Ready to eat my dust, Berkley James?" She bent her arms back behind her head and limbered up her shoulders before dipping into a few lunges on the grass in front of me.

"Sure. As long as you don't cry when I run circles around you. Literally."

She stood up straight, the humor fading from her smile. "What's up with you? Still with the headache?"

"No." I dropped my foot and averted my eyes from her prying stare. "I'm fine."

"Yeah, right. Your insults lack their regular, ruthless charm. Is something wrong?"

I played with the cuff of my shirt and kept my mouth closed, concentrating on how the slinky tech fabric slid between my fingertips.

"Fine. Be that way. But you'll tell me, eventually. You always do."

"Probably." Except not yet. She'd be less than supportive of my decision to hold off talking to Josh. And she wouldn't be wrong, but I couldn't deal with her disappointment. "But right now, I'm going to show you what a real athlete looks like."

"Oh, it's on." Lane crouched down, hand poised on the ground like an Olympic runner waiting for the bang of the starting pistol. She launched forward and headed down the hill, deeper into the park, before she glanced back over her shoulder. "Try not to fall too far behind me."

I laughed and headed off after her, down the well-worn path that twisted along the riverbank. The last few rays of evening sun warmed my skin as the crisp smell of fall air filled my lungs and pushed down the busy thoughts in my head. Maybe a run was exactly what I needed. The tightness in my limbs eased as I moved. One foot in front of the other, stomping out my worries and cleansing my soul as I breathed out. Each step edged me closer to transcendence. Like how running should feel. Like soaring.

"So, are things getting any better with your dad?" Lane asked as she puffed alongside me.

"About the same." I scanned the opposite shoreline and sped up as I tried to outrace some unseen competitor on the other side. Maybe another girl like me, running to keep her thoughts from catching up with her. "It is hard enough that my mom's gone, but it's like I lost him too. He tries. He's just not the same person anymore."

Like I wasn't the same person anymore. The new version, more flawed and broken than the original.

"He'll come around. My mom was totally screwed up after my dad died, but look at her now. She volunteers, she's in better shape than me, and she even has a date next week."

"Yikes." I chuckled, thinking about Mrs. Mackenzie on a date.

What if Dad started dating again? I scrunched up my nose and banished the idea. "How do you feel about that?"

"It's fine. It's been a long time now, and she seems to like this Craig guy. I think he's a big dork, but it's better than her dating some hunky player that will break her heart."

"Do they even have hunks at her age?"

"I never really thought about it, but probably not. Besides, I'm glad she's out meeting people. It'll be easier for me to slip out of the house next year. Otherwise, she'd get me a job as a cashier at the supermarket so I could stay with her forever."

I laughed, or at least I let out a muffled attempt as my lungs struggled to hoard all oxygen to feed my haggard running breaths. "Sounds like some creepy horror movie."

"No doubt. Promise you'll come back to town now and again to check that I'm not locked in a cage in my basement or something."

"She wouldn't do that."

Lane's head swiveled my direction, her eyes rolling. "Clearly, you don't know my mother."

"I do, and I know she wouldn't put up with you that long. She'd have you slaughtered and buried in the backyard by Thanksgiving."

"Good point." She nodded and threw off her rhythm for a brief second. "I'll just live in your dorm room at Princeton."

"Sure, but I thought we were here to run. It looks like you're falling behind. Again." I lengthened my stride and surged ahead of her, trying to put this topic behind us. No talk of college with Lane, at least not right now.

Lane grunted and dropped her forehead until she pushed herself up beside me. "Not this time."

At the bend in the river, the path curved and forked in two directions. The left trail kept following the water in a scenic straight run into the glowing orange sunset, but without stopping Lane veered to the right and into the thick of the trees winding back up toward Cresthaven Drive.

"Maybe we should take the other path?" I called after Lane, but she'd already disappeared into the shadowy woods.

With an exaggerated sigh, I followed as the pending dark hung thick in the air. I sprinted to catch up and soon saw Lane's curls flopping ahead of me. Only a few rays of lingering sun pierced the dense canopy of branches above us, and a chill slithered across my skin as my sweaty shirt clung to my body in the cool shade. The established path narrowed as the partially barren foliage crept closer to hide any uninvited visitors that ventured through. Lane's bright-blue sneakers kicked up in front of me. Left. Right. Left. Right. A crow flew overhead and cawed. The mournful cry echoed through the treetops and rang in my ears. I sped up.

A slight breeze rustled the leaves in the bushes of the tree line and tickled along the back of my neck. I flinched, twisting my head as a heavy darkness settled between my shoulder blades. A hungry stare locked laser-sharp on my skull. I grabbed at my shoulder, but the feeling remained. Deepened. My breath came shorter. Sharp gasps as my heart hammered to keep up. I peeled my eyes away from the path and dared to look out. The air swirled around us. The dying fall forest writhed and beckoned on the crisp breeze as it whispered a hushed warning. *Go now*, it seemed to say. *Get out*. The crow returned and squawked at the rising moon just beyond the trees. The stare persisted, growing stronger on my flesh. An overwhelming feeling of being watched. Being judged.

My pace quickened again, but my toe caught Lane's heel. A sick weightlessness rose in my stomach as we tumbled sideways. My hands smacked the ground as dirt caked beneath my fingernails. The damp, musty smell of the leaves oozed up around me. A ring of trembling candle flames appeared in the dark as a green light glowed deeper in the shadows.

"Clumsy much?" Lane scolded as she brushed off her legs and fumbled back to her feet.

I shook my head. The candles and green light disappeared.

"Sorry." I grabbed my forehead but stayed sitting on the ground. The stare lifted.

Lane reached down and pulled me to standing. "What's with you?"

"Nothing. Just lost my balance." I brushed off my tights and scanned the trees again as I leaned forward on my toes, ready to run. Nothing but the wind. I rolled my head back and stretched. What was wrong with me? Maybe I still needed more sleep?

She crossed her arms. "Don't lie to me, Berkley. You suck at it."

Very true. "I'm fine. Honest. Just a little spooked being out here in the dark. That's all."

She didn't believe me, and she shouldn't with a lie that weak, but she relaxed then moved to the side to let me back on the pathway. "Well, the only way out is through."

I plastered on a fake smile. "Aren't you the philosopher?"

"I have my days." She picked a stray leaf out of my hair and tossed it to the side. "Let's get out of here."

Lane ran beside me the rest of the way. We stumbled on the uneven ground, neither of us able to be fully on the path as the thick brush picked and clawed at our sides. But she refused to slide ahead of me, and I couldn't let myself fall behind. Over and over, I watched each of my own feet land on the dirt and spring back out of view again until the rhythm calmed my anxious nerves. I looked up only once, regretted it instantly as the shadows grew longer on the horizon, then returned to studying my feet until the trees thinned and we emerged on a more open pathway. One last slice of the sun glowed red as it disappeared from the skyline. We ran in silence until we left the park and surfaced on the sidewalk near where we met earlier.

Lane doubled over, her hands on her knees, as her heavy panting puffed thin clouds in the cool of the evening. I did the same, watching my own breaths form and fade, then looked back toward the now dim park and trembled. I really needed to get a grip.

"Well, you almost had me," Lane said between gasps.

"Guess I'll have to practice harder."

We walked in quiet down the street, neither of us saying anything. As we passed, I counted the glowing circles from the streetlights that illuminated the pavement. Thirty-one ... thirty-two ... thirty-three ...

"So what really happened to you back there?" Lane cut through the lull of my silent counting. She crossed her arms tight to her chest and lowered her voice. "You can tell me it's nothing, but I saw your face. You freaked out."

"Not sure," I said. "I told you I had a bad dream last night, and I guess it got to me more than I had thought."

She rubbed her hand up and down my arm as she maneuvered herself to stare me right in the eyes. "You gonna be okay?"

"Yeah, I think so. I just need some sleep. Trust me, if it were anything to be worried about, I'd tell you."

"You'd better." She smirked and let my arm go. "I'll see you tomorrow. Get some rest."

I watched as she jogged up the street. The night breeze blew against my limbs and I shook. Cold bled through my core, like it had sucked all the warmth out of me. I gazed at the dark, quiet street and swallowed before bolting up the steps to my front door.

The television blared from the living room, and my muscles relaxed in the comfort that I wasn't alone.

"Is that you, Berkley?" Dad called from the other room.

"Yeah, it's me." I slipped off my running shoes, my socks glued to my skin with sweat. I held the shoes in one hand and went in to see him.

He sat in the armchair, staring at a football game. He'd been sitting there awhile. His slouch seemed too settled in, and the empty glass hanging from his hand by the rim screamed trouble.

"Good game?" I asked, not caring about the answer.

"Meh. Okay, I guess." He shrugged, never removing his eyes from the screen. "How was your day?"

"All right. Are you feeling any better?"

He finally looked over to acknowledge me. His brow furrowed in the whitish-blue light of the television reflecting off his face.

"This morning, remember, you said you were sick."

"Oh, right." He shifted to sit upright in the chair. "Had a rough morning. That's all."

"That makes two of us."

"Something wrong?" he asked, his gaze flitting back to the screen.

"Nothing to worry about." *Not like you would.* "I'm going to take a shower and probably go to bed. I'm pretty tired."

"Okay. Goodnight."

"Want me to put that back in the kitchen?" I pointed at the glass as I rushed forward to grab it.

He snatched it out of my reach. "Don't worry about it. I'll take care of it."

I'm sure you will.

Hanging my head, I retreated upstairs to my room. After stripping out of my sweaty clothes, I tossed them in the hamper. My skin radiated heat, but under my flesh froze ice-cold. I grabbed my robe from the back of my door and went into the bathroom, filling the tub with the hottest water I could stand. I stood swaying with my eyes almost closed, listening to the lulling sound of the water rushing into the tub. Such a soothing sound, like the babble of the creek in the woods behind my house ... where the green light swayed. I snapped my eyes open. I had to stop thinking about that stupid dream.

After flipping off the tap, I slid into the steaming water. Every inch of skin blanched red as it approached the surface. But it felt amazing—the numbness of the heat against the cold. Too much sensation, so it overloaded my senses to nothing at all. Soon my head swayed, woozy from the warmth. After I finished my bath, I dressed and slid under the covers, relieved to finally get some sleep, but instead I just stared at the ceiling.

Why couldn't I relax? Was this some cruel joke? I looked at the clock. Only 10:06 p.m. I sat back up, yanked my backpack off the floor and dumped it onto my bedsheets. The ratty *Macbeth* book stared up at me. Oh well. If anything had a chance of putting me to sleep, it might be this. I thumbed through the pages as the words all jumbled together. We could be spending our time learning about important things. Things that made sense. Not ridiculous plays about nonsensical things like witches. How would this ever apply to my real life? Except I would get a real 'F' that would drag down my GPA if I didn't at least try to figure it out.

I flipped open a notebook and dug around in my mess for a pen. No luck. I slid open my nightstand drawer and rummaged beneath the stacks of campus brochures and glossy fashion magazines. My hand grazed the bottom of the drawer, but instead of a pen, it touched a familiar sheet of thick stationery. I sighed.

The day I found this sitting in the middle of my made-up bed appeared as clear as yesterday. All crisp and cream with my name across the front in a beautiful black flourish. My palms itched as I decided whether to open it. I didn't know why, but alarms rang in my head as it lay there undisturbed. A letter addressed to me in the middle of the afternoon on a Tuesday. It couldn't be good.

I freed the letter from the drawer and tugged it out of the envelope. The folds of the paper had fuzzed at the edges, worn from the many nights I'd held it in my hands, scanning in between the lines for the real reasons why.

My Baby Berkley,

By the time you read this, I will be gone. I know it is a coward's way to leave a goodbye in a letter, but there isn't any other word for me right now but a coward.

Leaving you is the hardest thing I think I will

ever have to do. Knowing that I will never get a chance to see your smile, or hear your laugh, or watch you take over the world as you certainly will one day. You are the one thing in my life that I am the most proud of. The one thing I know I have done right.

The next little while will be difficult for you, and I wish I could make it easier. I wish I could sit there and hold you to get you through it, but I can't. I know it's selfish, but I need to start over, and the last thing you want in your life is me dragging you down.

I'm sure you won't fully understand why I must go, but hopefully one day you will. As adults, sometimes we start with the best intentions, but we end up in situations that we wouldn't have chosen for ourselves if we had the chance. I'm trying to find my way back to the person I was. The person I need to be. Please forgive me.

Take care of yourself, take care of your father, and be sure that no matter what you do in your life, I will always be thinking of you and will carry you in my heart forever.

I'm so sorry.

-Mom

Tears formed in my eyes, and I wiped them away before tossing the letter on the pile of school things on my bed. I didn't know why I kept torturing myself. She left us. She didn't want to be here anymore, but I couldn't let her go. I wanted to hate her—so badly. It would be easier that way. But I couldn't. I had so many reasons why I should, most she'd written herself, but she was still my mom, and I'd have given anything for her to change her mind and come running back. But she never did.

I used to think she would one day. I'd sit in the living room by the window to do my homework, telling Dad that I just liked the sunshine, but I was watching. Hoping, one time, I would look up from my algebra and she would be standing at the end of the driveway with her bags in her hands. But no matter how long I sat, she never came. Then Dad started drinking more often and camping himself in front of the television. Eventually, I stopped sitting in the window.

After putting the letter back into its envelope, I slid it back into the drawer until the next time I'd almost forget her and the universe needed to knock me back down. I opened the play and settled back against my pillow.

When shall we three meet again in thunder, lightning, or in rain?

Seriously? What would this ever teach me about the world?

FIVE

"**Y**ou've all worked hard this season, and I know if we keep it up, it will pay off. Now take care of yourselves, eat well, get proper rest, and I'll see you all back here for practice on Friday. Now get to class."

Coach Kruger crossed her arms as her satisfied grin beamed with pride at her prize senior volleyball team. The first team ever to get close to a championship for girls volleyball—girls anything, for that matter. We needed to be at our best. Except her simple instructions weren't as easy for me to follow.

I pushed myself off the gym floor and guzzled the rest of my water bottle. My stomach gurgled, already anticipating lunch before school had even started.

Lane nudged my arm with her elbow. "Feeling better today?"

"Ow." I rubbed the spot where she hit, the skin tender underneath my long sleeves. "A bit. Still totally exhausted, though. Maybe I'm coming down with something?"

I pressed my palm against my forehead. I didn't feel warm. At least not any warmer than running around a gym for the last hour made me. We pushed into the locker room, along with the rest of the team, and hurried to get ready for class. I slid my jersey over my head and slipped off the long-sleeved shirt underneath.

"What's that?" Lane scrunched up her nose and pointed at my back.

I tweaked my head to the side. An enormous bruise covered most of my shoulder and extended down my arm. I shrugged and continued to get dressed.

"Matches these though." I held out my forearms. Trails of smaller black and blue bruises stained my skin. "It's probably from when I fell in the woods last night."

Or at least I hoped so. Not one mark appeared on my flesh in the bath last night. No pain in any places where a bruise might appear. Nothing. But if I remembered my biology notes, it could take time for bruises to show up after violating the skin.

Lane tapped one of the bruises with her finger, and I winced. Satisfied, she pulled her hand away, but her eyes stayed glued to my marks. "Maybe you are sick, because I don't even have a scratch from that fall."

"Maybe." Or maybe something else was wrong? But what? I'd fallen in the woods and bruises formed because of it. This shouldn't be a mystery to solve, but the logical answer didn't seem quite right. I slipped my sweater over my head and hid my new contusions. More from myself than anyone else.

I shimmied into my jeans then reached for my shoes. A brown stripe of mud still tainted the side of the left sole. Leaning farther into my locker, I licked my thumb before rubbing the mark away. Or at least dulling it a little. It still didn't make sense how the mud even got there. I swore I'd left my shoes next to my gym bag in my closet last night, but this morning they'd been sitting near the front door, covered in mud. It took nearly twenty minutes to wash all the dirt and gunk out of the treads, and I almost arrived late to practice. Maybe I did leave them by the door and just didn't notice how caked they got after my run? Everything from the past few days faded in and out of focus as scenes blurred and twisted together in my exhausted mind. Maybe I just forgot?

"Berkley," Lane shouted as she snapped her fingers near my ear.

I jerked out of my thoughts and knocked my head against the locker door with a loud bang. *Ow!* I rubbed the sore spot on my cranium and backed up.

"What?"

"I've been calling your name for about five minutes. Did you fall asleep in there or something?"

"No. Just thinking, that's all." My mouth tried to keep talking but stretched open wider with a massive yawn—the mention of sleep too tempting not to ignore it. "However, a nap would be awesome about now."

"Yep. Coach Kruger is definitely on the warpath this week. I think my legs will fall off after all those burpees."

"But it will be over soon."

"And then we will be champions. Not like anyone around here but us will care." Grinning, she leaned against the locker bank. "Meet me in the courtyard at lunch?"

I slouched as I dropped to the floor to put on my shoes and avoid eye contact. "Can't. I'm meeting up with Josh for lunch today."

"That sucks. Oh well. Say hey to lover boy for me." She launched off the locker bank and stepped over me before heading out the door.

All the breath rushed from my body, and I melted down lower onto the floor. At least she didn't ask questions.

I gathered up my gym clothes and rushed off down the hall to my locker. My stomach churned as it begged to be acknowledged, but the hallways already buzzed with students, which meant I had zero time left to hit the cafeteria before class. As I tugged open my locker door, a sharp pain surged in my abdomen, and I clutched my side.

Okay. Maybe I could be a few minutes late for first period.

I slung my backpack over my shoulder and fished through it to find my wallet. Only two dollars in cash. That wouldn't buy much.

"Hey there, beautiful."

Josh appeared beside me and waved his hand in front of my face. I jumped with a short yelp, but he quickly wrapped a thick, muscular arm around my waist and pulled me close. When he pressed on the fresh bruise near my ribs, I winced.

"You okay?" His brow furrowed with concern.

"Just a bit sore. I fell on my run with Lane last night."

"Oh." He eased up his grip. "Did you want the team's trainer to take a look? Make sure you didn't do any serious damage."

He ran the back of his knuckle down the side of my cheek, and I sank into his touch. His slate-blue eyes bore down into mine, asking wordless questions and pleading for me to answer. I glanced away and slunk out of his arms. I couldn't think when I looked into his eyes. That excited twinkle melted my conviction, like the first time he'd stared at me that way. I often wondered if he knew the effect he had or if he unconsciously knew how to make girls swoon.

"Thanks, but I'll be okay. I was just going to run to the cafeteria to grab a snack before class."

After maneuvering around him, I dug back into my locker, my hands searching my jacket for any extra cash. "But we're still meeting up at—"

My fingers plunged into my jacket pocket, and a crunching sound echoed in the dark metal locker. I yanked my hand out, a fistful of dead leaves crushed in my palm.

"Science experiment?" Josh glanced at my open hand and his eyebrow rose, clearly as confused as me. He shook his head. "And I forgot to text you, but I can't meet at lunch today. They wanted to run tape from the last Rockford game and work on some strategy. I'm sorry. But I'm free tomorrow?"

"Don't worry, it's totally fine." My body relaxed. One more day. I'd take it. "No big deal."

He clutched the sides of my sweater and tugged me close again. "I'm not trying to brush you off, I swear. It's just you know this game is important. Don't think I don't want to hear what you have to say, because I do."

"Absolutely." I tapped him on the shoulder and nodded. "It's all good, Josh. I can wait. I get it."

"That's why you are the best, Berkley James." His lips curled up. "And I talked to Coach the other day. He says that if I can impress the scouts over the next few weeks, I could go to any school I want."

"That's fantastic, Josh. Looks like it's all going to work out for you."

"Work out for me?" A dark scowl fell over his bliss. "Work out for *us*."

"Right, us." My one moment of relief floated away and crashed onto the dingy hallway linoleum.

"Our plan is finally coming together. You are going to love it in Texas. Hot and sunny all the time." He rested his forehead against mine, his warm breath stoking the fire in my burning cheeks. "I know how much you hate the snow."

I forced a smile. Texas. The elephant I'd been dancing around for weeks. I'm sure it would be amazing, and every time Josh talked about it, I wanted to go. I wanted to drift along on his excitement and enjoy the happy. Drown in it. But it wasn't my dream.

He tugged the drawstrings on my sweater, twisting them around his thick index fingers. "I can't wait for us to get out of here."

"About that. I ..." I paused, trying to summon the right words.

Josh took advantage of the silence and pressed his lips on mine. The leaf pieces fluttered to the floor like confetti as his arm twined behind my back, and I reached up to clasp my hands around his neck. His teeth grazed my lip as I evaporated into his kiss. I disappeared. Kissing Josh stopped time until I forgot who I was. And that was the problem.

"Get a room," someone shouted from down the hall.

Josh laughed against my mouth, the vibration almost as intoxicating, then he let me go. Time sped back up to reality. The bell rang.

"We can talk tomorrow. I really can't be late for class. Can't risk getting benched."

I nodded, and he gave me a quick peck on the forehead.

He stole away from me and swaggered down the hall. I watched him go, my head still cloudy. Why did he have to make this so hard?

Six

"Did I call you last night after I got home? Or text or anything?"

I slammed my books down on the picnic table, and Lane's water bottle jumped.

She dropped her pencil into the open spine of her textbook and leaned back, shielding her face from the sun as she stared up at me. "Good afternoon to you too. I thought you had a hot date for lunch today?"

I slid into the bench seat and gave her some reprieve from the glaring sunlight. "Josh had team stuff. But I'm serious, Lane. Did I say anything about going out after I went home last night?"

"Nope. Not a thing. Why?"

"Never mind." I rested my head on my books and crossed the question off my mental to-do list. Things still didn't make sense. The mud. The leaves. Even the bruises. Nothing major, but just enough to push me over the edge. Maybe I was losing my mind?

Lane smoothed the hair on the back of my head and leaned in close. "Are you okay, Berk?"

"Yeah," I mumbled into my textbook cover. "I've just been forgetting things lately. Or at least I think I am. No big deal. Probably just stressed out."

"Too stressed out to tutor me in chemistry this week? I have a test on Friday, and I'm so not ready for it."

I raised my head back up and brushed my hair out of my face. "Again? Why do you keep taking these classes that you hate, then get me to cram everything in at the last minute?"

"I do not. I actually opened the textbook this time and read a few things. Except the course work is crazy intense, and I'm having trouble memorizing all this stuff."

I shook my head. "Sure. Come over tomorrow, and we'll see what we can do. But you are the one who needs to do the work. I'm not even taking chemistry this semester."

"Sorry, super genius, I'll be sure to thank you when I win my first Nobel prize."

"You'd better." I laughed and reached into my bag. The ugly version of *Macbeth* stared back at me. I flipped the book onto the table at Lane. "How are you in English? Want to swap?"

She picked up the copy and thumbed through the pages. "I can try, but not typically my thing. I'm more of a technical writing kind of girl. Let me proofread your papers, but I'm not so great on the content part."

"Me neither." I stole the book back and tucked it inside my binder.

A sudden coolness fell over my back as the sun dropped away and a dark shadow cast over the table.

"Hey, Ethan." Lane smiled and closed her textbook. "I thought you were going to hit some balls with Rayhan and Oscar today?"

He flopped down beside me, and the picnic table shook. "I was, but Rayhan tripped down the stairs and sprained his wrist, so we bailed."

"Hmm. Sounds like clumsy seems to be going around these days." Lane's eyes darted toward me as a smirk lit on her lips.

I frowned and cast her my best evil stare.

Lane laughed. "I know it's because you two can't stand to be without me. Berkley canceled her plans to come bask in my radiance too."

"Yeah. That's it." Ethan shifted in his seat and pulled out a bag of potato chips.

The salty smell wafted around my head, and my mouth drenched with saliva. My lunch hadn't even had time to digest yet.

Ethan noticed my ravenous stare and tilted the bag my way. I snatched up a few and popped them in my mouth. Lane glanced at Ethan, and he shrugged. I stole another chip.

"It's perfect timing anyway. Berk and I were talking about a study session at her place tomorrow night. You in?"

"Sure, but isn't there that pregame party at Squire's?" He swayed closer to me. "Aren't quarterback girlfriends required to be all rah-rah and stuff?"

"Very funny." I leaned over and brushed against his arm. "Besides, Josh never goes to those. He has his rituals, and he doesn't go out the night before a game."

"I guess I don't understand the riveting and complicated world of football relationships." Ethan chuckled and offered me another chip. "And I'm perfectly fine with that."

I pointed the chip at him. "What? No romance drama in the baseball world? We tell you all the juicy stuff about our lives. How come we never hear about any girl trouble from you?"

"No, I just don't talk about that stuff, and you two would never let me get a word in edgewise if I did. Besides, you need to have a girlfriend to have girl trouble. Last time I checked anyway."

"Weren't you dating some Bethany girl over the summer? Why don't you ever mention her?" I popped the chip in my mouth and grabbed for another.

"Because we broke up."

Lane smirked. "You mean she dumped you?"

"No, I broke up with her, thank you very much. I just wasn't feeling it, so I thought it wasn't right to string her along."

Lane rolled her eyes and laughed. Loud enough that people in the courtyard turned to stare. "Just not feeling it? Wow. Way to open up, E."

"If it's not working, it's not working. End of story." He shot her a nasty glare.

"Okay." I nudged my shoulder into his, and the sour look on his face softened. "Then maybe we should try to fix you up with someone."

He shot to the far end of the bench and tossed his hands in front of him in defense. "Oh no. Please don't."

"Why not? Please? You're a catch, Ethan. Right, Lane?"

Lane shook her head and looked down at her hands on the table. "I really don't think that's a good idea."

"Ignore her. Trust me, you have so many things going for you, Ethan. You're smart, thoughtful, good looking—"

Ethan scoffed. "Said the girl dating a Renaissance statue."

"Not everyone is into that. You're just a different type of attractive. You have great hair and deep, mysterious eyes." I looked him over. He did have gorgeous eyes. They weren't like Josh's—that exuded his thoughts and feelings across his face—they were subtle. Locked. Like a puzzle to solve that hinted at an amazing prize inside. And soft lips of deepest crimson. They looked soft anyway. Perfectly kissable. Perfect like ...

I shook my head, a little dizzy from too much sunlight. "And you have a sexy smile. Tons of girls are into that. I think it's super hot."

Shades of red exploded in his cheeks, bleeding down toward his neck.

"Plus, you're tall. Girls like tall guys. And you dress well," I continued.

"So, any girl who wants a dorky, preppy guy, I'm her man." He thrust the half-eaten bag of chips at me and then backed away from the table. "I think I've had enough of your unsolicited advice. Bye, Lane."

I pulled my legs up and over the bench then swiveled around. "Don't be mad, Ethan. I'm just trying to help."

Ethan sighed and covered his face with his hand as he knelt in front of me. He placed his hands on my shoulders and stared up through his thick eyelashes. His eyes darkened as he narrowed his gaze and cut the light out. "I'm serious, Berkley. Don't. I'm perfectly happy with the way things are, and I don't want your help. If I decide to make a move, trust me, you'll be the first to know. Okay?"

He watched my face, waiting for me to relent.

I slouched. "Fine."

He let me go then bolted toward the school.

Lane shook her head. "You can't do things like that to him, you know."

I turned around and settled my legs properly under the table. "Like what?"

"Flirting with him. He might get the wrong idea."

"I was not flirting. I was trying to build up his confidence. Besides, we've been friends for like eight years. Wake up, Lane. Girls can be friends with guys and there be nothing romantic about it."

"You're absolutely right. Girls can be friends with guys, just like I'm friends with Ethan. But you can't."

"And why not?"

"Are you seriously that blind?" Lane stretched across the table as if someone might hear her. "He likes you. Like likes you, likes you. How can you not know that?"

"Oh, c'mon, Lane." My blood pumped faster, flowing through my veins at record speed and burning my skin a shade of thick scarlet. *Ethan? No way. Really?* "What makes you think that?"

"That look he gives you. Big, wide-eyed, and goofy. Like a lost little bear cub."

"He does not."

"How he's always making some attempt to touch you. How he's always offering to do things for you. And why do you think he doesn't want you to set him up?"

That desperate look when he asked me to let it drop. Maybe he wasn't just embarrassed? I grabbed my forehead. *Total idiot.* "But I'm with Josh, remember? He knows that."

"Which is exactly why he'll never tell you he's into you. He's too nice. But if he doesn't stand a chance, if you and Josh break up, please try to spare his feelings."

"If we break up? What is that supposed to mean?"

"It means that next year Josh is going to be elbows deep at frat house keggers in the Lonestar State, and you'll be studying your face off at Princeton." Lane flung one hand out to her left and one as far right as possible, the space between them seemingly infinite. "I love you, Berk, but do you honestly think the long-distance thing is going to work out? You have seen Josh, right? He'll be fighting those big-haired pageant queens off him in no time. I like Josh, I don't want him to break your heart, but I'm scared for you."

"Thanks for the visual." I crossed my arms, wanting to be mad, to yell at her for being judgmental. But the picture she painted seemed too real. I couldn't let that happen. "Besides, I haven't heard about that scholarship yet. Maybe I'll end up south with him too. We could be together for the rest of our lives. You don't know what's going to happen."

"Oh no, you don't. I have known you for too damn long, and you are the smartest person I know. Like insanely smart. There is no way you are going to let this opportunity pass by. Unless ..." Grabbing both my shoulders, she forced me to face her. "You haven't told Josh that you aren't planning to follow him to Texas, have you?"

I scanned the trees in the courtyard, the sky, the graphic T-shirts on the guys playing soccer in the field. Anything for inspiration to get me out of this conversation. Lane knew me too well. Dangerously well.

"Berkley Emmalina James!"

"I tried, Lane. I was even going to do it today, but that didn't work out. Besides, he's got so much going on right now. There're scouts coming. There's—"

"Enough excuses. You need to tell him."

She wasted her breath. I knew it. I'd known it for months now. "What if he breaks up with me?"

"Then he breaks up with you. You will be just fine without him. We'll get some ice cream, some rom-com movies." She smirked. "We can slash his tires. Trust me, the world will not end."

I yanked myself out of her grip and stared down at the yellowing blades of grass. I blinked, fighting the twinge in the corner of my eye. Lane walked around the table and sat down beside me.

"I do love him, you know." I swiped my cheek with my sleeve, hoping she wouldn't catch me crying.

"I know you do. And maybe I'm wrong. Maybe you guys will work it out and be happy forever." She leaned over and hugged me awkwardly from my right side. "I also know that you are one of the few people in this stupid school that is ever going to make something of themselves, so I'm not going to let you walk away from your future awesomeness."

"How is it that you have so much faith in me?"

"You seriously need to give yourself more credit. How is it possible that you can be so smart and, at the same time, so bloody stupid? You're too hard on yourself. It's like you think you aren't allowed to have good things."

"Good things fade. Nothing lasts forever, you know."

"For the love of cupcakes, enough with the melodrama." She grabbed my hands in hers. "We're going to try something I learned in my life coaching class."

"Wait, when did you take a life coaching class?" I flinched in her grip.

She shook her head. "Whatever. Not important. Repeat after me. My name is Berkley James, and I am amazing. Say it."

"This is stupid."

She clenched my hands tighter. "Say it. I'm not letting go until you do."

"Fine. My name is Berkley James, and I am amazing."

"Now. I deserve to be happy and let good things happen to me.

And I'm going to stop letting people walk all over me and pursue the things that I want in life. Say it."

I glared at her. "I get the point. I don't need to repeat everything you say."

"I don't want you to just say it. I want you to believe it. You've had this dark cloud hanging over you for months now, and it's getting exhausting."

"Sorry, I've just been going through some stuff."

Lane dropped my hands and wrapped her arm around me, her head flopping onto my shoulder. "And you don't think I don't know that? She didn't leave because you weren't good enough, you know? You don't have to prove anything to anyone. You just need to let her go, and live your life."

"How?" The tears flowed, and I didn't bother to stop them. "How am I supposed to get up every morning and know she didn't love me enough to stay? What if I tell Josh and he leaves too? My dad's such a mess, he's practically gone already. You and Ethan might be the only ones I have left."

Lane's slender arm squeezed harder than a metal vise. "Then consider yourself lucky, because I'm not going anywhere."

SEVEN

"**D**ad, I'm home."

My voice echoed through the house and bounced back, unanswered. I roamed into the living room and then upstairs, greeted by one empty room after another. Oh well. At least he'd left the car parked out front instead of driving himself. One less thing for me to worry about.

I raced to the fridge and yanked open the door. Hunger struck again in the middle of last period and nagged at me for the entire walk home. My body seemed eighty pounds heavier as I dragged it down the sidewalk. Volleyball left me physically drained, plus the bustle of the day matched with the emotional exhaustion of my all-too-honest lunch with Lane and the relentless lack of sleep plagued me. A square cardboard box called from the second shelf of the fridge. *Yes. Leftover pizza.* One small victory for today.

After tossing three slices in the microwave, I poured a tall glass of milk and set it on the table. A stack of mail sat haphazardly in the middle, and I flipped through it. Flyers. A phone bill with a red past-due sticker on the outside. I cringed. *Not again.* I threw it down with a sigh, and a crisp white envelope addressed to me shook loose. The return address read The Marquis Moore Foundation in Chicago. My fingers trembled as I ripped open the envelope and slipped out the single letter.

Ms. Berkley James,

It is our pleasure to inform you that you have progressed to the inter-

view round of the Marquis Moore scholarship program. Your interview is scheduled on October 4th at 6 p.m. at the Riverfront Marriott.

We look forward to meeting with you, Ms. James.

Sincerely,
Arthur Marquis
Co-Founder, The Marquis Moore Foundation

I got it. I actually got it. Or at least I got an interview. Only a handful of applicants made it this far in the process, and this year I would be one of them. First year tuition to your school of choice. I pulled out my phone and automatically started to text Josh but caught myself before I hit the send button. He didn't know I'd even applied. I shut the window and group texted Ethan and Lane. Immediately happy faces and—*what was that, an avocado emoji?*— came pinging back. The microwave beeped and the alluring scent of processed cheese beckoned strong enough to put the letter down and travel across the kitchen.

The plate burned the tips of my fingers, but I attempted to take a bite anyway and scalded my mouth on piping-hot marinara sauce. I raced back and tossed down the plate before slamming back the entire glass of milk. I needed to get myself together. If the scholarship committee saw the stupid things I'd been doing this week, they'd probably rip up that letter in front of me.

After refilling my glass, I sat down at the table, fighting my pizza craving for at least a few more minutes. *I can't believe I got an interview.*

The kitchen dimmed as the setting sun disappeared behind a cloud. My milk glass cast a long, solid shadow across the table, and I shivered as the room dropped in temperature. I glanced out the patio door into the backyard. The tops of the trees swayed over the upper edge of the fence. Long wooden fingers gesturing for me to come closer. Coaxing.

I rose from the table and gazed out the glass. My limbs drooped as an invisible weight pinned them down. The same presence as before. The same stare watching me. I snapped the blinds closed and walked away.

EIGHT

Today needed to be a better day. My head still bobbed in my ocean of exhaustion, which seemed to get wider and wider every day, but at least I'd somewhat learned to function in my half-asleep haze. It didn't make sense. Again, I'd gone to bed at a reasonable time, and again, I woke up like I'd never slept a wink. Except this morning nothing seemed out of the ordinary.

As soon as my alarm buzzed, I threw back the sheets and headed to the mirror. I examined my skin. No new marks, just yesterday's bruises already starting to yellow and fade. Everything seemed to be where I had left it the night before, and the line of scotch tape line that I'd stretched across my bedroom door remained intact. My paranoia successfully defused.

Josh texted on my way to school, confirming our lunch date, so I went straight to class. I didn't need Lane and her inquisition about this, especially since it would all be over soon. She was right, and I hated that. But I needed to tell him and accept whatever consequences came with it. Maybe then I'd feel some relief.

I pulled out the *Macbeth* book and tried to make sense of the words on the page, but nothing seemed to click. Maybe my brain functioned too logically to comprehend this artsy stuff? The noise in the room turned up as everyone else started filing in. Ethan appeared in the doorway and smiled.

"Getting a head start? I told you it wasn't that bad of a story," he said as he made his way to his desk.

"Not sure about that, but my GPA can't take a failing grade in English."

He pumped his fist in the air. "Ah, but screw your courage to the sticking place, and we'll not fail."

I gave him a sideways glance and eased away from his desk. "What does that even mean?"

"It's Lady Macbeth. Act 1, scene 7. Never mind. You are in trouble, aren't you?"

I nodded.

"Well, I guess it's a good thing that you are staying in tonight to study, isn't it?"

"Yikes. You sound like my dad." I tossed the book on my desk. "Just a hint, you aren't going to impress the ladies that way. Unless you have a thing for girls with daddy issues."

Ethan blushed.

Dammit. I promised Lane I wouldn't mess with him, even though it was ridiculous to think that he liked me that way anyway. Ethan needed a certain type of girl. Someone smart and sweet and a little shy. He deserved that. A girl he could fall head over heels in love with. Someone who could make him obnoxiously happy. Guys like Ethan deserved that perfect love. Unfortunately, not a whole lot of girls at our school matched that description. Maybe in college, he might have more luck. I swallowed hard. Next year. I hadn't thought about the fact that he would likely go somewhere else too. I'd miss him.

He waved his hand in front of my face. "Earth to Berkley. Where are you?"

"Sorry." I snapped back out of my own head. "I was just thinking about something Lane said to me yesterday."

"That's fine, but I think you might have creeped out Patrick back there with your vacant staring." He laughed and started to get his books ready for class.

I spun around and leaned my back against my desk. "Are you still coming over tonight?"

"Wouldn't miss it. Besides, who else is going to help you pass English?"

Lane's voice rang in my head. *He's always offering to help you.*

"You don't have to help me, you know. Only if you really want to."

"I know that. But I do want to. If you fail, then I'll have to explain it to you twice." He laughed. "It's self-preservation, really."

"Okay then." *See, Lane, it's nothing. Just being friendly.*

"Besides, I have to start work on a history term paper. It'll give me an excuse to get ahead."

The door clicked shut, and I swiveled forward in my desk. I pulled out my notebook, determined to concentrate and nail this whole nasty Shakespeare experience.

"All right, class. Let's get back to it." Mrs. Franklin clacked across the floor and leaned against her desk at the front of the room. She slid the cuffs of her yellow cardigan up to her forearms and grabbed a copy of the play.

As she flipped through the pages, trying to find where we left off, I unzipped the front pouch of my backpack and reached inside for a pen. My hand grazed the pocket liner, and a cool dampness brushed my skin. I jerked my hand out. Sticky red goo covered my fingertips. My heart thumped harder until I couldn't hear anything but its beat. *What the hell?*

I peeked into the bag. A furry ball of blood-matted brown fur sat on top of my pencils. I screamed and chucked the bag off my desk. It smashed down, exploding my school supplies three feet in every direction. The hairball rolled out and slid across the floor, leaving a red trail of blood behind it on the beige linoleum.

"Berkley," Mrs. Franklin snapped as her eyes followed the bloody line from my desk to hers. "What is the meaning of this?"

I trembled and stared at my red-tipped fingers, her shrill voice cutting through the thump of my racing pulse. "Uh ... uh, I don't know."

Everyone in a two-desk radius jumped up from their seats.

"It's just a dead mouse," Daniel Sawyer called from the back of the room. He shook his head as he passed, then balanced the carcass on two pencils and deposited it in the trash can at the front of the room.

"Disgusting." Lowering her glasses to the end of her nose, Mrs. Franklin watched as Daniel dropped it in the black trash bag.

The class erupted into chatter, but I couldn't look away from the blood on my fingers.

"Enough, everyone." Mrs. Franklin cleared her throat. "I said, enough. Berkley, collect your things and go wash your hands. Also, go see the nurse. I don't want you getting rabies or something like that. Ethan, can you please let the janitor know to clean up the floor?"

Dazed, I stood up and headed for the door. My arms and legs shook. How did that thing even get in there?

Out in the hallway, I collapsed against the wall and stared at the white-tiled drop ceiling. The loud murmurs and gossip sounded muffled on the other side of the closed door. My breath came fast and short, my heart still pumping too quick to be healthy. It was just a mouse. Nothing to be afraid of. But what was it doing in there?

The door creaked open again, and Ethan emerged, holding my book bag out in front of him. He spied me standing beside the door and jumped. He splayed his open hand on his chest and exhaled.

"You forgot this," he said, holding the bag toward me.

I grabbed the top of the bag by the handle, trying to keep it as far away from my clothes and stained fingers as possible. "I'm not sure I want it anymore."

"Why did you have a mouse in there? Science lab sending out dissection homework or something?"

He laughed. I didn't. He stopped.

"Or maybe he just crawled in and couldn't get back out or something?"

I thought through his solutions, but they made even less sense than the ones I'd come up with in my head. "The bag is made of cheap canvas. He could have chewed his way out through that."

"Well, you can sit there and rationalize my suggestions away or you can go get that dead rodent blood off your hands."

I shuddered, still staring at the bag.

"Give me that," he said, snatching it away from me. "You go clean up and get your rabies checked, and I'll salvage what I can from your bag and toss the rest. Okay?"

"Thanks, Ethan."

"Of course." He paused. Just for a moment, but long enough for his light-hearted grin to melt away and something else to take command of his expression. Whatever it was eclipsed in his eyes, draping out the last bit of sun into laser-sharp seriousness. His mouth opened then shut again as he grabbed the back of his neck with his free hand and looked away. "Just go, deal with all that."

I nodded as a strange calm took over my limbs. A heavy energy settled over us, like an ultra-soft duvet. Wrapping me in comfort and keeping the bad things out. Shielding me.

"Ethan." I shook my head, and the words forming on my tongue scattered in the silence. With a loud sigh, I started to walk toward the office. "And I wouldn't get rabies from this. The virus transfers through the exchange of the infected animal's saliva, not blood."

"Whatever, science geek. Go." He shooed me away with his hand and headed the opposite way down the hall.

"I'M PRETTY sure you're going to be just fine," Ms. Hendricks, the school nurse, said as she doused my hands in rubbing alcohol and enough antibacterial lotion to sterilize a landfill. "But if you have any strange symptoms or start running a fever, go straight to the hospital, okay?"

I nodded and stared at my clean hands. Even after all the washing, they still seemed dirty. As if the blood left an invisible stickiness I'd never be able to wipe off.

"If you'd like, I can give you a few minutes to settle down before you head back to class. First period is almost over anyway."

"Thanks. I'd like that." I clasped my hands together and hid them between my thighs. From her or me, I wasn't sure.

Ms. Hendricks nodded and disappeared into the hallway, leaving the door slightly ajar.

None of this made any sense. The only way a mouse wouldn't have tried to escape a confined space would be if it was already dead or it died in the bag. If the mouse died from suffocation, there wouldn't be any blood, at least not that much. Did someone think it would be funny and put it in my bag as a prank? *Gross.* But that didn't make sense either. I'd gone straight to class, and the mouse wasn't in there last night. My stomach twisted, and for the first time in days not from hunger, as a dark idea swirled in my brain. What had I been missing over the last few days?

Nine

"I thought we were going to talk," I said, only partly serious, trying my best to get back in control.

My eyes closed as Josh's lips kissed up the side of my neck. Slow. Painfully and maliciously slow. His warm breath tickled along my earlobe in deep, haggard gasps that made my heart pound with the same frenetic pace.

The mouse incident clouded my brain all morning until I arrived at my locker for lunch, with Josh leaning next to it. His dangerous smile drew me in as my resolve to tell him about my Princeton dreams wavered even more. But I couldn't hold off any longer. The stress had clearly messed with my head, and I needed to think straight again. To be me again.

"*You* said you wanted to talk," he whispered. "I didn't actually tell you what I wanted to do."

He pulled his knee up onto the seat of the car and put his arm around my back, bringing me closer. It didn't take long for me to fall into the easy rhythm of his kisses. His lips blended the perfect mix of sweet and strong. He pushed the tip of his tongue into my mouth, and I knitted my fingers in the hair at the nape of his neck, my other hand grabbing onto his bicep. He pulled me tighter, and the muscles of his arm flexed under my fingertips. All those nights of football practice had served him well. He moved to sit straight again, and I yelped as he seamlessly yanked me onto his lap. I caught his eyes flick open and saw raw desire, much more intense than our actions permitted.

"I can't wait," he said in the small spaces between kisses. "Next year I can spend every day with you like this."

I froze. He kept pressing at my lips, but I couldn't get my brain and my body to function together.

Josh stopped and sat back against the upholstery. "What's the matter?"

Now or never. Although, "never" did seem like a great alternative. "That's what I need to talk to you about."

He slid his fingers through my hair and rested his palms against the sides of my face. "Are you sure you want to talk about this now? Or can we talk later?" He smiled with a delicious hint of mischief and moved forward to kiss me again.

I sat up. "Yes. I need to do this now."

His face drained of color as his hands flopped down by his sides. My skin cooled at the absence of his touch.

"I've applied to Princeton."

His nose scrunched up as he processed my sudden confession. "Princeton? Is that out east?"

I nodded. "I know it's not what you were thinking, but they have a really great program that I want to get into."

"What about all that talk about us being together next year?" He rubbed his face with his hands. "I've been busting my ass trying to get a spot on the Texas State team, and you said you would be there with me. Getting out of this town. Us. Together."

"I know, but it's an Ivy League school, Josh. I met with the principal and the guidance counselor, and they think with my grades, I stand a solid chance. And there is this scholarship that I have a chance for that will pay for most of my first year."

The lustful look in his eyes faded to confusion. "Wait. How long have you been making these arrangements? When were you planning on telling me?"

"I'm telling you now." I leaned back, trying to give him more space, and smashed my shoulder blade into the driver's seat. "I've been trying to tell you for a while, but I haven't been able to find the right time."

"And making out with me in the back of my car with no one around was a perfect time?"

"No, I wasn't planning for that to happen."

He flopped his head back and stared at the roof. "You never are."

"What is that supposed to mean?"

Josh grabbed my waist and dropped me down on the seat beside him. "You know exactly what I'm saying. You haven't been the most affectionate lately, if you get what I mean."

"Are you seriously getting pissed at me because I stopped sleeping with you?"

"That would be awesome, but I'm not getting my hopes up anymore. I'd be happy with a kiss I didn't have to initiate. You won't do anything with me anymore."

He banged his head against the car seat, and dust motes drifted around in the sunlight. I watched them, silently trying to figure out what to say, but words wouldn't come.

He rubbed his forehead, then grabbed the bridge of his nose while he squeezed his eyes closed. "What did I do wrong?"

"Nothing." I sighed and stared out the window. Leaves fluttered down around the car. Beautiful colors. Romantic, even. A total waste. "I've just been dealing with a lot of stuff."

"I can see that. Lots of stuff that you haven't bothered to tell me about. I'm supposed to be your boyfriend, Berk. You should be able to talk to me."

"I know, but you have all your football stuff going on and the scout coming. I didn't want you to have to deal with it right now. Besides, I hardly ever see you, since you are always with your guy friends. It's not like I'm going to be all over you if I haven't seen you."

"And why not? No one else's girlfriend seems to have a problem with it."

Excuse me? The temperature in the car dropped a thousand degrees, and my hands shook. "You didn't just say that. What have you been telling your friends about me, Josh?"

"Nothing. I just hear what the other guys are saying, and it's a lot less junior high than what we have going on."

I grabbed the handle and tried to open the door, but it wouldn't budge. Josh leaned over and clicked the lock up to let me out.

"I can't believe you would say that to me," I shouted back through the open door.

"I can't believe you hadn't already figured it out. We used to be all over each other. You couldn't wait to see me. Then all of a sudden you just stopped, and I've been doing everything I can not to be the jerk who asks."

"Well ..." I crossed my arms and jutted my hip to the side. He made sense, but I didn't care. Not right now. Not like this. "You're being a jerk now."

A low growl emitted from his throat as he tossed his head back again. "No. I'm just trying to be honest, like you haven't been with me. Maybe they'll teach you how at your fancy-ass Ivy League school." He slammed the door closed and sat in the back seat of the car with his head in his hands.

I stared at him through the window for a few minutes. How dare he? Maybe if he'd told me before, we could have avoided this mess? My cheeks burned. Wait. Maybe if I'd told *him* earlier, it wouldn't have come to this. When I reached for the door handle, he didn't move. I paused ... one second ... two seconds ... then retracted my hand again. *Forget it.*

That wasn't how I'd pictured our conversation going down. Not once in the million times I'd run it over in my head. Sure, he would be mad. I'd expected that. But I didn't expect that the whole thing would turn around on me. That was definitely not part of the plan. A hollowness grew in my stomach, but I pushed it down and marched across the parking lot, heading back toward campus. The warm sun prickled my skin and fueled my stride as I pounded down the pavement, pumping rage through my limbs. After a few blocks, Josh's blue Charger streaked by me and skidded into the school parking lot. Stopping to cross my arms and stare, I watched him barrel into his parking space and strut into the school.

Ugh. Did he even care about what happened?

But the longer I stood watching, the more the anger subsided and let the truth seep into my brain. He was right. One hundred percent. I had pulled away from him—probably months ago. He didn't have to be so mean about it, though. I gripped my head in my hands and stared at the cracked sidewalk. What was wrong with me? I should be the luckiest girl in town. After all, I was the all-American cliché—dating the high school quarterback. The drop-dead-sexy, muscles-carved-from-marble quarterback with a future as bright as the midday sun. And he wanted to be with me.

Things were better before. We'd been inseparable. But then everything got so complicated in my life, and he started making plans I didn't feel I could say no to without losing him. And it's not that I didn't want him back. Every time I saw him, I wanted to rush over and wrap myself in his arms and disappear, but when it came to being alone with him, I choked. So he would prattle on about his team, and I would nod and smile, and then we'd kiss politely, and both walk away unsatisfied.

The school bell echoed on the crisp air. I gasped as the weight of everything pressed down on my chest, my breath short and labored. How come I never realized this before? I'd really screwed everything up.

TEN

"**B**efore you even consider touching me, are you rabies-free?"
Lane asked, making the sign of the cross with her fingers.

I shook my head and opened the front door wider to let her in,
even though I kind of wanted to slam it on her instead. "I do not
have rabies. It doesn't work that way. Why don't people get this?"

Ethan chuckled and followed in behind her, carrying the chilly
night breeze with him. "Told you, Lane, she's touchy about her
rabies."

I scowled at Lane as I closed the front door. She chuckled
and patted me on the shoulder as she led Ethan toward the back
of the house. I shook my head and followed them into the
kitchen.

Lane placed her books on the table and took her favorite spot
near the patio door. She sat down and pulled her feet onto the seat
of the chair. "Do you think it's safe being in here with all the mice
running around?"

"It was probably a field mouse that got in through the garage or
something. Besides, now it's in a trash bag casket in the dumpster
behind the school. I think you're safe." At least that's what I'd
convinced myself had happened. Any other explanation asked too
many questions I didn't want the answers to. "Anybody want
anything? Chips? Pop?"

"I'm okay," Ethan said as he took the spot across the table from
Lane.

"Just water for me," Lane said.

I opened the refrigerator door and pulled out two bottles of water. "Really? You're the reason I made sure we had cola in the house."

"Superior athlete diet, remember?" She flexed her left arm and kissed her imaginary bulging bicep.

Ethan tossed his head back and laughed. "Oh yeah, the one you told me about right before you scarfed a bag of M&M's."

She shrugged. "Don't knock it until you've tried it."

"Maybe some other time," I said, as I dumped the bottles into drinking glasses and returned to the table. As I settled in my seat, I turned to Lane. "Okay, so what did you want me to help you with?"

"She needs more help than you are qualified for." Ethan chuckled without looking up from his history book.

"Nasty." Lane launched her pencil across the table and hit him right in the shoulder.

"Ow ... that didn't hurt at all." He tossed the pencil back, and it landed in her lap. As he reached down into his pocket, he frowned. He patted his other leg then dug through his backpack. The frown deepened. "I'll be right back. I forgot my phone in the car. Might need to call the police if Lane keeps assaulting me."

She stuck her tongue out at him as he walked by, and he lurched toward her and barked.

Sighing, I shook my head. "It's like babysitting."

"Whatever. We're just having a little fun. What has you more uptight than usual?"

I picked at the coil of my notebook, carefully concentrating on sliding my fingertip over every metal loop. "I told Josh about Princeton today."

"Finally," she said, rolling her eyes. "How did he take it?"

"I'm not really sure. We ended up having a massive fight, but I'm not sure if it was because of that or everything else."

"What else did he have a problem with?"

I put my elbows on the table and rested my forehead in my hands, the whole scene flashing through my head and bringing back all the awful feelings I'd been trying to push down all after-noon. "I'm not sure I want to talk about it."

"And why the hell not? I know you, Berk. It will sit there and poke at you until you end up going crazy and telling me about it anyway. Might as well save us both the time and spill."

She was right. I hated when she was right. "Fine. He was upset because we hadn't been spending too much 'quality time' together lately."

"You sound like a middle-aged woman." Lane cackled and pounded her fist on the table. "Be direct. Josh is pissed because you aren't putting out."

Ugh. It sounded so awful. "I like my explanation better."

"I'm sure you would. It sounds less like it's your fault."

"No, my version doesn't sound so crass." I slumped closer to the table top, my shoulders deflating even more at Lane's mocking. "Besides, I know it's my fault."

"And why do you think that is?"

"I don't know. Maybe because I've been so scared to tell him about Princeton that I kind of cut him out altogether."

She put her head on the table close to mine so I couldn't hide anymore. Her jade eyes sparkled with sympathy, even though her tongue cut deep. "You mean cut him off altogether?"

"Whatever." I tilted my face closer to hers and finally let the reality sink in. "I don't know what's the matter with me. I mean, I should be happy. Shouldn't I?"

"Look, do you want to know what I think?" Lane brushed my hair down the side of my face. "Sometimes these things just happen. I mean, Josh is a good guy. He's nice, friendly, looks hot in a tight T-shirt, and can throw a long bomb with the best of them, but maybe he's not the one for you anymore. People change, Berk."

I blinked to fight the awkward tears threatening to fall. "I wish they didn't."

"Said the girl who just tossed a poison-laden monkey wrench into her BF's life plan. It's going to be okay. You'll see."

"I owe you one for this, don't I? Telling it to me straight, even if I don't want to hear what I need to."

Lane smiled and tapped my cheek. "You sure do, but I know you'll pay up. Besides, let's call it even for your support sessions when Owen Karkenhoff broke up with me last year."

She gagged as Owen's name fell off her tongue, and I shuddered remembering the drama that boy caused. So much trouble.

"I just feel like it's my fault. I know I should have told him about Princeton, but he was so pumped about Texas State that I couldn't bring myself to disappoint him. I didn't want to hurt him."

Lane shrugged. "I don't know what to tell you. I think the first thing you need to figure out is why you chose Princeton in the first place."

"It's Ivy League, Lane."

"Oh, I get that. But when Josh came up with this idea of you running off to Texas, why didn't you tell him then? And when you were doing all these interviews and things, you didn't happen to mention it. It seems a little odd that you kept something so big in your life from him."

I closed my eyes, and the memories flitted around in circles like a carousel of bad choices. I had kept it from him. I'd done everything to keep him from finding out. And why, so I didn't have to explain that I wasn't sure that he saw me for who I was anymore, instead of just the sophomore with zero life plan? Such a coward. "He wouldn't understand."

"How do you know that? You never gave him a chance to."

Ouch. The truth stung. I banged my forehead on the table. "You're right, Lane. I've been a bad girlfriend."

"No, you're not a bad girlfriend. You just want different things, and you fear what that means. You two used to be a super couple. It was so bloody cute it made me gag every time I saw you. But when was the last time you spent any time alone with him?"

I raised my head to speak.

"And in the backseat of his car at lunch does not count."

I stopped short and tried to think. Honestly, I couldn't remember. Was I that horrible of a person?

"See. Somewhere along the way you and Josh found other interests."

"Well, what exactly are you guys studying?" Ethan appeared in the doorway to the kitchen, his eyes wide, watching us.

Lane sat up straight in her chair. "Chemistry, silly. But I think Berkley is learning a lot more than I am."

·⁺·★⁺ (·★⁺·.

I READ the same sentence about twelve times, and it still didn't make any sense. Lane scribbled formulas in her notebook, the tip of her tongue sticking just past her lips as she concentrated on her writing. If she kept this up, she might actually pass. Ethan tapped his pencil on his textbook, his eyes flitting back and forth as he read each paragraph and moved down the page. It would be rude to interrupt him, but he said he'd help. I opened my mouth to speak, but a creak echoed from the front hall instead.

"Hi, Mr. James," Lane said as Dad walked into the kitchen.

Dad stumbled a step as his head jerked back, likely not expecting guests. His bloodshot eyes narrowed as a crooked grin graced his chapped lips. "Nice to see you, Lane. Ethan, how's it going? Still playing baseball?"

"Well, we're done for the season now, but I'm sure I will play again next spring." He looked at me, confused.

"Right, right, it's football season now. Speaking of, where's Josh?" He sauntered over to the counter and removed a tall glass from the cupboard.

"Josh had practice tonight," I replied, watching him as he pulled out a bottle of vodka and half-filled his cup. I glared at Lane, and she shrugged.

"Then why aren't you all out cheering him on? Show him some

support." He took a large gulp then closed his eyes as he swallowed.

Wow, he isn't even watering it down anymore.

"I have work to do. We can do things apart, you know." I held up my textbook, strategically waving it across Lane's eyeline to my father.

"Beginning of the end." He shook his head and refilled the glass before walking toward the living room. "Don't work too hard. Go out and have some fun while you're still young."

"Yikes," Lane mouthed to me once she heard the TV volume increase in the other room. "Is he always so philosophical?"

"No, that's a fun new trick." Staring down at my notebook, I tried to read what I had written, but it was pointless. I ripped out the page, crumpled it up, and tossed it into the middle of the table.

Ethan looked at me, then Lane, then back again. "Did you need some help with something?"

"Sure." I rubbed my hands over my face. "I don't get this Shakespeare stuff. The words are total nonsense."

"I'll bet you understand it more than you know. You just need to think it through. Concentrate a little," Ethan said with a wary smile.

Right, concentrate. How could I do that with my father drinking himself into oblivion in the next room?

Ethan slid his chair closer to mine, and I saw Lane smirk in my periphery. I scowled at her.

He bent over my textbook. The heat of his body close to mine prickled along my skin. "What part are you working on?"

I cleared my throat. "Me thought I heard a voice cry 'Sleep no more! Macbeth does murder sleep,' the innocent sleep. Sleep that knits up the ravell'd sleave of care. The death of each day's life, sore labour's bath. Balm of hurt minds. Great nature's second course. Chief nourisher in life's feast."

He glanced up toward the ceiling as he seemed to process the passage I'd butchered. "Okay. So, what do you think it means?"

"I have no idea." I sank my head into my arms. "All this talk of sleep is exhausting. I wish I could get some rest one of these days."

Ethan leaned closer and nudged his shoulder into mine. My head flopped over on his shoulder. I rested there for a second, then realized what I'd done and shot straight up again. Ethan gazed over and smiled while Lane's jaw dropped to her chest. *Get it together, Berkley.*

"Kind of. Macbeth can't sleep either because he feels guilty. He's saying that he thinks he will never go to sleep again."

I rubbed my hand over my face as my eyes drifted shut for a second. *Sleep would be nice.* "I understand how that feels. But I don't need all these crazy words to say it."

"No, you just whine," Lane added.

"Sorry, guys, it's just been a rough few days."

"It's okay. I'm kind of scienced out anyway." Lane shut her book and stretched her arms over her head. She nodded at Ethan. "Ready to get going, professor?"

He glanced down at me, and I nodded.

Tilting his head to the side, he waited a few seconds, watching. Maybe waiting to see if I'd change my mind. But after my dad's show, I kind of wanted to be alone.

After several achingly long seconds, he blinked and broke his silent interrogation. "Sure."

They packed their things and headed for the door. I followed, lingering in front of the opening to the living room from the hall.

"I can try to help you with that English stuff tomorrow, if you want? I have a spare in the afternoon. Or maybe I could come by after school?" Ethan flashed a sympathetic smile as he shrugged his jacket on over his broad shoulders.

I nodded. "That would be great. But maybe we could meet at the library or something?"

"She can't," Lane interrupted. "Volleyball practice tomorrow, remember?"

I smacked myself in the forehead. "Shoot, I forgot."

"Yeah, looked like your head was somewhere else." Lane smirked. "I'll be right there, Ethan. Can I just talk to my girl for a second?"

"Sure. See you, Berkley." He headed out the door and disappeared down the driveway. His car alarm beeped somewhere out in the shadows.

Lane stepped onto the front step and grabbed my hand, ushering me outside. I pulled the door shut and crossed my arms close to my chest. The fall air nipped at my cheeks.

Lane stared out into the night until Ethan's door thunked closed. She sighed, her breath swirling in soft clouds from her lips. "Are you going to be okay, Berk?"

"Yeah. I'm just tired." The words coaxed a yawn, and I covered it with the back of my hand. "Besides, Ethan said he'll help me with English tomorrow. No worries."

"Stop it." Lane put her hands on her hips and glared. "You can't lie to me. You look like a complete wreck. And we didn't finish talking about Josh. Plus, it's not like you to struggle this much with schoolwork"—she leaned in closer—"and your dad looks like he's fallen off the rails."

"I'm dealing, I guess. Josh and I are at a stalemate until we talk again, and he'll be out of town for the game, so I probably won't hear from him until the weekend. And the school thing is just that I can't seem to concentrate."

"And?" Lane nodded toward the living room window.

The last bit of life drained from my limbs as my head dropped to my chest. "I don't know what to do about him anymore. I think it's getting worse."

She rested her head on my shoulder and hugged me tight. "If you ever need anything, you know you can just ask me, right?"

I drifted into the smell of her apple shampoo, letting the familiar sensation numb the uncomfortable ones. "Of course, but it's not fair for me to come to you with my crap all the time."

"I'm your best friend. That's what I'm here for. Besides, I have tons of stuff I need to make up to you from over the years."

"Thanks," I said, as she finally let me go. "But you don't need to."

"I know." She gave a soft half-smile, then brushed her hands along the arms of her coat. "Hopefully, I don't have rabies now."

"Go home." I laughed, and pushed her toward the front walk.

She teetered down the steps and jogged into the hazy glare of Ethan's headlights.

I took a deep breath as the car drove up the street and disappeared around the corner. As I leaned against the wooden door, the low rumble of the engine faded in the distance, replaced with the faint whistle of the wind through the treetops. Nothing dared to move. The night's stillness blanketed over the world as if it understood that, for even just a moment, I needed the calm. I glanced up at the small sliver of moonlight peeking behind a thick, dark cloud. My silent confidante. Giving me my space, but still watching. Always watching.

Just like Lane. Even though I thought I'd played it down, I guess things looked as awful as they seemed. I understood she wanted to help, but I had no idea how. If I did, maybe I could help myself. Everything felt so impossibly hard. And I was just so exhausted.

Goosebumps pebbled along my skin, and I retreated into the house. The television roared in the living room with what sounded like a hockey game, the distinctive sound of the announcer blasting in my ears. I cringed as each excited cheer smashed against my eardrums. Sometimes I wanted to march in there and throw the stupid thing out the window.

I went back to the kitchen and tried to read *Macbeth* again. Sleep no more. How appropriate. But if his insomnia stemmed from guilt, what did that make of me? I didn't feel guilty—at least I didn't think so—and I sure hadn't killed anyone. At least that I was aware of. I shuddered at the memory of the mangled mouse in my bag during English. Could I have had anything to do with that? No way. Not possible.

Dad stumbled back into the kitchen, his glass empty, and his red face puffy. "Your friends gone?"

"Yeah. They'd had enough for the night."

He glanced at his watch, pulling it closer and farther from his face as he focused. "It's only nine o'clock, Berkley. You're a teenager, you should be out living it up. Not sitting at home poring over those books."

"I need to do this. I want to get into a good school next year." *And get out of this house.* "I can't risk failing anything."

"You won't fail." He pulled a bottle of rum out from the cupboard, and it clanked against the countertop.

Great, he's mixing tonight.

"I'm not so sure," I muttered as I tapped my pen against my notebook.

"Of course you won't. Your mom, she was so smart. I'm sure you picked up her genes."

I trembled. This was the first time he'd referenced her in months. It either meant that things were getting better, or much, much worse.

The mouth of the rum bottle clinked against his empty glass.

I stared at my notebook and swallowed. "Are you sure you should have any more this late in the evening?"

He glared at me and kept pouring, a little more than normal. Likely for spite.

"I mean, you haven't been feeling so great lately, maybe you could slow it down a bit."

"I don't think it's any of your business what I do, young lady. I'm the adult here, I decide what is right for me. Got it?" He dropped the bottle back down to the counter, and I jumped at the smacking sound.

It added to the pile of things pressing on my nerves. Every little thing building like another marble tossed in an already overfilled jar. The rancid smell of stale liquor. The harsh tone of his slurred voice. The collection of broken promises and necessary lies as his life turned south and kept racing downward. My tired brain popped into overdrive.

"No, I don't 'got' it." I slapped my open hand on the table as I rose to my feet. "I'm worried about you. Ever since she left, all you have done is sit around this house and drink. It's not healthy."

He stared at me aghast, as though I'd hurled my textbook at him instead of just words. "It's been hard without her around, and sometimes I need a little help to relax. Stop trying to be such a smart ass."

"Don't you think it's been hard on me too?" I swung my arm in the air, my limbs acting on their own. "Don't you think I miss her?"

"Miss her?" He jerked his head back as his face screwed up into a harsh scowl. "She left us. She walked out that door and never looked back, leaving me to pick up the pieces and take care of you. No, I don't miss her. I hate her, and you should too."

"You don't mean that." Dad blurred into a haze as my tears welled, but I refused to let them fall and give him the satisfaction. "You're just drunk and angry."

"And you're a know-it-all. Maybe you take after her more than I thought."

I sat back down, unsure of what to say. He'd never truly listen. Not in his current state anyway.

"That's right, hide your head in your books. Walk away from your problems."

I couldn't hold it in any longer. The teardrops splattered onto my notebook, spreading the blue ink into cloudy starbursts.

"Hey, hey, don't cry. I didn't mean it." His voice softened, and he let out an exasperated sigh. But I wouldn't look up. Not like this. His footsteps lumbered across the linoleum floor to the far end of the table as his shadow darkened over my head.

"I'm sorry. You picked at me, and I guess I got worked up. I do the best I can around here, you know, but sometimes it feels like it's never enough."

"Just go watch the game," I said, between sobs.

He rubbed his forehead with his hand and stood motionless across from me. Minutes passed, and I refused to look up. He withdrew to the living room.

I pulled my hand into my sleeve and tried to dry my eyes, but the tears came too fast. Grabbing my books, I headed up to my room then fell onto the bed.

Why did he have to be such a jerk? He never used to be this way. Before she left, he was one of the best people you could meet. He was warm, caring, considerate, everything a little girl would want or need from her father. Then she left, and he changed. He was a bitter man now. She had broken him in ways that I couldn't understand, or maybe he was letting the real him shine through, and Mom had kept him in check all these years.

But I knew the true cause. His new friend alcohol spoke for him. I knew people worried about him. They would see me at the store or on the street and ask about him, then give me that sad face like he had been the one who left. But all of that wouldn't matter much longer. I was going to get into Princeton, or wherever, and get the hell out of this town, out of this house, and out of this life.

ELEVEN

Beep. Beep. Beep.

Morning already? Why did it feel like I'd just gone to bed? I slammed my hand down on my nightstand as I reached for my phone.

Owww!

Pain surged up my arm, wave after wave. I yanked my hand back and cradled it next to my chest while I tossed aside the blankets and slithered into a sitting position. Holding out my throbbing hand, I gasped. Beads of fresh blood pooled from a jagged gash that sliced across my palm.

I scrambled to my feet and backed against the wall, staring at my hand. *What the hell?* I grabbed my head. Burnt-sienna-colored flakes drifted onto my arm. I forced my eyes to look up, and I screamed. Smears of dark blood streaked across my bedsheets. The pillows. The duvet. All painted red.

Falling to the floor, I scanned the room. Two eyes stared at me from the closet. I screamed again and cowered back, but I had nowhere to run. Sweat broke from my brow and trickled down my cheek. I stared harder, and the eyes stared back.

My eyes. My own reflection in the mirror, but I barely recognized it. Matted hair clung to the head of the other me, and everything about her was covered in blood; her face, her pajamas, even the skin on her arms. I rubbed my flesh with my healthy hand, but it flaked off and fluttered to the carpet. *What happened to me?*

I tried to think, but I couldn't focus my thoughts. Clearly, I'd done this to myself. It had to be. Maybe I'd cut my palm last night and didn't notice? Rubbed a sharp corner on my bed frame or against the edge of the nightstand, and I'd been too exhausted to feel the pain? That had to be it. What other explanation could there be?

I glanced around the room as my heart banged against my ribs. Pounding harder and harder each second that the reality of this massacre settled in. My chest ached. I might pass out. With my good hand, I ripped the sheets off my bed and rolled them into a ball on the floor to make the panic subside. More bloodstained clothes lay in a pile in the corner. Almost hidden. I gasped and held my hand over my mouth so I didn't scream again. *I hope all this blood is mine.*

I peeked out the door down the hall, but nothing moved. No sound. Even after all my screaming. Dad must be good and passed out. Tiptoeing into the bathroom, I stripped off my pajamas and turned on the shower. I bit my lip to keep from yelling as the hot water hit the cut on my hand. The blood tinged the water flowing into the drain a bright crimson, like a murder scene of a horror movie. When it finally ran clear, I turned off the water and wiped the fog from the bathroom mirror to inspect the rest of me for any remaining red stains. All clear. I fumbled under the bathroom cabinet and found a roll of gauze as well as some medical tape. I wrapped my hand over and over then struggled to tape it down with my left hand.

Much better. Out of sight, out of mind. Then I collapsed on the toilet seat as the cold porcelain tank dug into my naked back.

Inhale. Exhale. Inhale. Exhale.

It did little to stop the tilt-a-whirl of thoughts racing through my brain, but it slowed my pulse and my breathing enough to stand. I searched for every explanation, but they all came back to the same place. What had I done?

I snuck back into my room and slipped on some clothes before flipping through my phone. No texts sent or received. No incriminating photos. Nothing except for the stripe of dried red across the screen from when I'd shut off the alarm. My body deflated. I opened the phone again and dialed Lane.

A muffled yell came from outside my door. I clicked off the phone and ran into the hallway.

"Berkley," my father yelled from the kitchen. "Berkley!"

I sped up, the air plunging colder and colder as I descended the stairs.

"What?" I yelled back, barging into the kitchen, then stopped short.

All the cupboard doors lay wide open, and various colors of smashed glass shards were scattered across the floor. The kitchen chairs were flung to different corners of the room, and the patio door swung wide open in the wind.

Dad crouched in the middle of the mess, still in his jacket and the same clothes from the night before.

Gasping, I backed out of the room. "What happened?"

"Thank God, you're safe," Dad said as he rushed over and pulled me into a hug, his day-old whiskers scratching against my forehead.

"I'm fine, but what's going on?" I mumbled into his shoulder.

"Someone broke into the house last night." He released me and looked back at the mess. "I just got home, and the front door was open. The living room is destroyed too."

I tiptoed around the shattered glass and shut the patio door, hugging myself to keep warm against the fall chill. "Did they take anything?"

"I'm not sure. The car is gone." He grabbed one of the askew chairs and set it back at the table. "I had hoped you had just taken it early this morning, but I guess not."

With the door closed, my nostrils burned as the stench of alcohol filled the room.

"I'll get a broom," I said, skulking into the hallway, hoping for some fresher air.

The open closet door hid me from the kitchen, and I slapped

my hand over my face. Did I do this? I looked at my sliced hand, and my stomach turned. There was no way that I could not have heard that amount of noise right beneath me. And why the smashed liquor bottles? If this had been a break-in, thieves would probably have just stolen the booze. Warm saliva built up in the back of my throat, and I swallowed hard. Shaking my head, I reached for the broom. On the left side of the closet sat the red fire extinguisher. My mind flashed to the night in the woods, and I knelt to inspect it. The safety pin dangled from a chain down the side instead of blocking the trigger as it should. A thin, dry froth covered the end of the nozzle. This canister had definitely been used. I squealed and smacked my hand over my mouth to smother the noise. Was this really happening?

"Don't touch anything yet," Dad called from the kitchen. "The police are on their way."

I grabbed the broom, slammed the closet door, and rushed back into the kitchen. After propping the broom against the wall, I disappeared into the living room. The glass top of the coffee table sat spidered with the remnants of a broken vase sticking out of it. The couch lay flipped over, and someone had rammed the armchair into the wall, leaving a large hole in the drywall.

The cut on my hand twinged. Maybe it remembered being here, but I couldn't. Except it had to be an actual break-in. I wouldn't have done this to my own home. *Would I?*

I crept around the pile of books strewn across the floor to the fireplace. A broken frame lay on the brick hearth, and my eyes filled with tears. I had hidden this picture behind all the others on the mantel, hoping that Dad wouldn't get rid of it. When Mom left, he'd thrown out anything he could that reminded him of her. But I still needed her, even if he didn't.

The three of us at Disneyland—Dad, Mom, and me—on our trip to California, eight years ago. We all looked so happy, smiling at the camera. Dad looked so young with his dark, wavy hair. And Mom, the only one not facing the camera. She was staring right at Dad. The look of awe on her face, like all she saw was him.

A tear fell and splattered on the broken glass inside the frame. As I clung tight to the picture, the end of the frame dug into my bandaged hand. Blood oozed from my cut again. I yelled and dropped the picture frame on the stone hearth, shattering it further.

Dad rushed into the living room. "What's wrong?"

"It's nothing," I said as I whipped my hands behind my back and tore off the blood-soaked gauze. "I just cut my hand on some broken glass."

He walked closer and inspected my injury. We locked eyes, worry stinging through his stare, then he looked down again. My hand jerked in his, ready for him to expose my lie. Instead, he sighed.

"That's pretty nasty. Maybe you should stay out of here until the police arrive, okay?" He pulled me into another hug as I held out my arm, trying not to bleed on him. "When I finally felt that things were starting to get better, something like this happens. But don't worry, we'll get through it."

"Thanks, Dad."

"Go clean yourself up. I'll call you when they arrive."

I ran upstairs and put my hand under the tap. The hot water stung, but at least it seemed to slow the bleeding. I wrapped a towel around my arm and sat down on the toilet seat, staring blankly at the eggshell-painted wall ahead of me. What had I done? Could I be responsible for this mess? And to make matters worse, now I'd lied to my dad. Sure, it had gotten me out of explaining why I had a gaping hole in my hand, but it gave me an uncomfortable tight feeling in my chest, like someone had put my torso in a vise. Like I couldn't breathe. And what was I going to tell the police? I couldn't lie to them too. Could I?

The thunk of a car door closing came from outside, and I rushed to haphazardly bandage my hand before it started bleeding again. I walked down the stairs slowly. Two officers stood in the kitchen talking with Dad, their hands on their hips, puffing out their regulation police jackets. Dad waved his hands and paced back and forth in the tiny space that didn't have any broken glass. He looked much older from here. The lines on his face etched deeper than I'd ever noticed. His hair gleamed with a slight tinge of gray at the roots. My imaginary torturer tightened the vise another notch, and my breath hitched in my throat.

Dad noticed me watching from the stairwell and rushed over to usher me into the kitchen.

"This is my daughter, Berkley."

"Hello, ma'am," the taller officer said, nodding respectfully. "Your father says you were in the house when the break-in occurred."

I nodded, feeling heat rise up my neck and into my cheeks.

"And he said you didn't hear anything going on downstairs?"

I shook my head, unable to form words.

"Must be a pretty heavy sleeper?" the other, less fit officer commented, looking me over a little too carefully.

"Yeah." I cleared my throat. "I mean yes, I'm a heavy sleeper."

"Could sleep through a tornado, this one," Dad added in my defense, putting his hand on the back of my neck.

"Do you mind if we look around?" the stocky officer asked.

I winced every time their big, black boots crunched across the shards of glass on the linoleum floor. Each step ripping through me, scratching at my conscience.

"And you said only the car was taken?" an officer called from the living room.

"As far as we know."

"Well, Mr. James," the taller, nicer officer said as he came back into the room. "We are sorry for the trouble this has caused you, but if no one saw anyone it will be much more difficult to catch the perpetrator."

Dad rubbed his hands over his face then glared up at the ceiling. "I understand."

"We'll canvass the neighbors and put a watch out for your car, but if you hear or remember anything, or if you find anything missing"—he pulled a business card out of his shirt pocket—"please give us a call."

"We appreciate it, thank you," he said as he walked the officers to the door.

"And you can let your insurance company know that you filed a report, so they can deal with the damages."

The tall officer tipped his hat at me and smiled, while the other lingered a little longer, staring me down. I already didn't like him. I glanced at his badge. Officer Shipley. I'd have to remember that name.

After they left, Dad closed and bolted the front door, then leaned against the wood and let out a giant sigh.

"You should probably get to school, kiddo."

I froze. I couldn't remember the last time he'd called me 'kiddo'.

"It's okay, I can stay and help."

"No, no. I don't want you to get behind at school. Gotta keep that GPA up if you are going to go to a good college next year, right?"

Sober Dad seemed remorseful. Almost reasonable. Maybe we could actually talk. "Honestly, it's alright."

"Let me be the parent for once, okay?" he snapped, his calm demeanor broken like the bottles on the floor.

"Fine." I grabbed my coat and my bag from the front hall then stormed out through the garage.

TWELVE

"'Out, damned spot! Out, I say! One: two: why, then, 'tis time to do't. Hell is murky! Fie, my lord, fie! a soldier, and afeard? What need we fear who knows it, when none can call our power to account?'" Mrs. Franklin held an open copy of *Macbeth* in one hand and swung her open arm wide through the air as she spouted gibberish words at the front of the classroom.

I opened the door slowly to avoid any creaking and crept along the side wall.

"Miss James, how lovely of you to make time for us today," she said, without looking up from her lecture.

"Sorry," I mumbled as I avoided eye contact and dashed to my desk.

Her heels clicked on the linoleum as she walked over to stand in front of me.

"Now," she said with her bright-red lacquered lips as she glared down at me through her wire-rimmed glasses. "What does the blood symbolize in Lady Macbeth's monologue from Act 5, Scene 1?"

"Uh ..." I pulled out my book and flipped through the pages to find the reference.

She sighed loudly as I tried to read the scene. The ornate words not processing in my brain fast enough—or at all.

"Anyone?" she asked, tapping her foot on the floor.

A flutter of movement behind me ruffled the tiny hairs on my neck.

"Yes, Ethan," Mrs. Franklin said.

"The blood symbolizes Lady Macbeth's guilt over the murder of Duncan and Banquo."

"Very good." With a contented smile, she clicked her way back to the front. "But why does she feel guilty? She didn't kill them."

My shoulders dropped as I settled into my chair.

"Because she knows it was her fault. Even though she didn't actually kill them, she caused it to happen." Ethan's confident voice boomed behind my head. He truly did understand this nonsense.

"Excellent. Now if you could all turn to that particular scene, we can dissect it further." She tapped her finger on the board where she'd written the page reference in big, bold numbers.

I opened my book to the appropriate section, considering I'd been searching about two acts off. I stared at the numbered passage as if it were written in some foreign language, only a few small words that I recognized jumping off the page. Why was this even relevant? Mrs. Franklin's words fell away as she had found a new victim to torture. Math I understood, science I understood, I could even handle flowery, self-involved novels with deep imagery and theme, but Shakespeare was just beyond me.

"Hey," Ethan whispered behind me.

I leaned back in my seat without turning my head. I'd captured enough of Mrs. Franklin's attention for one day.

Ethan's breath fell warm against my neck as he leaned toward me. "You okay?"

I nodded, still facing forward to avoid any unwanted attention.

"Why are you so late?"

I bent my bandaged arm behind my back so he could see.

"Damn, Berk," he whispered a little too loudly.

Mrs. Franklin stopped mid-sentence and looked at us. I sat up, rubbing my arm against my spine and stretching the other in the air as I let out a fake yawn. Satisfied, she continued her lecture.

"One of the fascinating things about this scene is that Lady Macbeth's monologue is performed while she is sleepwalking.

Throughout the play, she is portrayed as a very strong, female character, but in her sleep, she unloads all the thoughts and feelings that she conceals during the day. Shakespeare takes advantage of this altered mental state to show us her deepest, darkest emotions. The compulsive washing of the blood, or guilt, off her hands lets us know how she genuinely feels."

I chuckled to myself. I definitely knew what compulsively washing blood off your hands felt like, since I'd been doing it all morning. But did Lady Macbeth have to wash her sheets, her pillows, and her clothes too?

In thick black pen, I wrote 'SLEEPWALKING?' across the top of my notebook page. Would it be possible for me to have done that much damage to my own house without waking up? I mean, this all seemed crazy. But I couldn't help thinking about the fire extinguisher in the closet. Could that night in the woods been real, not only a dream? Maybe that green light did something to me? I put my head in my hands and flinched when I touched the bandages. This was ridiculous. Even if it were true, who would believe me?

The bell rang, snapping me out of my erratic thoughts. I gathered up my books and hurried out the door, Mrs. Franklin's eyes boring through me the entire way. Ethan stood in the hall, leaning next to the door, waiting.

"Okay, what happened?" he asked as he shifted in front of me and refused to let me pass until I provided him with an answer.

"Our house got broken into last night. And I cut my hand on the glass, cleaning up the mess. I guess I'm a pretty big klutz." It sounded reasonable as I said it out loud, but my stomach churned.

Wrapping his arms around me, he squeezed. "Seriously? Are you okay? I mean, I know the hand, but really? That's kind of scary to have someone walking around your house while you're sleeping."

"Um ..." I mumbled into his jacket.

He let me go, and his cheeks flushed. "Sorry."

"It's fine." I straightened myself. "I'll be all right." *Except that I won't.* "And thanks for saving my butt in there."

"Don't worry about that. I know you said that this stuff wasn't your favorite."

"It's okay, I just don't get it. I guess it's an acquired taste."

"Well, if you need any help, you can come over to my place tonight, and I can try to explain it to you."

"Oh." It was my turn to blush.

"Besides, I'm sure you could pay me back with some calculus tutoring. Mr. Finnegan is determined to kill my GPA." He gave me an encouraging grin, but his eyes still analyzed my every move as if looking for a weakness. Or maybe he just expected me to break down from all the drama.

"Sounds like a good deal, but I can't tonight. I have practice, then I need to deal with stuff at home."

"Right, Lane said that last night. Volleyball finals this weekend." He smacked his forehead. "I completely forgot."

"Yep, that's it." I leaned to the side and glanced up and down the hallway. "Have you seen Lane today?"

He shrugged. "Nope, I haven't seen her all morning."

"Okay, I should go look for her. If she hears about the break-in from someone else first, she'll freak."

He placed his hand on the side of my face and gazed down at me, his dark brown eyes heavy with concern. "I really am glad that you're okay, and if you ever need anything, all you have to do is ask."

My throat dried. The warmth of his palm on my cheek jolted through my bloodstream. A connection. A reaction I didn't expect nor have time to process. His stare flexed wider for a moment, as if he sensed my confusion, then narrowed as he drew it in and locked it away.

Dropping his hand, he flashed a sympathetic half-smile then turned around and headed down the hallway.

I exhaled hard. I needed to find Lane—now.

Thirteen

I tightened the bandage on my hand then tugged my volleyball jersey over my head. The locker room had cleared out five minutes before, but I wanted to catch Lane before practice started. Except she never showed. Eventually, I gave up and paraded into the gym, careful to keep my sleeves pulled over my hands. Girls sat around the cold gym floor, stretching and chatting. Still no Lane, though. Where could she be?

Tweet! Tweet!

Coach Kruger blew her whistle, and everyone huddled around the bench.

"Okay, team, we don't have much time left. Finals are tomorrow. Is everybody ready?"

"Yeah," we yelled in unison.

"Great. Now we need our game to be tight. Controlled hits. Everybody low. Got it?"

The group murmured their agreement.

"Okay, everyone run five laps, then grab a partner and do some warm-up rallies."

Tweet! Tweet!

I joined my team and started running around the edge of the gym. It seemed much harder than a few days ago with Lane in the park. I kept getting more and more run-down. My body ached as I pushed forward, begging my brain to make me stop. A few more lousy nights and I'd probably just lie down on the floor and stay there for a week.

But what was going on? I needed to talk to Lane. She was the only one I knew that would listen to me, even if I was insane. And there was a good chance of that. I still hadn't figured out how I'd explain it to her, but at least she would listen. Where was she?

I bent over and put my hands on my knees, gasping for breath. Five laps shouldn't be this hard.

"Heads up," Lane shouted, and tossed a volleyball at me.

I bolted upright, quick enough to volley it back.

She laughed then returned it to me.

"I haven't seen you all day. Where have you been hiding?" I bumped the ball to Lane, wincing as it hit the outside of my injured hand. Fortunately, it didn't hurt as bad as I thought it would.

Leaning to the side, she hit the ball. "Did you miss me?"

"Very funny." I knocked the ball back with my healthy fist. "I really need to talk to you."

"Yeah, I heard about the break-in. Did they take anything?" She volleyed.

I bumped. "That's what I need to talk to you about."

"What, you and Josh got a sex tape that might go viral?" She laughed and struck the ball again.

"It's not a joke. I think something weird is going on." The volleyball veered to the left, but I managed to get under it before crashing into the wall. It sailed back over Lane's head.

She reached her arm behind her and spiked the ball toward me. "You can buy me a smoothie after practice then."

I lunged forward and lost my balance, hurtling headfirst toward the gym floor. Instinctively, I put my hands down to break my fall. The jolt of pain shot right through my palm and up my arm. "Owwww!"

Everyone stopped and stared as I pulled myself to sitting. I tried to ignore the spot of blood on the floor, but from the wide-mouthed gape on Lane's face, she'd already seen it. I closed my fist and put it in my lap, awkwardly trying to get up without calling attention to my injury.

Lane ran over and grabbed my wrist. A dark spot of red grew in the center of the white gauze. Lane ripped the wet bandage off, her face contorting in horror as she looked at the gash.

A small crowd gathered around us, including Coach Kruger. I struggled against Lane's grip to hide my hand, but Coach charged forward and pulled my arm away from Lane.

"Berkley, what happened to you?" she asked as her jaw dropped open.

I swallowed. "I cut my hand cleaning up some glass." It sounded honest. I had repeated the lie so many times today it had even started to feel true.

Coach shook her head and sighed. "I can't let you play like this."

"It's just a minor cut, it will get better." I yanked my hand out of her grip and cradled it near my chest, away from everyone's prying stares.

"I'm sure it will, but that's a huge slice. It needs to be cleared by medical if you want to be in the finals."

"But what if ..." I trailed off, not wanting to say the words.

"Then you can't play."

I winced as her words socked me in the gut.

"Trust me, I don't like it either, but your best chance is to get it looked at. You might need stitches, and it looks like it's infected." She snapped her fingers and motioned to Lane with her arm. "Take her to the nurse, then hustle back."

Lane nodded and put her arm around me, leading me out of the gym.

"Did you seriously think you were going to get away with that?" she asked as she clicked the gym doors closed behind us.

"I hadn't really thought about it." I closed my hand, so I didn't have to look at the cut. "I just knew I couldn't miss practice."

She turned toward me and clapped her hands on my shoulders. "For someone so smart, you sure do stupid things sometimes."

I twisted away from her and stared at the bulletin board of posters near the gym office, trying to keep my emotions in check. "Thanks a lot."

"I mean, you need to take care of yourself. I know you've been going through a lot lately, but you need to let things happen. You can't control everything."

"Oh, I know." I nodded my head. "I'm starting to understand that far better than you think."

Her brow furrowed, and she squinted her eyes into questioning slits. "Does this have anything to do with what you wanted to talk to me about?"

I nodded. "But that can wait. Get back to practice, and we can talk about it after."

"Screw practice. What is it?"

"Trust me, it's a long story. It can wait an hour." I swiped my hand through the air, dismissing her, as I jerked my head toward the gym doors.

"Okay." She backed away from me, still seeming uneasy.

"I promise. Now go."

I SAT on the gym bench, watching my team scrimmage. My feet swiveled from side to side and my arms tensed every time one of my teammates made contact with the ball. I should be out there, not sitting on this stupid hunk of wood watching everything I worked for happen without me. Besides, a few good spikes would do wonders for my mood right now. Work all my problems out through my focused fists. Except instead I looked down at my hand wrapped in more stark-white gauze and cringed.

Ms. Hendricks said I could get away without stitches, as the spot on my palm would be too hard to suture properly anyhow. She glued the wound shut, but not before cleaning it with what I assumed must have been hydrochloric acid. Pain surged up my arm, and I had to bite down on the shoulder of my jersey to keep from screaming. After giving me some butterfly bandages, she wrapped up my wound, promising that if I took proper care of it, my hand should be okay soon. But I needed to be better now.

Tweet! Tweet! Coach Kruger blew her whistle, and the girls began cleaning up the equipment. They all laughed and smiled. Excited to be playing. Not knowing what it felt like to sit on the sidelines. I closed my eyes and tried to swallow my emotions. *It's not their fault your life is falling apart.*

A stray volleyball rolled across the floor and landed in front of my feet. Danielle Sanders ran over to pick it up, her auburn ponytail bobbing back and forth as she ran.

"How's the cut?" she asked, cocking her head to the right.

I waved my mummy hand in the air. "All patched up." I picked up the volleyball and gave it a lopsided toss.

She jutted left and caught my awful throw, then rested the ball on her hip with her arm, still staring at me. "Did they say how long you're out?"

"Nurse says a week, but I think I'll be fine to play tomorrow."

She squinted and glared at my hand. "Do you think that's a good idea?"

"Absolutely. It'll be all right, I just have to think positive and everything will be fine."

"That's the spirit." She giggled and gave a fist pump in the air. "Did you get hurt today? I didn't notice it last night, but then again, I wasn't looking for it either."

"Huh?" I grabbed the side of my head and narrowed my stare. "Last night?"

"Don't you remember? I saw you at the gas station on Cumberland. After Squire's party."

My limbs shook, but I clenched them tight to mask the vibration as I stared at her, unsure of what to say.

"I was with Becky and Sarah," she continued, giving me a confused glare.

My brain whirled, trying to process the information, but nothing came up.

"Yeah, sorry. I forgot," I lied.

"Not surprised. You seemed kind of preoccupied. You didn't even acknowledge us until I walked up to you at the gas pump. Becky thought you were just being a snob."

"I was getting gas?"

"That's what you do at a gas station." She tossed her head back and laughed.

I fell back against the wall, my head still spinning. "Sorry for not being nicer, I've had a rough couple of days."

"Sounds like it. No worries." She clamped both hands on the ball and twirled away, her ponytail swishing from side to side.

"Hey, Dani," I called after her.

She spun around.

"Do you remember about what time I saw you last night?"

She paused, her eyes rolling toward the ceiling. "About eleven-thirty, quarter to twelve?"

My entire body vibrated as everything clicked in my brain. Until now, I'd carried doubt that nothing really happened, but Danielle had seen me when I thought I was asleep, and to make matters worse, I had been the one to steal our car. Not some criminal.

Warm spit gathered in the back of my throat, and I bolted into the change room. I skidded through the lockers and slipped on the damp tile as I raced into the bathroom stall. As I dropped to my knees with a painful jolt, I puked. My body convulsed over and over, spewing everything out of me. My lunch, my fear, my constant panicked stress. As if my flesh couldn't hold it in any longer. I crossed my arms on the toilet seat and rested my head on them. The putrid cocktail of stomach acid, stale urine, and toilet bowl cleaner made me gag more, but there was nothing left to purge.

"Berk," Lane called from behind me as she raced into the stall. "You okay?"

I rolled back onto the floor and leaned against the metal bathroom stall partition. "No. I think I'm in big trouble."

Fourteen

"Nuh-uh. You are totally making that up."

Lane played with the straw in her triple berry smoothie and gawked at me like a kid seeing their first penguin at the zoo.

I polished off the rest of my own drink with one long gulp. I purchased the small one, not wanting to risk another trip to the bathroom floor, but my stomach needed more. It always needed more. "I wish I were."

"So, let me get this right." Lane dropped her elbow on the table and swung her pointed index finger toward me. "You had some weirdo nightmare about a green light, and now you are out sleep-walking all over town?"

"Keep your voice down." I leaned close to the laminated table top and peeked over the edges of the booth. No one stared or even looked our way. Too busy with their own Friday night plans and totally disinterested in ours. Besides, if anyone overheard they'd likely think Lane was retelling some obscure horror flick or something. "You probably think I'm crazy."

"No, not at all."

"Thanks, but you are allowed to think I'm insane. I do."

She patted my head like an adorable kitten, or maybe a disobedient child. "Really, I don't. I just think you're stressed out."

"What?" *Stressed out? No way. Not with this much trouble.*

"Think about it. You said you weren't sleeping and you have all this stuff going on, so I'll bet you are completely stressed out. I've seen it on TV. Some sort of state. Fugues or something. People just black out and don't remember anything but are fully functional." She pulled her feet up in the booth seat and leaned against the wall, taking up the entire bench, as casually cool as if she were recounting the plot of her favorite novel. "Since your mom left, you've been super high-strung, and with all the other crap in your life, I wouldn't blame your brain for wanting to take a walk without you weighing it down."

Ouch. The words stung, prickling along my skin. "I thought I was handling my mom leaving pretty well. I guess I'm failing at that too."

"Hey, you aren't dropping out of school or huffing household cleaners from a brown paper bag, so I would say you are taking it like a champ. Besides, are you sure your dad didn't smash up your place? He was certainty keeping hydrated when we were there. Maybe he had some fit of rage and wrecked the joint. Maybe he just doesn't want to admit it."

I slouched back in the booth. Possibly. It made more sense than my green light theory. I picked at a fraying edge on the white gauze around my hand. A few drops of red already bled through the thick layers of cloth. The skin of my palm itched underneath. "But what about my injury?"

"Like you said, you could've cut it on your bed frame or something."

"The dead mouse?"

"Could've been anything or anyone. Didn't have to have anything to do with you."

I closed my eyes and let the thoughts sink in. Coincidences. Just a bad string of coincidences.

"But what about Danielle and the gas station?"

Lane wrinkled her nose and stared into the bottom of her cup. "Hmm. That one's trickier. Maybe it wasn't you? Like one of those doppelgänger situations, and your lookalike was too polite or confused to correct her when approached."

"A little too convenient, Lane."

She shrugged. "Sorry, but it's all I've got."

I glanced up at her pathetic attempt at a smile, but it didn't cheer me up. I'd tried to come up with explanations before and failed. How did I honestly expect her to come up with something more realistic?

Something flickered out the window behind Lane's head.

I jumped up and slammed my knees against the table, keeping me pinned down.

"What?" Lane twisted around to follow my stare.

A girl stood in the parking lot. Long, dark hair. My height. Dressed entirely in black. I leaned across the table for a better look, and her head tilted my direction. Her eyes widened as her stare pierced through the glass and locked right on my face. The burn of scrutiny seethed in my cheeks.

"Do you see that?" I pointed through the window. "That girl?"

Lane dropped her drink on the table and climbed onto her knees to face the window.

The girl shook her head and bolted off into the night.

"Where?" Lane asked as she pushed her nose against the glass, a foggy ring forming around her face. "I see nothing."

I flopped back in my seat. "She's already gone."

That stare. The weight of it heavy on my shoulders, boring its way through my skull as if trying to squeeze out what was inside. It didn't feel as strong as the one from the woods, but I had no doubt it was directed right at me. My mind reeled with so many new questions. Who was she? If only she'd stood closer, I might've recognized her face, but the haze of the parking lot lights masked her features. But more importantly, what did she want?

Lane snapped her fingers in front of my face. "Hello, Berkley."

"Wait. What?"

"Seriously, you need to give yourself a break, girl. Weird dreams. Seeing things. You've totally hit your limit." She propped her elbows on the table and held her chin as she leaned closer to my side of the booth. "I'll tell you what. I'm sure you're just having a rough patch. I'll sleep over at your place tonight, and if you decide to go for a stroll, I'll wake you up."

"I'm not sure it'll be that easy. If Danielle was right, and I really drove to Squire's and then a gas station last night, I doubt shaking me is going to do anything."

"Fortunately for you, they don't give tickets for sleeping and driving. More fortunately, I'm not opposed to pinning your scrawny butt down and pouring a bucket of water over your head until you blubber like a goldfish."

It might work. Probably not, but what options did I really have? I cast a glance out the window into the night, but only a bunch of cars looked back. I shivered. I had to try something.

"How did I get so lucky as to have you as my best friend?" I said.

"You must have done something right in a past life. I'm just happy it wasn't something worse."

"And what could possibly be worse than blacking out for twelve hours a day?"

"From the puking, I thought you were going to tell me you were pregnant," she said as she shredded the loose threads on the booth seat.

"We both know that's so not happening." Not with Josh, anyway, and definitely not with anyone else.

"I wouldn't expect you to kiss and tell. You don't seem like that kind of girl."

I shook my head. "Is there anything I've ever managed to hide from you over all these years? You know I would tell you."

"Yeah, I know. I just wanted to hear you say it." She took another sip from her cup and winked.

FIFTEEN

The alarm wailed, and I yawned. Carefully, I slid my bandaged hand to the nightstand and grabbed my phone to stop the noise. I peeled my eyes open slowly, unsure what terrors I might face this morning. My stare darted around the room. Everything looked okay, and thankfully, no blood this time. I exhaled a huge breath and sank into my mattress. So much better. Stretching my arms over my head, I squealed as blood started pumping through my limbs. My joints seemed stiff. Sore. But maybe it meant that I stayed in one spot for an entire night. Except the haze of exhaustion still painted a cloud over everything.

My stomach grumbled, and I sat up against the headboard.

A face gaped at me from across the room. I yelped. This time the eyes didn't belong to me and my mirror.

Lane sat in the corner of the room, staring back, her cheeks ashen and eyes wide. She held her knees taut to her chest with white-knuckled hands. Unmoving. Unblinking. So unlike Lane.

I sprang from my bed and crawled across the floor. Her body tensed as I knelt in front of her, her gaze following my every movement and her lips silent.

A hint of bruising shadowed around her left eye. Likely a full-on shiner before long. I tried to smooth her hair away from her face, but she twitched and pushed herself farther into the corner.

"What the hell, Lane? What happened to you?"

"You don't know?" Her whispered voice shook.

"Of course not." I sat back on my feet, giving her some space.

Her body eased a fraction but still sat as rigid and cold as a bronze statue. "It was you, but not you." She blinked and wiped her hands over her face. "You've got a big problem."

THE TOASTER'S THIN, wavy elements glowed yellow, then orange, until they flared the brightest vermillion. I stared harder, hypnotized with their brilliance, and doing anything to avoid looking over at Lane. To escape the guilt that pooled in my chest and pressed against my lungs, stealing my breath. To ignore the truth for a few more minutes.

The toast popped up, and I flinched as I snapped out of my thoughts and into the act of slathering peanut butter thick on both slices with a hint of blueberry jam in the center. Exactly how she liked it. I crept back to the kitchen table, my steps slow and unsteady as Lane lowered the ice pack from her eye, and the sickening shade of blue torture came into view again. I swallowed against the thickness in my throat and eased into the chair beside her, then slid her the plate. She nodded. Still no words. None since I peeled her off my bedroom floor.

She bit into the toast, and the loud crunch echoed in the silence between us and prickled up my spine.

I rubbed my damp palms down my thighs, then slid to perch at the edge of my chair. "So, what happened?"

Lane took another big bite before flopping back in the chair. She swiped a stray dollop of peanut butter off her lower lip and licked her thumb, then dropped her arms beside her. "I'm still trying to figure all that out."

Her nostrils quivered as she took a deep breath and rolled her stare toward the ceiling. I inched closer. Lane had never been this quiet—ever.

"Am I the one who ..." The words formed on my tongue, but stung too much to set them free. Instead, I pointed at her face and frowned.

"Yeah. You've got a much better right hook than I would've expected with those toothpick arms." She flashed a smile, but it faded too fast to be real.

My hands shook in my lap, and it spread through my body. A vibration flowing through my limbs, trying to get me to do something. Anything. But what exactly could I do? "I'm so sorry, Lane."

"It's okay. I know it wasn't your fault." She grabbed my shaking hand and squeezed until it stopped. "But something is definitely wrong with you."

The shaking moved inside as my organs tensed and ached. "What did I do?"

"It was totally creepy. You lay sleeping for about fifteen minutes, then you woke up again. No tossing and turning, just sat straight up, got out of bed and dressed super fast, like you were late for something. At first, I poked you to wake you up, but you swatted me off like a pesky fly. I yelled your name, I grabbed at your hood, I even smacked your face a couple of times, but you didn't care."

I flexed my jaw and brushed my cheek with my fingers. A deep ache tingled in the muscle. *Made sense.*

"I ran to the bathroom, filled a bucket with water, and tossed it over your head. Except instead of waking up, it only pissed you off. You grabbed my arm and flung me across the room like I was a stuffed bear."

Lane released my hand and twisted her arm up under the kitchen lights. Five smaller circular bruises dotted her bicep. Five determined fingertips stamped on her flesh.

Warm saliva built in my mouth, but I swallowed it back down. I grabbed my forehead as I gawked at the bruises. "You know I'd never hurt you on purpose, right?"

She tucked her arm back down at her side. "Oh, I'm not done. After you cast me aside, you changed your wet clothes and headed for the door. I raced up and stood in your way, but it just seemed to make you madder. Eventually, you stopped trying to dodge me, then wound up and smoked me right in the eye before booking it out the door. I followed you, but you ran too fast to catch up. Faster than I'd ever seen you run before. I barely got a block before you disappeared. And that's not even the screwed-up part."

"Of course it isn't." I launched up from my chair and paced behind Lane. The treetops over the fence blustered in the wind. Taunting me. Teasing. What secrets had they witnessed over the past week? What did they already know? "What else happened?"

"I didn't know what to do, so I just waited. You'd said before that you always ended up in your own bed, so I figured you'd come back eventually and I could deal with you then. I'm not sure how long you were gone, but it must've been a while, because I dozed off on the floor. Sometime later I heard a noise and woke up. Your lamp was on and you were sitting on your bed in your pajamas staring at me. You didn't speak, but when I looked up you tilted your head to the side at some crazy unnatural angle. Almost like you'd snapped your head off your neck and glued it back on crooked. Plus, you had the most messed-up expression on your face."

She shuddered hard enough to shake the chair, and it squeaked against the kitchen tile. She looked over her shoulder as the blood drained from her cheeks. "You were smiling. A big, broad grin that stretched across your whole face. But not a happy smile, a sinister one, like a murdery supervillain-before-he-blows-up-the world type grin. And your eyes. I couldn't see them. Your eye sockets just glowed. Bright, like blood-red laser beams."

"What?" I glanced at my murky reflection in the patio door glass and pulled at my eyelids. No laser beams. Nothing unusual. "Are you sure it wasn't just the lamplight?"

"Maybe. It was all kinds of hazy at that point." She shrugged and twisted around in the chair to face me. "It creeped me out. And it felt weird around you. Cold and dark, like a dingy base-ment. Except you didn't care. After you got bored staring at me, you just switched off the lamp and went to sleep. But I couldn't, so I just sat in the corner and watched you until the sun came up."

"How did you know I wasn't going to hurt you when I woke up?" The thought settled into my brain and itched there until I pushed it down.

"I didn't, but as soon as you spoke, I knew it was you. You didn't look any different when you had left the house, but you were definitely not the same person. I can't really explain it; you just carried yourself differently. Stronger, quicker, sharper. Like an animal or something."

"And I'm guessing not a bunny."

"Hell no, more like a bloodthirsty panther."

Pacing again, I ran through Lane's story over and over. It didn't make any sense? None of it. How could I just change like that? "Do you still think I'm only sleepwalking?"

"I don't know. I've never actually seen someone sleepwalk before, so I have nothing to compare it to, but it was seriously weird."

I pressed my head against the cool patio door, but it did nothing to slow the spinning in my brain. "Great. What am I supposed to do now?"

"First, I think we need to figure out where you go when you're like ... well, that." She wiped her hand in a circle through the air.

"And what's that going to do?"

"Where you go might help us make sense as to why you are doing what you're doing."

I banged my head on the glass, the thump reminding me that I was indeed awake and this wasn't a twisted dream. "Don't you think I might need some professional help?"

"Like a doctor?" She scrunched up her face. "Maybe. Problem is, I don't know what you need, other than a leash."

"Nice, Lane. Real nice."

"Hey, you have no right to mock me today. After what I just went through with you, you owe me big time." She crunched down on her toast again, her appetite speeding back as she let this story off her chest.

"It just doesn't make any sense. I mean, how am I supposed to think that I walk around and not have any clue about it?"

"Hell if I know," Lane mumbled with her mouth full.

I clutched my stomach as it growled with jealousy. Pulling myself off the patio door, I strode back to the table and leaned my hands on the top. "Think about it logically."

She rolled her eyes. "Here we go."

"If I were to go out and talk to people, I would have to register my memory to be able to recognize them. And pain is a response that the body sends to the brain as a survival mechanism, so why wouldn't the infliction of pain cause me to wake up? The cut on my hand is really deep. I should have felt that."

"Maybe you felt it, but you just didn't care."

"But why not, though?" I paced again. Faster and faster, each hot lap decreasing in size and increasing in speed. Intense enough that I might take flight. One more strange thing to add to the list.

Lane pushed away from the table and jumped in front of me. She grabbed my arms and forced my eyes to meet hers. "Easy, Berk. We don't know anything yet, and making guesses isn't going to solve anything. Why don't we go to the hospital and get you checked out? Maybe there is a perfectly reasonable explanation for this, we just don't know what it is."

"Maybe." Sighing, I pulled out her grip.

"I'll go with you. Just let me get—" She slapped her hand on her forehead. "Shoot. Volleyball championship game this afternoon. How about we go after?"

"Right." This whole thing had my head so messed up, I completely forgot. "Do you think Kruger will let me play?"

"Not if Ms. Hendricks didn't clear you, but maybe." Lane grabbed my hand and unraveled the gauze.

Bright-red splotches appeared after the first layer came off, each layer growing darker and thicker. Fresh smears colored my palm, almost hiding the cut beneath them.

"I must've ripped it open again when I was ... well, wherever I was."

Lane wrinkled her nose and turned her head away. "Plus, it's kind of starting to reek. There's no way they'll put you on the court like that."

I ripped my hand away and fell into my chair. The cold air against my palm stung, and my arm throbbed as a reminder. Closing my eyes, I tried to regain focus. Everything seemed to be spinning out of control. A carnival funhouse of nightmares, laughing and poking fun at me on every turn. Spinning around and around until I screamed, or threw up, or both.

"Why does it feel like everything is falling apart, Lane?"

"It's not. I'll come back after the game, and we'll get it all sorted out. You'll be just fine. I promise. And while we're at the hospital, we'll get them to patch that hand up properly."

"Do you mind if I come watch?"

She rubbed her hand across my back. "Of course. You're still part of the team, I just didn't think you'd want to."

I nodded and stroked my knuckle over each of my eyes to catch the few tears that had already formed, but I refused to let fall. "No, I think I want to be there."

"Good." Lane nodded hard and sharp, then sat back down in her chair. "But could you please go clean that cut? It's starting to make me nauseous."

Sixteen

"I'm sorry to do this, Berkley. You know we need you out there on the court, but I can't afford to take a risk like this with you." Coach Kruger cupped my shoulder as her lips fell into a sympathetic frown.

I sighed, my body shrinking and sinking into the floor. "It's okay. I understand."

Except I didn't. My logical brain knew it was for the best, but the rest of me deflated like a popped balloon. The whole team stood dressed and ready in their uniforms, stretching their legs along the wooden benches, getting ready for the biggest game of their lives so far. The smears of greasepaint our captain Becky convinced them to wear under their eyes for intimidation looked ridiculous, but I suddenly wanted so badly to have those marks on my skin. To be a part of this. I should be here. I deserved to be here. But, of course, I couldn't.

Lane scrunched up her face as she deduced Coach's answer from the far side of the bench.

"But I'd be more than happy to have you sit here and help out, if you want? Be a real inspiration from the sidelines."

I glanced at the wooden bench and winced. "I think I'll watch from the stands. I don't want to be a distraction." Especially if I broke down bawling in front of the team.

"Well, cheer hard. These girls will need everyone on their side that they can get." Coach gave me a reassuring fist pump.

I forced a smile as I passed the row of my prepping teammates and headed for the stands.

"No go?" Lane asked as I grabbed my coat and bag from the end of the bench.

Shaking my head, I gave her a playful punch in the shoulder. "Good luck."

She trembled as a flicker of what looked like fear flashed in her eyes when my fist connected with her arm. *Great. I've got a lot to make up for.*

I trudged up the steps and took a seat in the middle of the crowd. Typically, fans never came to volleyball games, but we'd never made the finals before either. Out on the court, the teams rallied and warmed up, waiting for the big game to start. I slouched, wishing I could be out there with them. I'd practiced so hard, even making the starting line. And now—just like that—gone. Lane better be right about the hospital being able to help because I couldn't take much more torment. My limbs ached. My brain functioned in a fog most of the time. And now I didn't even have control over my body. All the things I'd built over time were falling down around me, and I didn't know what was even wrong to be able to stop it. What did I do to deserve this?

"What are you doing here? Aren't you supposed to be lighting up the court?"

Ethan jumped beside me from the row above, and the bleachers shook. A few people gave him some fierce side-eye, but he ignored them and took the empty seat next to me. I sat up taller and forced my happier smile again.

I held up my bandaged hand. "Welcome to the injured reserve list. What are you doing here?"

He unzipped his coat, revealing his navy-blue 'Property of Henstridge Ram Athletics' T-shirt, and leaned back in his seat. "You and Lane always come to my games. Why wouldn't I come out to yours?"

"Oh. Thanks. That's really nice of you." A warm tingle flitted through me as he flashed his infectious grin, nearly cheering me up.

"I would've liked to see you play, though. Lane said you were actually a decent setter, which is high praise coming from her."

"Yeah. Me too."

He nudged his shoulder into mine. "Sorry. I didn't mean to upset you."

"No, it's not your fault. It was a game-time decision, so I'm still a little disappointed." I shook my head. "Unless you know how to go back in time, there's not much you can do about it."

"Nope. Not one of my superpowers. But it's cool of you to stay and watch. It must be hard."

"Kind of. But at least now I'm not sitting up here alone and sulking. I have you to sulk with me."

"Anytime." His head swiveled as he scanned the crowd. "But didn't Josh come to watch you play? Or did he bail when he knew you weren't on the roster?"

Josh. Great. Another problem I need to fix. "No. I doubt he's coming. He would've just got back from Rockford this morning, and besides, I don't think he wants to see me right now."

A whistle squawked, signaling the start of the first set. Danielle served the ball over the net. A bunch of orange shirts chased after it and rallied to a spike back. Lane got under the ball and put it back over the net.

"That sucks. But I'm sure you will guys will figure it out," Ethan said as he watched the play.

The whistle blasted again. Point for the Maplecrest Cougars. I slumped down in my seat.

"Actually, I'm not sure we will this time."

"LET'S GO, RAMS!" Ethan cupped his hands around his mouth and yelled at the court.

He winked at me. I laughed again and grabbed my side as I struggled to catch my breath.

"Should we try to start the wave one more time?" he said.

"No. Please don't." I waved my hands in opposition as the chuckling subsided. "Our pathetic two-man wave hasn't worked the last four times. I think we should give up."

He shrugged. "Fifth time's a charm."

Ethan tossed his arms over his head and started to stand. I tugged on his arm and pulled him back down to sitting but kept my elbow linked with his to avoid another attempt.

"Easy now, Ram Boy. I think everyone has had enough of us for today."

"If you say so." He squeezed my arm under his and flashed me a wide, tooth-baring grin.

I shook my head. "I do say so."

"Fine. Besides, I really just wanted to make you smile." He rocked sideways and knocked me off balance. "I hate seeing you unhappy."

"Well, thank you." I smiled back, as large as I could force my muscles to stretch.

His goofy expression refined into something quieter. Deeper. "Anytime."

Heat pulsed under my skin, spreading up my neck and through my limbs. A whistle blasted to start the fifth set. Two sets per team already. I whipped my head back toward the court.

Lane served to start the game. The Cougars answered back. We rallied.

"What's going on after the game? Did you guys want to do something after?" Ethan asked.

My eyes followed the bouncing white ball. Back and forth. Back and forth.

"Lane is taking me to the hospital. I have to ... get my hand checked out." I thrust the bandaged hand up as if to remind myself.

"No problem. But maybe after that then?"

I glanced over. His stare caught mine.

"We could watch a movie, or order pizza, or even study."

"I don't know. I'll have to check with Lane. She didn't sleep much last night, and after this she'll probably be exhausted."

His eyes widened, and I fell into the hypnotic swirl of the soft golden flecks that circled in his ember irises. They shone brighter than ever. Open for once, telling me things instead of keeping them hidden. His hand slipped into mine, his thumb running across my knuckles and sending a shiver up my arm. Electric, like touching a live wire. Sparking my draining battery back to life. My brain told my hand to pull away, but my fingers refused.

He leaned closer and whispered, "Maybe you could just come over then?"

"I..."

Ethan's lips twisted. Silent. Waiting. Hoping I would meet him halfway.

Words jumbled in my brain. I knew what I needed to say, but I couldn't force it out. The thought of being alone with Ethan charged through my mind in a way it shouldn't. A way that made my throat dry up and my knees weak.

"Maybe—"

A tickle broke down my face. Red splattered on the back of my hand and splashed on Ethan's fingers.

He pointed at my face. "Uh, Berkley, your nose is bleeding."

I clamped my hand over my nose and rushed through the stands, tripping over people's feet and collecting scowls on the way down. I scrambled down the hallway and burst through the bathroom door. Blood oozed through my fingers. Droplets speckled the floor as I ran into the stall and unwound a healthy wad of toilet paper. With the paper secured around my face, I locked the door and sat down on the toilet seat, my head down and my nose pinched at the bridge.

Just great. Maybe I really was falling apart. Or maybe destiny was giving me a sign. If I hadn't started bleeding out all over Ethan, what would I have said next? What would I have done? Lane warned me that Ethan might think of me as more than a friend, but

I should've been able to shut him down. What was wrong with me? I was with Josh. And it was Ethan. I wasn't allowed to mess with Ethan.

The tail of paper from the toilet roll dispenser fluttered as a gust of wind blew from the direction of the bathroom door. A faint squeak of rubber on the tile floor echoed in the tiny room. I sat up straighter and pulled my legs up. No one needed to know I'd left that mess of blood out there. Not until I had a chance to clean it up.

A pair of black boots walked past the stall, squeaking, as they headed down to the far end of the bathroom. The boots stalked back and stopped in front of the stall, the toes facing the door. I held my breath.

The fine hairs on my arms stuck up as a chill rushed through my body. After several minutes of stalemate—me on the inside, and someone on the outside—I made a move. I slipped one leg slowly down to the floor. The boots didn't move. I slid the other down. Again, no movement from the boots. I reached back and flushed the toilet. The boots ran. I threw open the door. A flash of black disappeared out the bathroom door. The chill returned and ran all the way down my back into my legs. They trembled.

I tossed the bloody toilet paper in the trash and quickly wiped the floor, careful to keep one eye locked on the bathroom door. Blood stained my hands and face. I washed them in the sink as the pink-tinged water circled the drain and disappeared. Another day, another sink full of red on my hands. I gave one more wary glance around the bathroom then, seeing nothing, walked out.

SEVENTEEN

Red and white ambulance lights flickered in the dark outside the waiting room window. Another stretcher wheeled through the lobby and past the swinging doors into the depths of the hospital, a sacred place Lane and I had yet to breach.

I clicked the power button on my phone. Five hours already. A town the size of Lethe shouldn't take this long for emergency services. Maybe if we hadn't gone for burgers with the team to celebrate their amazing defeat over the Cougars, we would've missed the rush.

Lane flipped through a magazine from another decade, giggling to herself at the hideous fashion from times past. I rubbed my hand. The cut ached, and I flexed my fingers to keep the blood pumping through my palm to help heal the wound. How much longer did we need to wait?

I glanced out the window again. The EMTs puttered around the outside of the ambulance, then jumped back in and drove away. Maybe if I'd tried calling them instead, I could've gotten in quicker. My ears popped, and my mouth dropped open as an enormous yawn escaped my lips.

Lane dropped the magazine in her lap. "What are you doing?"

"What?" My mouth opened again and yawned.

She pointed at my face. "That. Don't tell me you're getting tired."

"Sorry, Lane. I haven't been sleeping. What did you expect?"

Her lips pursed into a hard line, and she chucked the magazine on her chair as she launched up to her feet. "Hang on."

She marched up to the admitting counter.

I chased after her, hoping she wouldn't make a scene, but still hopeful that she would make some progress.

"Hello, ma'am. I know you've got a lot to do, but we've been sitting here for over—"

She glanced at me.

"Five hours," I mouthed.

"Five hours. And my friend needs to see someone soon, or you are going to have a problem on your hands."

The clerk removed her glasses and clasped her hands in front of her. "What exactly is your friend's problem?"

"She's having trouble with sleepwalking."

The woman behind the counter laughed. "Then keep her awake."

"It's not that simple. She can't control when she falls asleep, and then once she does we won't be able to control her. Do you understand me?"

"Oh, I understand you, but do you understand me?" She focused her laser beam stare and locked it between Lane's eyebrows. "Was your friend in an accident?"

"No," Lane responded.

"Does she have any broken bones?"

"No."

"Chest pains? Is she in labor?"

"No."

Without even the slightest hesitation, the clerk fell into her canned speech that she'd probably used a hundred times before. "Then I'm sorry, but your friend is not on the priority list, so you will have to take a seat and we will call you when a doctor is available."

Lane swung her arm to the side, nearly slapping me in the chest. "She can't wait. There is going to be a scene if she isn't treated soon."

"Look. I know you're worried about your friend, but there was

a five-car pileup just outside of town, and those people need imme-
diate care. Unless you would like to explain to their families why
we can't save their lives and put their bodies back together so your
friend can catch a nap, I'd suggest getting her a cup of coffee and
telling her to hang on."

My head fell to my chest. I turned to leave, but Lane's hands
balled into fists.

"Now listen, lady—" she started.

The admitting clerk stood up and leaned toward her window, a
vein starting to throb in her neck. "No, you listen. If you don't get
away from my counter and settle down, I will have you both
removed from here and your friend will not get to see anyone. So I
would suggest you go back to your seat and wait for your name to
be called."

Lane narrowed her glare but bit her tongue and did as she was
told, storming back over to our seats by the window.

"Thanks for trying," I said.

"People drive me bonkers sometimes."

I yawned. "Hopefully, someone will come soon. I'm getting
tired."

"Oh no, you don't." Lane grabbed me by the hand and walked
me over to the bathroom. She locked the door and ran the cold
water. "Put your head under there."

"What?"

"I need to keep you awake. Put your head under there."

Cold wafted off the stream of water, filling the sink. "Lane, it's
freezing."

"I don't care. You were the one who came to me saying that you
needed help, so I'm helping. Get moving."

I sighed then tied my hair up in a ponytail. I stared at the water
running from the tap into the dirty sink with who knows what
germs on it. The coolness of the water radiated, and it chilled my
fingers on the edge of the porcelain. *Here goes*.

I dunked my face under the water and choked on my own

scream. Cold. So cold. Icy. My skin might just freeze right off my bones. I closed my eyes and tried to count to ten slow. *One ... two ... three ... four ... enough!* I yanked my face up and shut off the tap. "That hurts."

"Well, I didn't think it was going to be fun, but do you still feel tired?"

"No, actually."

"Then I guess it worked." Lane patted my shoulder and jerked her head toward the door. "Let's get back to our seats. I'm sure my friend at the counter would take any chance to skip your turn."

I stretched and scrunched my face, checking to see that I could still move it and to work out some of the cold paralysis. An elderly couple had swooped in while we'd been in the bathroom and stole our seats, so we moved between a lady with a baby and the vending machine.

Lane flopped down in the chair and exhaled audibly. Sitting beside her, I stared out at the dark-gray carpet that lined the room. Rips and tears made intricate patterns to follow and keep me entertained. My jaw tickled and stretched as another yawn came on. I turned away from Lane and let it out.

"Did I see you sitting in the stands with Ethan during the game?" she asked.

I nodded and blinked. Once, twice.

"Weird that he didn't stay after. Oh well, at least we didn't have to explain where we were going."

"Good point." Plus, I had more explaining to do than I wanted to. "Maybe we should've driven to the next town to see if they would've been faster."

"Yeah, maybe."

I yawned again, but it came too quickly to hide.

"Oh no." Lane jumped in front of me and stared me in the eyes. "Look at me, Berk. You need to stay awake."

"I'm trying," I said, yawning again. "But I'm just so tired."

My eyelids drooped. Heavier. Thicker. Lane's face moved in and out of focus.

Smack!

Lane slapped my face. The lady with the baby launched from her seat and rushed across the room. My lips tried to form words and failed. I yawned again. Just ... so ... tired.

Eighteen

"**B**lood pressure looks good. No fever. Vitals look normal." Dr. Benson ripped open the Velcro pressure cuff and slid it off my arm.

I slipped my shirt sleeve back down to my wrist as my phone vibrated in my back pocket and crinkled the white sterile paper on the examination table. I peeked at the notification. Josh again. "So, what do you think it means?"

Dr. Benson sat down on her wheeled stool and slid back toward the desk. After writing my blood pressure on my file, she flipped through the other pages, looking over the years of medical data. "It means you're a perfectly healthy young woman and there's no physical reason why you are having the symptoms you are indicating."

Clang!

Lane blushed as she picked up the metal lid of the tongue depressor jar off the counter.

Dr. Benson shook her head. "Can you please stop playing with the supplies?"

She shrugged and looked at me. "Sorry."

"Now are there any other reasons you think you might be experiencing somnambulistic episodes? Any changes in your diet? Stress levels?"

"She's definitely been stressed out. Tell her, Berkley." Lane leaned against the wall and crossed her arms.

"Yes, Berkley, but before you do, can I ask that you please meet your friend in the waiting room?" She glared at Lane.

Lane's eyes popped open wide, but I nodded, and she slipped out the door.

"She's just looking out for me," I said as the door closed and the cheap Van Gogh 'Starry Night' print rattled against the wall.

"I'm sure she is." Dr. Benson wheeled closer to inspect the new layer of bandages she'd applied to my hand. Sterile and freshly glued again. "But I'm serious, Berkley. Is there any reason you can think of that might have caused this behavior to suddenly appear?"

Closing my eyes, I breathed deep. The scent of bleach and antibacterial soap burned my nostrils as the green light appeared in my memory. The light grew bigger and bigger, blinding out the flames of the candles in my mind. "I guess I have been stressed a lot lately. I haven't been sleeping, or at least I'm not feeling rested. And then there's school, and my mom left, and—"

Dr. Benson raised her hand. "Slow down. I get it. And what does your dad think about all of this? Have you talked to him?"

I twisted my fingers together in my lap. "My dad's very busy. I don't want to bother him with any of this."

She scooted closer on the stool and placed a hand beside me on the table. "Is there anything you need to tell me? Anything you say is in 100% confidence, you know that, right?"

I glanced toward the door Lane had escaped through. "No. It's fine. Just the sleepwalking trouble."

Her stare scanned me over, scrutinizing every single inch. I sat up straighter and held my head up again.

Dr. Benson wheeled across the tiny room and pulled out a small prescription pad. "I'm going to prescribe you a mild sedative. Extremely low-dose. Non-addictive. And only for the next seven days. Then I want to see you again, but at my clinic."

After scrawling out the words, she ripped off the sheet, handing it to me but just out of my reach. "In the meantime, do you have someone you can talk to? I can recommend a great counseling program if you need."

I shook my head, and her serious tone dropped to a frown.

"Please don't be looking for a quick fix to this problem. Sometimes issues like this take time and commitment from you to make it better."

"Of course I want to get better." I took a deep breath, letting the oxygen flow through my bloodstream. "I do."

She extended the prescription the rest of the way, and I took it from her hand. "My receptionist will be in touch about setting up your follow-up appointment. If this persists, I will not prescribe you anything stronger until you are referred to the proper mental health program. I also suggest speaking to your father and letting him know the problems you are having. If he doesn't know, he can't help. Understand?"

I curled the prescription in my fist and jumped down from the table. "Absolutely. Thank you."

Scooping up my bag, I rushed toward the door.

"And, Berkley."

I froze as my pulsed pounded faster, my hand resting on the doorknob. So close to free. "Uh-huh."

"Take it easy, okay? And remember mental health is important and nothing to be ashamed of."

"Got it. Thanks, Doctor." I whisked open the door and rushed out.

"DO you really think this will work?" I studied the small, green pill in my hand and glanced up at Lane.

She pulled her knees onto my chair and gripped the side of the desk before spinning around in circles. "I don't know, but it's worth a shot. Dr. Uptight seems to think so, and she said that you have nothing wrong with you."

"What about the things you saw? Like my red eyes and stuff."

Lane grabbed the desk and stopped herself, but my head kept whirling.

"Maybe you were right, and it was just the lamplight. Plus, there has to be a reasonable explanation."

"All right, here goes." I swallowed the pill and washed it down with a glass of water before crawling into bed. "Thank you for being here. Sorry I ruined your weekend."

"Never mind that. I've always wanted to chase after you two nights in a row and spend the rest of my Sunday afternoon waiting at the hospital again."

"I know you're trying to be funny, but I'm seriously grateful. You could've just ditched me."

"I could've, but I wouldn't do that. Besides, you stayed with me every night for almost a month after my dad died."

I closed my eyes. That time seemed so long ago.

"Yeah, but you never tried to punch me," I said.

Lane shrugged, then walked over and sat beside my head. She brushed my hair back over my ears. "I'll stay as long as I can, but I need to go home at some point. Are you sure you don't want to tell your dad? Just in case?"

"Why? I don't want to make any more problems for him. If there is something seriously wrong with me, I might make him worse, you know? I don't want to be responsible for that."

She melted lower into the mattress, pressing closer to me. "He's your dad, Berk. He needs to be responsible for you."

"I know, but I just can't."

Sighing, Lane rolled her eyes. "Fine. But maybe think about it. I don't want something bad to happen if I could've done something about it."

"I promise I will. But thank you for coming with me today." I slid my hand into hers and squeezed.

She gave me a sympathetic smile.

My phone vibrated on the nightstand. Lane snatched it up and flashed the screen at me. "It's Josh."

I yawned. "I don't know if I can deal with him being mad at me right now."

"Good idea."

She put the phone down, but it vibrated again. Longer.

Lane clicked the green phone icon. "Hey, Josh. It's Lane ... Yeah, she's not feeling that great right now. Maybe you should just talk to her tomorrow. Uh-huh ... Yeah, okay ... Sure."

She shook her head and handed me the phone. I slipped my arm out of the covers.

"Hi, Josh."

"Hey, Berkley. I heard you're not feeling well. That sucks."

"Yeah, well, I'm hoping I'll feel better soon. How was your game?"

"Good. We won. But I've been thinking about you all weekend, and I really want to talk. I still love you, Berk, and I want to see if we can figure this out."

My heart pounded beneath my blankets. "Yeah. I'd really like that."

"Okay. Then I'll talk to you tomorrow. Get some sleep, and I hope you feel better."

The phone line clicked, and I slid the phone back on the nightstand.

Lane's brow furrowed as she stared down at me. "That's an annoying smile. What did he say?"

"He said he wants to figure things out."

Lane frowned and glanced down at the phone. "Are you sure that's what you want?"

"Why wouldn't it be?"

"I don't know, because you hid your entire life from him for months." She tapped the back of the phone. "I just lied to him for you right now."

"True." I crunched my knees up to my chest as a pain dug deep in my gut. "But he knows now, and he wants to work things out. It's going to be okay. I'm going to get this sleep thing figured out, and everything is going to go back to normal."

My lips pulled tight into a smile, but Lane didn't smile back.

"Get some sleep, Berkley. Deal with tomorrow, tomorrow."

I closed my eyes. Lane's fingers tickled the side of my head as she stroked my hair. *She'll see. It'll all be better tomorrow.*

NINETEEN

Weightlessness. Falling. My stomach lurches, and my limbs flop loose. I try to scream, but nothing comes out. My lips don't respond to my brain. My body doesn't respond either. Trapped inside a fleshy cage I can't control.

Through the windshield, the lights of the sky blur together. Dashboard indicators. A stereo dial. All points of context in the dizzying dark.

I beg my head to turn. It ignores me. All I see is the windshield as I twist and turn through the sky, heading to who knows where, and who knows how far down.

No other voices fill the space. No perfumes or hints of sweat. I'm alone. At least I think so. I struggle against my vocal cords. No sound. Just the rush of the wind as I glide. An airplane without wings.

Inevitably, the car hits bottom. The metal of the body groans as it smashes into the ground. It rolls and pitches as it flips over and over until landing with a dull thud on the tail end. Flames flicker behind me. Oranges and yellows reflecting off the broken pieces of glass around me. The pungent vapor of gas burns my lungs. Breathing is agony. My mind runs through the possible scenarios. One likely outcome—when the fire hits the tank, the entire vehicle explodes into oblivion.

I want to scream. I want to bust open the door and run away from this ticking time bomb. But I can't. I sit and watch my hands as they try to move the car with the steering wheel. I silently yell at them, but they are not my actions. Not my hands anymore.

The flames behind me grow higher and higher in the rear-view mirror.

My unresponsive body claws at the door handle, trying to get it open. It doesn't budge. The frame crumpled on impact. My body slams against the stuck door. The pain detonates in my shoulder, but I can't stop it. Every impact brings blinding pain. I can't stop.

The door finally bursts open. My body flees from the car. A hiss. Louder and louder.

Boom!

The explosion rages at my back. The hot, burning force pushes me forward to the ground. My muscles relax. Safe. For now. The car razes, but I survive. Resting my head on the dirty ground, I look up at the brilliant stars. The light fades, and once again I plunge into darkness.

TWENTY

The strange dream replayed over and over in my head. I even thought I smelled smoke billowing off my body as I showered and dressed for school. A side-effect of the sedative, maybe?

But for the first time in days, the haze in my brain lifted, if only a little. The sun shone brighter through the window. The sky seemed a deeper shade of blue. Maybe things would be okay.

I headed into English class and dropped into my desk. After pulling out my copy of *Macbeth*, I laid it out in front of me with a notebook and a pen. It might be my least favorite subject right now, but if the universe had decided to give me a second chance, I was going to grab it with both hands.

Right as the bell rang, Ethan slipped into class and headed for his desk. I smiled as he rushed past, but he didn't even look at me, probably too concerned that he might be late. Something he never did. At least, not that I could remember.

Mrs. Franklin rose from her chair and called everyone's attention with her trademark three sharp claps. "Everyone please turn to Act 4, Scene 1. Today we are going to go back and revisit my favorite characters, the witches. In this scene is where Macbeth further ..."

Mrs. Franklin's voice droned on, but the words disappeared into the noise of my own thoughts. I turned my body slightly to the left and leaned toward the desk behind me.

"Hey," I whispered.

No response. Maybe he hadn't heard me. I scanned the room,

but no one seemed to have noticed my lack of attention. I swiveled myself more.

"Hey," I whispered louder.

The girl beside me looked over, but Mrs. Franklin just kept on going.

"Hey," Ethan finally responded.

"Why so late this morning?" I asked.

"Busy." He didn't look up from his notebook.

I sat still for a moment. Then I tried again.

"What did you do last night?"

Mrs. Franklin drummed her index finger on my desk. "Miss James, please keep your conversations for after class."

"Yes. Of course." I righted myself in my seat. Why wasn't Ethan answering? Things got weird at the volleyball game. I knew it, and clearly so did he. What had I done? My foot tapped as I beat an uneven rhythm on my notebook with my pen. Was this class ever going to end?

FINALLY, the bell rang. I grabbed my books and bolted for the door, trying to get some reprieve from the stifling air choking me in the classroom. Too much talk of Shakespeare and not enough talk from Ethan. What was going on? A fresh breeze rushed at my face as I hit the hallway. Like yanking my head out from underwater. No longer drowning.

I leaned against the wall and waited for Ethan. His curt responses seemed off. Wrong. I hoped it wasn't my fault.

Everyone cleared out of the room, but still no Ethan. I glanced back through the door as he bolted past, nearly knocking me over, and headed off down the hallway.

"Ethan," I called, waving my arm in the air.

He didn't stop.

I raced up behind him and caught the crook of his elbow, tugging him to me. He glanced over his shoulder, his eyes wide and cheeks scorching.

"What's up with you today?" I asked, not letting go as he shifted his weight from foot to foot like he might run if given the chance.

"Nothing. Just forget about it." His head wobbled as he looked around at anything but me.

"No. Not until you tell me what's going on."

He wrenched his arm free. "It's nothing, Berkley. I've just got to go."

"Nice try." I stepped in front of him, my hands on my hips to make myself as wide and impassable as possible. "Something is totally bothering you, so tell me what it is, and I'll leave you alone. Are you mad at me?"

"I'm not mad. I'm ..." He scowled, then stretched his head toward the ceiling tiles. "Fine, I'll talk. But not here."

He glanced back and forth down the hallway then charged into the now empty English classroom. He ushered me in with a wave, staring out the tiny door window as he clicked it shut behind us.

I sat on the closest desk, swinging my feet an inch above the floor. "What's with the covert ops?"

"What?" His brow furrowed.

"Never mind. What's going on?"

Rubbing his hand across the back of his neck, he directed his gaze down at the floor. "It's about Saturday. I know I need to explain, but I thought you were still upset because you didn't answer my texts on Sunday."

"I was busy. I didn't answer any texts." More like I avoided all texts, trying to keep from answering Josh or my father. "If anything, Saturday was my fault."

A brief snippet of that day in the stands flashed in my memory. Staring into his dark eyes. Watching his lips move so intently. Both of us moving closer than we'd ever been before.

Too close. But nothing happened. Why was he being so dramatic?

"No, it's my fault. I asked you to come over." His face blazed bright, like the spark of a firework before it exploded. "But I didn't plan on anything happening. I wouldn't do that. Then we were kissing, and things kept moving faster, and you didn't seem like yourself. That's why I stopped. I don't want to be some rebound guy to you."

He took a step closer and reached his hand toward me. "I hoped I'd be more than that."

"More than what?" Kissing? I never kissed Ethan. I'd remember if something like that happened. I was at the hospital with Lane until I ... oh no. I slapped my hand over my mouth and gasped. "What time did I come over?"

He raised an eyebrow. "About eleven."

"Omigod." My throat tightened, and I struggled to breathe, like the air had actually gained mass. I launched off the desk and paced the line of linoleum tiles, refusing to look at him. Could I really have kissed Ethan? If so, what else might I have done? "And then what happened?"

He shook his head. "You just left. But you seemed angry, so I wasn't sure what to say this morning."

The room spun. I'd kissed Ethan, and I didn't even remember it. I kept pacing, trying to mine deep into my brain and pull out the memories, but they wouldn't come. The walls seemed to close in. My breath came harder and faster. I needed to be out of this room. I needed to think.

"Slow down, Berk." Ethan placed his hands on my shoulders and held me in place. He glanced down with his familiar, calming stare. So trusting. So honest. "I don't want you to think that I'm not interested, because I am. Trust me. It's just that everything happened so fast, and you probably just broke up with Josh, and—"

"We didn't break up."

"Oh." His eyes widened, and he stopped rambling.

My stomach twisted into knots as the gravity of the situation weighed on his expression.

He dropped his arms to his sides. "Then—"

"I have to go." I pushed past him, ripped open the door, and booked it down the hall.

TWENTY-ONE

Pick up, Lane. Pick up.

I stared at my phone screen, hoping for a miracle, but it just kept ringing.

Lane seemed to have disappeared. No one said they had seen her when I asked, and I wasn't about to ask Ethan. If anyone other than me could find Lane, it would be him, but I couldn't deal with that right now. Maybe she'd slept through first period? I had put her through a rough weekend, but this week was about to get worse. So much worse.

I went to Calculus and watched the minutes tick by on the clock until the bell rang, then bolted straight to her locker and waited. But she never showed. Ripping open my bag, I took out a piece of paper, wrote a quick note to call me immediately, and slid it through the slotted vent at the top. A strange shadow loomed behind me. I whirled around and smacked straight into Josh.

"Whoa, you scared me." I placed my hand over my racing heart and steadied myself.

"Funny, I thought maybe you had forgotten about me altogether." He held his lips tight, his narrow stare boring through me, leaving a cold, empty hole.

"I don't get it. What does that even mean?"

He placed his hands on the locker bank behind my head, trapping me between his hulking arms. "It means, have you been cheating on me?"

"What? You're insane. Why would I ever cheat on you?" I leaned forward to try to kiss him, but he jerked away.

"You said you were sick, but a few guys on the team said they saw you out last night. And they saw you last week at Squire's party. You said you always hated those things." His jaw clenched, and the muscles in his neck started to throb. "Please tell me they are making this stuff up and you aren't seeing someone else."

"I'm not. I wouldn't do that to you." I reached up to place my hand on his cheek, but my fingers shook, and I yanked it back down by my side. Except if what Ethan said was true, maybe I would?

"Really? And why would they lie to me?"

"I don't know." Nor did I know where any of the football team would've seen me last night. One more mystery to solve. "But I'm not seeing anyone else either."

"I don't know who to believe anymore, Berkley." He wiped his hands over his face and groaned. "I find out that you've been hiding all this college stuff from me for months, then the guys are saying you lied about being sick, and even Brett said you were all over that friend of yours, Ethan, at the volleyball finals."

My stomach hollowed. So all that wasn't in my head. It had all been too much, and I knew it. "I told you I didn't want to lie about Princeton, and I really was sick. Plus, Ethan just sat with me at the game. No big deal."

"A game you were supposed to be playing in, except you didn't because of this." He took my wrist and held my bandaged hand up between us. "You didn't even tell me that your house got broken into and that you were hurt. I had to hear it from someone else."

My pulse pounded in my temples as Josh piled up the lies and tossed them at my feet. "I knew you had a big game and didn't want you to worry."

"You're supposed to be my girlfriend. I'm supposed to worry when bad things happen to you. But everyone else knew. Your teammates. Your friends. That Ethan guy that you're always hanging out with. Just tell me the truth."

Ethan. I'd kissed Ethan. Or at least he thought I did. I couldn't remember anything to know the truth. Maybe there were others? I shuddered. Maybe there were a ton of things I didn't know about myself over the past week.

"I ..." I looked at the ceiling, hoping for an answer. "Nothing is going on."

He yanked his cell phone out of his jacket pocket and unlocked the screen. "And if I ask him, he'll tell me the same thing?"

"Don't do that." I reached for the phone, but he wrenched it back out of my grasp.

"Why? Scared of what he might tell me?"

"No." *Yes.*

"I must be pretty stupid. I spent all weekend feeling awful about getting mad at you. Then you wouldn't return my texts. You keep lying to me. I thought you loved me."

Josh slammed his fist into the locker behind me, leaving a small dent with his knuckle, and headed off down the hall.

"What the hell, Berk?" Lane said as she rushed up beside me.

"Someone told Josh I'm cheating on him, and he thinks it's Ethan."

"What?" Her mouth dropped open as her bag slid down her arm to the ground. "That's ridiculous. Nothing's going on with you and Ethan."

Collapsing against the locker bank, I held my head in my hands. I couldn't even think straight. How had this gotten so out of control?

"No," Lane gasped. "Berkley, you didn't."

"I don't know. I don't remember anything. But Ethan says I went over there Saturday night and we kissed, and now Josh is going to kill Ethan if he finds out."

"We need to find him before Josh does." Lane grabbed my arm and dragged me down the hallway. "I thought I saw him studying in the courtyard. If we cut through the gym, we might beat Josh there."

··*·(·*···

THE COOL, fall air whooshed against my face as I swung open the double doors into the courtyard. Sunshine blasted across the square and danced on the heads of students gathering near the picnic tables. Specifically, our picnic table.

"I think we're too late," Lane said as she grabbed my hand and we ran toward the commotion.

Ethan sat, oblivious to his fate, face down in his algebra textbook as Josh approached with the stealth of an elephant stampede.

He flipped Ethan's binder off the table onto the ground. "You must think you're pretty smart. That I wouldn't find out."

Ethan glanced up, then crept around the picnic table to get his book. His eyes stayed locked on Josh and his entourage with every careful motion as he crouched, then stood again. "About what?"

"About you and Berkley, jackass." Josh stepped forward and pushed Ethan in the chest, sending him stumbling back a few feet.

I cringed, the weight of my mistakes crushing against my ribs as hard as Josh's hands must've slammed against Ethan's.

Ethan raised his hands in surrender. "Listen, Josh. It's not what you think. I didn't know you were still together. I thought you'd broken up."

My breath caught in my throat, and I struggled to breathe. *No, Ethan. Don't.*

"You mean you wish we'd broken up." Josh shoved him again as the small crowd grew and gathered closer around them. "You've always been sitting around on the sidelines, just waiting, haven't you? I tried to ignore it, but it was all here in front of me. Well, I guess you've had your shot now, how does it feel?"

I pushed my way through the crowd and rushed in between them. "Enough, Josh. Leave him alone."

Josh stopped his advance and glared down at me. Fire flickered in his eyes. A red rage burning out of control, and I'd been the one to light the match. "Get out of the way."

"No." I crossed my arms and planted my feet. "I'm not leaving. Just let this go."

He stepped to the left, and I followed, cutting him off. He bobbed right. I shadowed.

"Fine." He tossed his hands up and pulled his head back. "I've only got one more thing to say to him anyway."

"What's that?" Ethan sighed.

I dropped my arms to my sides and gave him a few inches of freedom. He took full advantage and stormed past, nearly knocking me over.

Josh's fist made a dull thud noise as it connected with Ethan's face, and Ethan dropped backward onto the ground and grabbed his eye. The crowd made a collective groan. Josh smirked at me then did some macho false start toward Ethan, making him twitch on the ground.

Heat blasted through my limbs as I clenched my fists. "What the hell was that? Did you really need to hit him?" My head spun as a tornado of emotions tore through my body. Ripping me apart and smashing everything I'd ever built. And it was all my own fault. My eyes stung as the crowd distorted into a watery haze. "I tried to tell you this is just a big misunderstanding. Can't we talk about this?"

The crowd waited silently for an answer; the stares flipping from Josh's face to mine and back.

"I don't think so. All you seem to want to do anymore is talk. Doesn't seem to get us anywhere." He puffed out his chest like some prize rooster.

"Then maybe you need to listen." *Why did I say that?* A darkness surged through me. Muscles separating from bone. Soul from body. A clarity as the clouds lifted off my brain for the first time in a long while. "It's over, Josh."

He laughed. "Uh, yeah. That's pretty obvious."

"I mean, it's been over for a while now. Except I didn't want to admit it." The tears dried as the darkness solidified in my bloodstream. Thick and strong. "We should've broken up a long time ago. But I couldn't handle the thought of losing you."

Josh's face dropped, the words hitting their mark. Not as a weapon, but as a truth. A long-overdue truth I hadn't been able to face. I didn't want to go to Texas because I didn't want to be with Josh. I still loved him, but it wasn't enough anymore. Full stop.

The tough-guy, rigid stare slid back into place and bored into my forehead. "Well, you've lost me now. I don't need a cheating liar like you anyway."

I shook my head. "Nice, Josh, real nice."

He shrugged. "Just saying."

The crowd laughed.

"I only wish I'd figured this all out before I risked injuring my throwing hand on your second choice's ugly face." He glared down at Ethan, still sprawled on the ground. "By the way, he's going to need some ice. Might want to get on that."

Josh pushed past me and headed toward the school, a satisfied smirk across his smug face.

"Do you not even care about the last two years?" I called after him.

He didn't turn around. "Not anymore."

I stood there and watched him walk away. A few guys high-fived him and patted him on the back as he swaggered off into the sunlight. After all, it was quite the punch—broke Ethan's face and my heart in one shot.

TWENTY-TWO

"Looks like you're going to have quite the shiner." Lane dug through her lunch and tossed an ice pack on the picnic table. "We can be bruise buddies."

Ethan raised his eyebrows and winced. "Great. How did you get yours anyway?"

Lane glanced over at me, her eyes widening. "Volleyball. But you've got to learn to stay on your feet when taking a punch, though. Square yourself to your opponent and don't lock your knees."

"And since when did you become the street fighting pro?" Ethan picked up the ice pack and eased it onto his eye. He flinched a few times but finally let it settle.

"Took a boxing class once. I still have their card if you want to get in on a few lessons. Mention my name and they'll give you fifty percent off your first class." Lane jumped up, then hopped back and forth like a prizefighter as she jabbed at an imaginary opponent.

"No, thanks. I think my brawling days are over," Ethan said.

I leaned across the table and wrapped an arm over my stomach, my gut aching just as awful as the skin swelling around Ethan's eye. "I'm really sorry about Josh. I didn't know he was going to do that."

"I'm okay, but"—he slid closer to me and whispered—"why did you tell him about ... you know?"

Lane slammed her hands on the table top with a loud smack.

"No point in being all hush-hush, I already know she tried to jump your bones."

Ethan's face flushed, and he bolted upright.

"Seriously?" I snapped.

Lane sat back down on the bench. "Look, E, Berk tells me everything, so there is little point expecting that I wouldn't have already heard."

"I guess I'm the only one who decided to respect your privacy." He pulled the ice pack down and tried blinking his bruising eye. A few red dots from broken blood vessels grew near his eyebrow, and I shuddered.

"I didn't tell him, exactly." I lowered my head. "At least I didn't mean to. It's complicated."

"I'm sure it is, but a heads-up would have been nice," he said.

"Some weird stuff has been going on with me lately, and ..." I glared over at Lane, hoping for her to jump in and help.

Instead, she sprang up from the table and knocked her knuckles on the wooden slats of the top as she hurried away. "This seems to be my exit. Talk to you two later."

I chased after her. "What are you doing?"

"It's about time you tell him, isn't it? The boy just took a bullet for you, so I say lay it all out there."

"I can't ... I ..."

I glanced back at Ethan; his head rested on the top of the picnic table. He deserved the truth. Lying seemed to have gotten me into this mess. I needed to set it right.

"Fine."

"Good. Come find me after." She patted me on the shoulder and walked away.

Dropping my head to my chest, I took a deep breath. This wasn't the way I'd ever want to tell someone something like this, but Lane was right. How come she was always right all of a sudden? I inhaled again and let it out super slow. *Now or never.*

I spun around and landed right into Ethan's chest.

"Whoa, don't sneak up on me like that." I stumbled back, and my ankle rolled to the side.

"Sorry." Ethan winced as he clutched my arms and steadied me back on my feet. "I just didn't want you to leave yet."

My pulse throbbed in my ears—but from the scare, the near fall, or the secrets I'd been keeping, I wasn't sure. "Yeah, there's something I need to tell you."

"Okay, but first, let me say thank you."

"For what? All of this"—I waved my hand in front of his swollen eye—"is my fault."

"Maybe. But you didn't just let it happen. You stood up to Josh, and that wasn't easy." He slipped his hand on my cheek, and I leaned into his warm palm. "You have no idea how much that meant to me."

And there it was. The look he'd given me at the volleyball game. The same one that hid beneath layers of panic as he told me about the late-night visit I couldn't remember. The one Lane had been watching for months now. So raw and piercing it stole my breath.

I cleared my throat. "Please don't say—"

His lips pressed against mine, and I swallowed the words trapped in my mouth. I didn't need them anymore anyway. Ethan had a confession to make.

In that kiss, he told me everything. The years of waiting for that perfect moment, the longing, the heartbreak. The way his lips moved slow and careful as he tasted this kiss and savored it. The slight slant of his neck and the pressure of his fingertips on my skin. Perfect, in a meticulous way that only studying and dreaming and wishing of the other person could make so right.

I placed my hands at his neck, just inside the collar of his jacket, as his pulse pounded against my palm. I fell into him. Into his arms. Into his kiss. The rhythm, the cadence, in impeccable time. As if somewhere, something inside me had been waiting for this too.

The sensation flowed through my body in waves. Warm at first, then building hotter, scorching my senses, until I couldn't stop. I pushed up on my toes, craving more. Needing more. He followed my lead, but his jaw tensed beneath my unrelenting mouth.

A moment flashed through my brain. The familiarity of these same lips crushed against mine. Except darker. Wanting. Wrong. My limbs froze as snips and cuts of memories spliced with the sensations of the now. Saturday night. A twisted version of myself devouring Ethan's honesty and corrupting into something deplorable. A massive mistake.

I pushed my hands into his chest and jerked my head to the side. The disturbing urge drained from my bloodstream. "I can't do this."

"What's wrong?" Ethan gasped and pulled his face away, the euphoria of the kiss fading fast as confusion set in. "I thought this was what you wanted? That's what you said."

"I did?" My head spun as I replayed the conversation from this morning, but nothing matched up.

"At my house on Saturday. You told me—"

"Stop. Ethan." My stomach hollowed. "I don't remember."

He ripped his hands off me as if my arms were fire. "You don't remember?"

I shook my head. "No. I don't remember going to your house. I don't remember what I said. I don't remember anything. That's what I needed to talk to you about. There's something wrong with me."

"I'm such an idiot." Ethan clutched his face and backed up. "If you regret it, fine, but just tell me. Don't lie or make up some story, Berkley. This is embarrassing enough."

He stared at the ground as his shoulders crumpled in toward his broad chest. The harsh truth biting down on him, hard enough to draw blood.

"It's not a lie, it's—"

A silhouette stained the grass beside us. I glanced up. A girl.

Black hair. Black eyeliner. Black boots. The same black boots I'd seen at the volleyball game. An icy chill ripped down my spine. The memory so clear. The nervous writhing of my stomach as those boots stopped outside the stall and waited for me.

"Excuse me," the shadow girl said as she took a cautious step forward. "You're Berkley James, right? You live down on Piper Street?"

I crossed my arms and jutted my hip toward the unwelcome intruder. "Yes. Why?"

She glanced over her shoulder. Two other dark-clad girls stood under the shade of an elm tree and beckoned her with their hands. I looked again. Memories folded upon memories as a face crisped in my brain. Outside the smoothie shop. I'd seen one of them staring at me through the window.

The shadow girl's face blanched, and she stepped back. "Never mind. I should go."

She glanced at Ethan then turned to run.

I caught her by the arm. "You and your friends have been following me."

Ethan stormed past us. "I'm leaving."

"No, Ethan. Wait." I lunged after him, but the girl in my grip twisted and tried to escape. I held tighter. "No, you don't. Why have you been chasing me around?"

I watched Ethan stomp off toward the school, and a sharp stinging rose in my chest.

Relaxing my grasp on the shadow girl's arm, I pushed down the pain and turned to her. "Okay, I don't know who you are, but—"

"My name is Orianna." She ripped her arm out of my hand and shook it out. "Not that I should bother telling you now, but did you see a green light in the bushes behind your house last Monday night?"

My heart thumped faster, which I doubted was even possible. I closed my eyes and pictured the eerie light swaying in the darkness. Lunging toward me. My hands gripped into fists as phantom pain cramped in my stomach where it had slammed into my flesh. I tensed and ripped my eyes open again. "How did you know about that?"

She hung her head, and a few inky box-dyed strands fell in front of her face. "Because I was there."

"Wait a minute." I narrowed my stare. "You were there? I didn't dream that?"

She shook her head as deep crimson bloomed in her cheeks.

The sharp pain in my stomach deepened. "What did you do to me?"

I lunged forward, and Orianna jerked back.

"Nothing." She threw her open palms up in surrender. "It wasn't like that. We didn't expect that to happen."

"You didn't expect *what* to happen? What did you do to me?"

She took another cautious step back. "We didn't do anything to you. At least not on purpose."

My knuckles clenched tighter. Enough to nearly break through my skin.

"The three of us"—she nodded toward her waiting friends near the tree—"me, Kassia, and Dabria, were doing a harmless equinox ritual when—"

"A what?" I shook my head, trying to make sense of her crazy. Too many words. Not enough logic.

"An equinox ritual. As part of our practice, we celebrate all things to do with nature."

"Your practice?"

"Yes, we're witches. But—"

"What?" My eyes bulged, and I blinked to knock them back into my skull. "Witches? Like hocus pocus and all that? Yeah, right."

Orianna dropped her hands to her hips and glared. "Whatever. Not the point. We were out in the bushes, doing our ritual, then we heard you coming and hid. But then the green light appeared, and you started yelling, so we took off." She stared back over my shoulder.

Her monochromatically dressed crew glowered at us. Their stares hung on my shoulders, rooting me to my spot. They couldn't really be witches, could they? Witches didn't exist. They were fairy tales to scare little kids into behaving. Except regardless if these girls were insane enough to believe they actually were witches, it didn't change that they saw what happened to me. They knew. My skin flushed as heat bubbled up through my veins. They knew this whole time and never said a word.

"My sisters didn't want me to tell you," Orianna continued. "They figured it was your own fault for interrupting us."

"What was my fault? What happened to me that night?" I shouted.

She trembled and stepped backward. "Maybe this was a mistake."

"No, no." I tried to keep my voice calm so she didn't shut down again. "Please tell me what you know."

"I need to go," she said and tried to run off toward her group.

I grabbed her by the arm again, but she squirmed free and kept running, her black boots kicking up behind her. I gave chase, but the three of them disappeared back into the school before I caught up. For a witch, she ran like a cheetah. Maybe she should be playing soccer instead of make-believe. Maybe if she did, I wouldn't be in this mess.

After leaning against the tree and giving it a solid slam with my fist, I yanked my phone from my pocket. My fingers shook too much to text, every word coming out completely wrong until I gave up and dialed. It rang twice.

"So did you tell him?" the voice chirped on the other end of the line.

"Not now, Lane. I need your help. Someone knows what happened to me."

Twenty-Three

My fingers grazed the metal knob as the library door flung open from inside. I jumped out of the way as the edge zinged just past the end of my nose, the shock increasing the tempo of my already hammering pulse. Splaying my hand over my chest, I struggled to catch my breath. I'd had enough surprises for today—maybe even for the next year.

Lane sped by me into the hallway then halted, her sneakers squeaking against the worn tile floor.

She spun around as her hair flopped against her forehead. "You're here. Finally. What took so long?"

She tucked her curls back behind her ears and grabbed my hand.

"Sorry, I ran here as fast as I could, but—"

I swallowed the remaining words back down as Lane yanked me behind her. The harsh fluorescent lights swirled around my vision as I focused on following without tripping over my own feet.

"Where are we going?" I called after her. "Don't you want me to tell you the rest of what happened before class starts?"

She glanced back and shot me a crooked, mischievous smile over her shoulder. "No need. I'm going to hear it from the source."

Lane weaved us back and forth, earning scowls from the increasing number of students that flooded the senior hall. Lockers slammed behind us. Metallic pinging added to the annoyed mutterings as we passed. The school bell squawked, signaling the end of lunch, as we flew over the steps into the junior and sopho-more wing.

Finally, Lane slowed and shifted to walk beside me. She squeezed my hand and smiled. "Now, the way I see it, if neither of us knows this girl and her creepy friends, then they likely aren't seniors, but they clearly go to school here if they've been stalking you without being called out."

"Excellent theory, but how's that going to help us find them?"

"Peek into every classroom in this school until we catch a glimpse, then wait for them to come out. Starting right here." She stopped in front of a closed door and pointed. In the window, students shuffled into their desks. "I'm sure it shouldn't be too difficult to find three girls who look like vampires or whatever."

"Witches, Lane. They said they were witches." I shifted back and forth on my toes as I scanned the inside of the classroom. No sign of Orianna or her friends. "But aren't you worried about getting caught skipping class?"

She rested her head on my shoulder as she linked her arm in mine and hauled me farther down the hall. "Oh, my poor, innocent child. How do you think things get done in the world, by everyone doing exactly what they're supposed to do all the time?"

"I'm betting you're going to say no."

She nodded. "Precisely. Do you think Ethan would come help? We need a tall guy to look in the top windows."

I wriggled out of her grip as warmth rippled across my skin. The devastated expression on Ethan's face crept into my brain, even though I'd tried to push it down. "He's probably busy."

Lane stopped short, dragging me backward as my feet kept moving. "What did you do?"

"Nothing." The rush of heat flooded from my limbs to my face, signaling my lie in scarlet across my cheeks. I dropped my head to my chest and stared at my shoelaces. Memories of Ethan's lips drifted across my own. I sighed, trying to straighten out the thoughts in my head, and failed. "I just didn't get a chance to tell him everything yet, so he won't exactly understand what we're doing."

"Sure. Sure." Her hands slammed to her hips as her piercing stare plucked at my emotions like guitar strings. "You're lucky we have work to do, otherwise I would torture it out of you. Now, you take the left side, I'll take the right, and hopefully, we can come up with something before the bell rings."

We searched through every classroom we could access. Students stared and pointed; plus, a few times we caught the attention of the teacher, and I'd been certain we were busted. Except neither of us saw any of the girls, and they should be pretty easy to spot considering they were dressed from bangs to boots in black.

"This is hopeless, Lane. They probably took off as soon as Orianna confessed." I leaned against the wall and slid down to sit on the dingy floor with my knees pulled into my chest.

I rested my head against my crossed arms and sighed.

Lane plunked down beside me and flung her arm over my shoulder. "What kind of name is Orianna anyway? I'll bet her name is really Ashley or Jessica or something basic like that."

"Probably. But that doesn't mean she doesn't know what happened. The witch thing is obviously fake, but she's the only one who's been able to tell me anything about that night." I peeled my head up and pressed my palms against my temples. "It just feels like everything is spiraling and I can't make it stop spinning."

"Well, then, I guess we need to find them. But if I was a horror-movie-monster wannabe with an angry senior chasing after me, where would I go?"

Lane nudged me with her shoulder and stroked her chin like an old-time villain.

I shook my head. "I have no idea. Maybe hiding out in a basement somewhere."

"No. That's the first place we'd think to look." She grabbed my arm and pulled me to my feet. "If they're smart, they would go to the last place anyone would expect. Come on."

She ran down the hall, and I struggled to catch up as I kept looking into all the windows of the classrooms as I passed, just in case we'd missed something. She sped up and ran out the side doors toward the football field. The looming scoreboard grew larger as the head of the Henstridge Ram in the center watched our every move. Sure enough, as Lane had predicted, three black-clad figures appeared on the bleachers as we approached.

Lane ducked behind the rows of metal seats and signaled for me to keep quiet.

"How did you know they would be here?" I whispered.

"Football fields are where the shiny, happy people hang out. Didn't think it would be their scene, which means it's the first place they would go if they were trying to avoid us. You go that way"—she pointed left—"and I'll go this way. They won't be able to escape."

I nodded, and we took our positions. As soon as I went topside on the bleachers, the trio stood and moved to run, where they got the surprise of Lane at the other end.

"Boo!" she yelled, as they backed away from her.

The girl closest to Lane tripped and toppled over onto the remaining girls, knocking them all against the metal bench with a series of loud bangs that echoed in the crisp autumn air.

"I've told you everything I know. Just leave us alone. We don't want any violence," Orianna said as she squeezed herself out of the middle of the pile. She stood, holding one open hand toward me and the other toward Lane.

"Violence? We weren't going to beat you up," I said, ignoring Orianna's warning and closing the gap between us.

Lane cracked her knuckles and stared each of them down like my hired bodyguard. "Well, she wasn't going to."

I shook my head at Lane, and she stood down, but not without sticking out her lip in a pout.

"I just want some answers," I said. "What's wrong with me?"

"Other than the fact that you don't know anything about personal boundaries?" A girl with a messy black bun sticking out of each side of her head thrust her hands on her hips and scowled at me. She pushed to her feet and squared her stance as her stare narrowed and her left eye rolled back in a creepy, menacing way.

A chill slithered over my skin, and I shuffled a step back. *If all this was true, did they know how to curse people?*

I cast my eyes away from her and cleared my suddenly dry throat. "Look, since you all did whatever you did to me, it's been a complete nightmare. I've been sleepwalking. Doing weird messed-up things in the middle of the night. I think I even trashed my own house."

"And you think that it's our fault?" The angry girl tried to lock eyes with me again, but I turned my head and refused to let her. Orianna hung her head.

I eased closer, my shadow looming large and dark over her. "Of course I do. Besides, why would you bother to tell me? And none of this strange stuff happened until after I got beamed by that green light."

The girl beside Orianna snickered and turned her head toward the sun, a pair of oversized black sunglasses covering most of her face. Her amber skin glowed in the light as she flicked her wrist toward me. "Beamed? Not quite. It totally knocked the crap out of you." She flipped her glossy black mane over her shoulder and laughed. The other two glanced at each other and joined in. Cackling together at my misfortune.

Lane stomped her foot on the bench, and the clash of metal rang across the football field. The girls shrank closer together with angry glares, but they stopped laughing.

I closed my eyes and inhaled deeply through my nose to settle the seething anger growing in my chest. "Didn't you think it might be important for me to know that some mystical glow stick blasted me? Why didn't you tell me sooner?"

The three glanced at each other in silence, as if waiting for someone to make the first move.

Orianna eventually sighed and gazed back up at us, likely pulling the telepathic short straw. "We were scared. We'd never seen anything like that happen before, and we didn't know what to do."

"Plus, we thought you were dead," the glamorous one chimed in as she examined her ebony manicure.

"Dabria!" Orianna scolded.

Dabria shrugged as her lip curled up in a half-smirk. "Well, we did. You just lay there after it hit you, so we weren't sure if you were alive, and no one wanted to check if you were still breathing."

"Instead, you just left her there!" Lane shouted. "What kind of psychos do that? You didn't think to call the police or anything?"

Their snarky smiles deflated.

Orianna dropped her head to her chest. "We went back for you that night. But by the time we got there, you were already gone. Then you actually showed up at school the next day, so we thought everything was fine."

"It's definitely not even close to fine." I jutted my hip to the side, blocking more of their escape, and stood taller as my silhouette swallowed them, the scorching sun at my back.

"We know." Orianna rubbed her hands over her face then looked to the other two girls for support, but no one volunteered. She huffed into her palms then dropped her shoulders in defeat. "Everything seemed to be fine for a while, but then we heard about the break-in, and then the scene in the courtyard today with your boyfriend happened. It looked like the light and your sudden bad luck weren't just a coincidence. Besides, you've kind of been looking terrible lately. All tired and sick and stuff."

I cringed but quickly shook it off. *Great. Everyone's noticed.*

"Plus, your aura's super dark gray," Dabria added.

I shook my head and blinked. "What?"

"It means that your body and spirit are not well. Like you're going through some kind of crisis or something," the angry girl with the puffy buns said. "And it sounds pretty accurate to me."

"Enough, Kassia," Orianna reprimanded.

The girl's back straightened, rigid and ready as if to argue, but her plum-painted lips stayed closed.

Orianna stared her down for a few seconds, then sighed. "Dabria can read auras, and she saw yours. That's when we knew that something had gone wrong and we—"

Kassia cleared her throat.

"*I* decided we needed to reach out to you. One of our first rules is 'An ye harm none, do what ye will,' so I didn't think we could stand by any longer."

Lane stomped her foot on the bleachers again. "In English."

"Do no harm, and she was speaking English, half-wit." Kassia uncrossed her arms and leaned toward Lane.

Lane growled.

"Okay, then you can fix it?" I asked, trying to get back to the point.

"No. We don't even know what happened, let alone how to fix it," Orianna said.

I tossed my hands in the air and turned away, trying to push down the rage bubbling through my bloodstream. "Then what good are you to me?"

"We know someone," Orianna's voice continued behind me, but softer. Cautious. "We have a mentor who might be able to help, if you will go see her."

My shoulders sank. A mentor? *Great.* This whole witch thing kept getting weirder. Plus, it just meant one more person I had to tell the truth to. *Fantastic.*

"Sounds good. Call her up," Lane answered for me.

I glanced back over my shoulder. Lane kept her distance from the witches, but her glare made it clear she only needed a second to start causing chaos.

Orianna nodded. "Okay. Meet us after school at Divina Tea on Kennedy Street."

"No. How do I know I can trust you? After all, you've already screwed me over once," I said. "I want to go now."

"Calm down, or we won't help you at all." Dabria scoffed and stuck out a full, pouty lip.

Orianna stepped in front of her and gazed up at me through her dark lashes, her sea-green eyes clear and calm. "If we give you our word, then we will honor it."

I wanted to argue. I wanted to scream and make demands, but the words stuck in my throat. Sharp and needling at my nerves until I could only nod.

The group gathered close together, like a murder of crows ganging up against a predator, then waved for me to move out of the way. I obliged and watched them descend the stairs and head back toward the school.

Lane's mouth dropped open as I let them pass. Her arms flew up in confusion.

I shook my head and dropped onto the bleachers, my head in my hands. Lane plunked down beside me, the metal rumbling beneath my thighs.

"Do you think any of this is true?" I asked. "That they really might be—"

"Total witches?" Lane stared after them then shook her head. "I don't know, but I'll bet you a hundred bucks that at least one of them is really named Ashley."

Twenty-Four

A small bell jingled overhead as a rush of rich, spicy notes of chamomile and cinnamon wafted out into the street. I breathed them in. It didn't smell witchy. Not that I knew what something witchy would smell like, but I doubted it would've been like that. The air from Divina Tea smelled like a comfort, not a curse. A warm hug for your nose.

Lane raced up behind me, her sneakers thumping loudly on the pavement. "Hold up. We can't go in yet. We have to wait for Ethan."

"You invited Ethan? I haven't told him about any of this." I let go of the door and stepped back onto the sidewalk. The toastiness of the shop faded fast, and I pulled my jacket tighter around my chest. "Besides, even if I had, I doubt he'll come."

"Why? Because you stomped on his heart with Josh's football cleats?"

The chill spread faster through my limbs, and I shivered. "He told you that?"

"Not in those exact words, but that was the gist of it." She pushed herself up to sit on the back of a bus bench along the edge of Kennedy Street. "You didn't think you were the only one who trusted me with their secrets, did you?"

"And it looks like you are doing an outstanding job of keeping them too."

"Hey, I always keep things quiet, but that one wasn't a secret, since you were there and all." She planted her elbows on her knees and rested her chin on her hands as she flashed a devious smirk.

I refused to give her the satisfaction of eye contact. Instead, I studied the scalloped edges of the jade and periwinkle awning hanging over the tea shop window. People inside sat at small tables, sipping their drinks. They laughed. They frowned. Oblivious to the broken girl and her snarky best friend standing outside.

"Also, since you punked out from telling Ethan about what's been going on, I did you a favor and filled him in," Lane added.

I let out a sigh. The steam of my warm breath swirled around my head as my shoulders deflated. "I'm not sure if I should thank you or be super furious."

"Don't get all dramatic, you know you would've dragged this out forever. Besides, he's worried about you and wants to help. I didn't really see a point in lying to him."

"You're probably right." No. She was right. The sick feeling in my gut knew it. "But I didn't 'stomp on Ethan's heart,' as you so nicely put it."

She wagged her finger at me. "You knew full well that he liked you, yet you let him kiss you."

"What?" I cringed and thrust my hands to my hips. "I did not just let him kiss me."

Lane laughed and jerked forward, nearly falling off the bench. "Keep telling yourself that. But I guess it isn't really letting him kiss you if you kiss him back like that. Not going to lie, that was a pretty heavy make-out to have on school property."

I covered my face with my hands and growled into my palms. "Is there anything he didn't tell you?"

"Oh, that part I found out from Danielle and Kaitlin during sixth period. They had video. The natural sunlight gave the whole thing a nice romantic glow."

She waved her arm in front of her, drawing an invisible rainbow through the sky as she fought to choke back more laughter.

My cheeks burned against the cool early-evening air. "Fantastic."

She dropped her hand into her lap, and her smile disappeared.

"So how I see it is that he likes you, you like him, and you totally shut him down."

"Did you completely miss the part where less than twenty minutes before, I broke up with my long-term boyfriend in front of a large crowd of people?"

"We both know that your relationship was on the decline anyway. Even your alcoholic father figured that out. All I'm saying is that you shouldn't toy with him if you're into him." Lane crossed her legs and straightened her back. "Or even worse, don't toy with him if you aren't into him."

"I don't know how I feel right now. I don't even know if I'm thinking clearly anymore."

"Well, part of you is. Why do you think you showed up at his place in the middle of the night? Something locked away in that brain of yours knows." Lane launched off the bench and marched up to me, her finger pointed at my head.

I jerked to the side and put more space between us. "I can't deal with this right now. I need to figure out what is going on with this whole sleepwalking thing, then maybe I can worry about this."

"Fine. Can I ask him out then?"

"What?" I shook my head. "I can't believe you would ask me that."

"See, you do like him." She waved her hand in the air as she glanced over my shoulder. "Hey, Ethan, just talking about you."

I spun around as Ethan crept our direction. He stuck his hands deep in his pockets and dropped his head toward the pavement the second I caught his eye. An apology formed on my tongue, but I knew it wasn't enough, so I swallowed it back down.

"Now, let's go meet the Wicked Witch of the Midwest, shall we?" Lane grabbed the door and ushered us both into the café.

·:·*·☾·*·:·

A BLAST of heat hit us as we walked through the door, but the soothing qualities did little to ease my trembling limbs. The idea that my sanity hung on the actions of a bunch of self-proclaimed witches pinched and poked at my stomach. Or maybe I was just hungry again. Ethan tagging along didn't help much, either. The second he walked down the sidewalk toward us, it opened a box in my brain I tried to keep shut. At least for now. He was Ethan. My friend. Right? Nothing more. Except as he brushed my arm to head deeper into the tea shop, my lips twitched, remembering far too many things I needed to forget right now.

"Sorry." Ethan looked back over his shoulder, his dark eyes wide and far away as he positioned himself on the other side of Lane, away from me.

I opened my mouth to speak, but nothing came out.

In the back corner of the shop, Orianna swiveled in her seat and waved us over, as if we couldn't see her and her monochromatic crew amongst the cluster of white and seafoam-green tables in the cute little space.

Lane shot me a last reassuring glance, and I nodded as I marched over to their table. Both she and Ethan trailed behind me.

"Thanks for showing up." I leaned over the table and forced out the words without the scornful tone I desperately wanted to add.

"We promised, and we don't go back on promises," Orianna replied.

"No, you just leave people for dead in the middle of the bush." Lane crossed her arms and wobbled her head like a poor impression of a boxer.

I stared Lane down, and she shrugged. The other girls glared at her, clearly not appreciating her lack of tact. Not that they deserved any. Ignoring them, she fidgeted with the meticulous display of tumblers and teapots in rich fall colors of crimson, mocha, and terra-cotta behind her.

I grabbed an empty chair at a nearby table. "So, what exactly are we doing here? You said you were going to get some help."

Dabria drank from her glossy black, star-patterned tumbler, then clasped it in her hands. Her stacks of silver rings clicked against the metal. "That's what we're here for, to meet with our mentor. We figured it might be easiest if we brought you to her instead of trying to explain your problem ourselves."

"Your spiritual mentor works at a tea shop?" I asked.

"Actually, their 'spiritual mentor' owns a tea shop." A sweet, melodic voice drifted toward the table as a tall woman glided closer, making air quotes with her fingers. "But I much prefer the term 'guide'. Less of a power dynamic."

Orianna smiled as she approached, and even Kassia seemed to lose her scowl and sit up straighter.

"Blessed be, Sage," the witches chimed in unison.

"Blessed be, girls. Who are your friends?"

The woman slipped a green apron over her head and mussed her thick blond waves. She didn't blend in with Orianna and her sidekicks. In fact, she radiated sunshine in equal measure to the three girls' broody darkness. In just a white T-shirt and jeans, she emitted power. Strength. But that could be the heels on her amazing knee-high sable suede boots.

Lane nearly dropped an adorable copper French press as she stared at the newcomer. "Wait. Do they actually write Sage on your chai latte, or is that just your pretend witchy name?"

I elbowed her in the side. She glared at me.

Sage sashayed behind Lane and rearranged the display, correcting every product into its perfect spot, then stood back and inspected her handiwork. "First off, I prefer a matcha. Second, yes, Sage is my actual name. My *witchy* name is Lucretia." She turned to Orianna. "Please tell me this one isn't thinking of converting?"

She shook her head.

"Thank the Goddess," Sage said, staring up to the ceiling, then dropping herself in an armchair, legs crossed and statuesque. "So what brings you by? I didn't think we were meeting until next week."

Orianna moved to a seat next to her and leaned close, her black hair creating a curtain between us. "We have a problem."

Sage sat up and exhaled sharply, a disappointed frown turning down her full rose lips. "I told you, none of you are ready for spell work yet."

"That's not it." Orianna glanced back to Dabria and Kassia. They both nodded. She dropped her arms by her sides and took a deep breath, letting it out slow. "We did a Mabon celebration ritual last week, but I think something went wrong."

Sage's expression hardened, and she nodded toward Lane, Ethan, and me. "Do you really want to be talking about this in front of them?"

Pointing at me, Kassia sneered. "She's what went wrong."

"You," Sage called. "Come here."

I trudged slowly from the safety of my little table and sat down beside her.

She took my hand and sandwiched it between hers on the plush arm of her chair. Her soft skin calmed some of my nerves, as her questioning stare zoned in on my face as if trying to read some ancient text from off my complexion. "Now tell me, what happened?"

I looked back at Lane and Ethan, and they shrugged. "It was late at night, and I ran out into the woods because I thought I saw a fire. All I found was a bunch of candles, but then this bright, green light came out of nowhere and just rammed me in the stomach."

She nodded, but her face didn't give away any emotions. "Then what happened?"

"Then I woke up in my bed. But now every time I go to sleep, my body goes off to do whatever it does, and I wake up the next day not having any idea what happened."

"Are you sure?" She squeezed my hand tighter and narrowed her stare. "You aren't just dreaming?"

"Oh, she's sure. We've both seen it." Lane nudged Ethan.

He nodded as his shoulders deflated around him, and he dropped his gaze to the floor. So Lane had really told him everything. I winced.

Sage patted the back of my hand and slid back in her armchair. "Hmm. All that from a Mabon ritual? Seems a little excessive."

Lane shot her hand in the air as if she were in class. Sage nodded in acknowledgment.

"What in the world is Mabon?" Lane asked.

"Fall equinox." Kassia rolled her eyes at Lane. "Seriously?"

Lane narrowed her glare, and Kassia ignored her.

"Okay, did you cast a circle first?" Sage asked, ignoring us outsiders again.

All the girls nodded in unison.

"Call the quarters?"

They nodded again.

"We did everything. Thanked the Goddess, thanked the Guardians, opened the circle again."

"Deosil or widdershins?"

"Deosil."

Lane opened her mouth.

Orianna raised her hand before she could ask. "Clockwise versus counterclockwise."

Sage rested her arms on the sides of the chair like a bombshell mafia don. She closed her eyes, and I looked at the others, hoping that someone would know what was going on. Nobody moved. My legs quivered, and I stared down at the scuffed hardwood floor. If she was a queen witch or whatever, what could she do to me?

"What's she doing?" I whispered to anyone who might want to answer.

"I'm thinking," Sage said without moving. "Which is a bit tough with you all staring at me like that."

"Sorry." I sat back in my chair.

"Okay." Sage snapped alive and slid to the edge of her seat.

"Did you ladies remember to cleanse the circle before you closed it?"

"We did," Orianna replied. "We almost forgot because Dabria remembered after she saw the broom sitting there."

"Wait, wait, sitting where? Inside or outside the circle?" she asked.

"It was outside, but I didn't leave the circle. I swear." Dabria lurched forward in her chair as she flipped her hand through the air.

Sage's eyes widened. "Did you just reach over and grab it, then?"

Dabria's flawless demeanor cracked as she nodded. "But just for a second."

"Then you broke the circle if you already closed it, and you have to cleanse it before it's closed." She pushed herself to her feet. An ugly grimace creased her lips and her forehead as she wagged her perfectly manicured finger at the girls. "That's it, no more rituals for you three without supervision."

Lane leaned down beside me. "Do you have any idea what this circle stuff means?"

Sage rubbed her temples and sighed. "Cleansing the circle means getting out all the negative energy out of the area."

"And you do this with a broom?" Lane snickered and tapped Ethan's arm, trying to coax him into her enjoyment, but he didn't follow.

"It's symbolic," Sage snapped at her. "And closing a circle is important to keep destructive energy out and positive energy in. Kind of like a mystical force field. If you break the circle, you leave yourself open to uninvited spirits."

Lane laughed and knocked the display shelf behind her with her elbow. The merchandise clinked, but fortunately, nothing fell. "Spirits? You're kidding me. Like ghosts and stuff?"

"Exactly, like ghosts and stuff," she mocked Lane's flippant response.

"So what does that mean?" I asked. I didn't want to annoy her, but this made no sense. Witches. Ghosts. Seriously?

Sage pinched the bridge of her nose and sighed. "It means that you are probably being affected by the spirit of someone who has passed on. They might be trying to settle some unfinished business or something through you."

"Why me? Why didn't it just jump into one of them?" I pointed at Orianna, Dabria, and Kassia. They all scrunched up their noses and turned away.

Sage closed her eyes for a moment and swiped her hair back over her sinking shoulders. "Who knows. Maybe the person knew you, or sometimes they just pick the most vulnerable person who's around. Were you doing drugs or something before you went out into the woods?"

"No," I barked, offended at the implication. "I told you, I had trouble sleeping and then saw the candles and thought it was a fire. Your mentees could've burned down my entire neighborhood. Shouldn't they be the ones in trouble here?"

"So you were stressed out and overtired. That would make you pretty vulnerable, wouldn't it?" Sage replied, her voice dripping sarcasm.

Whirling to face her, I snapped, "Are you trying to say this is my fault?"

"No, I'm just really upset about this whole situation." She paced in front of all of us. "It's a little bit of being in the wrong place at the wrong time, and a whole lot of people not following the most basic of rules."

The girls bowed their heads.

"Do you know how to get rid of a ghost, Sage?" Orianna dared to ask without looking up from the table top.

"In theory, yes. But I would want to make a few calls to some elders before I tried anything, just to make sure I had everything covered." She ground her fingertips into her temples again and glared at the three so-called witches. "Wouldn't want anything else to go wrong. Should be a few days." She waved at a customer standing by the counter. "I'll be right there."

Sage slipped her apron on as she rushed toward the back of the shop.

I chased after her. "So what am I supposed to do now?"

Sage stopped but didn't turn around.

"I'm going to fall asleep in a few hours and do who knows what because I'm infected with some sort of ghost that your followers called, and I am supposed to just sit around and take it until you're ready to deal with it?"

Lane's eyes widened. She rushed toward me, attempting to lead me back into my chair. "Calm down, Berk."

"No." I pushed past Lane and stood behind Sage. "I'm tired of not being able to control myself, and I'm tired of finding out all the people I've hurt after the fact, and above all, I'm actually tired. I'm completely physically and emotionally exhausted."

She spun around on the heel of her boot. Her mouth formed a hard line. However, I refused to back down. Tears welled in my eyes, but I couldn't give up. This needed to end.

"You're right," she said.

I started to argue but stopped, realizing that I got the answer I wanted to hear.

"It isn't fair for you to suffer for something that you didn't have any hand in creating. Our creed is to do no harm, and clearly, we have." Scrunching up her face, she swept a few stray blond strands over her right ear. "I'll do what I can as quick as I can, but that's the best I can do."

I stomped my foot. The rest of the patrons in the shop glared at me like I was a spoiled child. "That doesn't help me tonight."

Sage lowered her voice and put her hands on my shoulders. "You need to chill. The more out of control you are, the more the ghost can sink its teeth into you." She reached past me and grabbed a silver plastic pouch with a gold label. "Go home, drink this, and try to get ahold of yourself. There isn't anything else I can tell you."

I tossed my shoulders back and broke her hold on me. "Forget about it. It's not like you could really help anyway. Witches aren't real. Ghosts aren't real. This is all a bunch of nonsense."

Sage's jaw dropped for a second, then she jerked her head to the side and glared at me. She grabbed my hand and yanked me through the swinging door into the back of the shop. "If you don't like my interpretation, that's up to you, but don't you dare tell me what's real and what's not."

She leaned forward against the stainless-steel table in the middle of the room and closed her eyes, her eyelashes fluttering as her face twisted with concentration. Her grip on the table tightened, and her knuckles blanched.

A chill set over the room, and I swallowed as goosebumps pebbled across my flesh.

Sage whispered something so quietly I couldn't make out the words. The harsh lights of the kitchen flickered. Once. Twice. Three times. A spoon rattled against the metal counter, shifting back and forth until it started to spin. Faster and faster. I stared at it, mesmerized by the spinning as my feet stayed rooted to the floor. It spun faster, then faster still, then suddenly shot off the counter and clanged onto the tile floor.

Sage's cheeks paled as she lowered herself off her tiptoes, back to the floor. She opened her eyes and cast me a weak grin. "Believe me now?"

"I ..." The words wouldn't come. My pulse raced. Instead of answering, I threw back the kitchen door and ran.

TWENTY-FIVE

The cruel sun tormented me through the window, burning shapes across my bed and pinning me to my mattress. Groaning, I shielded my tired eyes with my pillow. What had I done now?

On the nightstand, my empty mug of tea stared at me. The gritty feel of it lingered on my tongue as well as the unfortunate dirt-like taste. Sage didn't explain what the tea could do, but maybe it had done something. A flash of Sage and her magic spoon flickered through my brain. There had to be a reasonable explanation for how she'd performed that trick, but I hadn't thought of one. It couldn't really be true. Could it? But if witches were real, that would mean that all the things she said—the bizarre things about being possessed by a ghost—could all be real too. I couldn't even talk to Lane about it. I'd bolted out of the café and bailed on both her and Ethan. I cringed. Ethan. Another thing I didn't want to think about. At least, not right now.

I rolled toward the side of my bed and forced myself to sit. My limbs ached, sore and rigid, like going twenty rounds in a cage-fight and never stopping. Or at least that's how I figured it would feel. A lump of clothes sat piled near the door. I hadn't worn them recently. My stomach twisted. Of course. Why did I honestly think today would be different?

Black rimmed my fingernails. I flicked my index finger, and flakes of dried brown mud fluttered out. At least it wasn't blood this time.

My stomach churned again. But this time it wasn't actually

fear or dread. The greasy smell of sizzling bacon lured me to my feet.

After grabbing my phone, I rushed down the stairs into the kitchen.

"Morning," Dad said as he scrambled eggs in a frying pan, the dreamy bacon sputtering beside him. "Thought it would be nice to have breakfast together for once."

"Yeah, sure." I gripped my forehead and blinked. Dad looked different. Better. His hair was slicked back, and although a decade out of style, still a thousand times more effort than usual. His clothes didn't carry the same hopeless wrinkle they had over the past several months. Perhaps the tea did have some sort of impact. Maybe I had woken up in a totally different dimension.

I slipped in behind him and took two plates out of the cupboard then cutlery from the drawer. "You seem like you're in a good mood today."

His smile morphed to a frown as he switched off the elements and carried the piping-hot frying pan toward the table. After serving the eggs, he dropped the frying pan in the sink, and it gave a sharp sputter as it touched the water inside. He snatched up the plate of bacon and sat down across the table.

I helped myself to a few slices as my stomach insisted that I take more. *So good.* The salty heaviness would hang on me until lunch, but it would be worth it.

Dad rested his hands on the table, his fingers laced together. "So, Berkley. Is there something you want to tell me?"

I froze, a forkful of eggs halfway to my mouth. This wasn't a change of heart; this was an interrogation. Unfortunately, there were far too many things I was guilty of, and I didn't even know where to start.

Lowering my fork, I pushed my plate farther toward the center of the table then crossed my arms over my chest. "I don't know. But I'm guessing you already have something you want to say."

He dug into his pocket, pulled out the bottle of sleeping pills, and slammed them down on the table.

I quivered.

"Can you explain these?" he demanded.

Exhaling, I tapped my dirty fingers on the table, trying to form the best version of a lie. I could always go with the truth, but that would not do. I already thought I was insane. Telling Dad I had severe problems or that I might even be possessed wouldn't go over well.

"I've been having trouble sleeping lately, so I went to the doctor for some help. They are low dosage, and I can't get any more without your consent anyway."

"And how exactly did you get these without my consent in the first place? You can't fill a prescription on your own from my health plan, and these are far too expensive to pay for outright."

"We called them in. The pharmacy thought it was you, and we said you'd given me permission to pick him up." I stared down into my lap as Dad smashed his fist against the table, making the cutlery jump.

"That's fraud, you know. And who exactly is 'we'?" He held his face in his hands and sighed. "Why didn't you just come to me?"

"It was Lane. Me and Lane. She's kind of amazing with voices, after some acting classes she took two summers ago." I dared to look up, but he still hadn't yet. "And I didn't want to bother you. You seem to have a lot going on already, and I didn't want to make things worse."

"You have no idea what I'm going through. Besides, that's not your concern. I'm supposed to be the one taking care of you, but it seems like I'm failing at that too. You never used to lie to me before."

"I never used to have to." I slapped my hand over my mouth as the words came flying out.

He looked up, his gaze hard as steel and sharp as a knife blade. "What was that?"

"Nothing."

"I thought so. I'm extremely disappointed in you, Berkley. I don't want you to go down a dangerous path."

Too late for that. And not like it mattered. What about him and his months of self-medicating? Didn't he realize what a hypocrite this made him? Or maybe, just maybe, he'd finally realized the damage his own behavior was causing to his life.

The words built up inside my mouth but stayed frozen on my tongue. Each one prickled and stung as they tried to escape. "Understood."

"You should probably get ready for school, don't you think?"

Wincing, I grabbed my head. "I'm not feeling so great all of a sudden. I think I'm going to stay home today."

"Skipping class? What did we just talk about?"

"What? Can't I be sick once in a while? You've been doing it at least once a week." I grabbed my fork and shoveled the rest of my eggs in my mouth, barely chewing before I swallowed.

Dad scoffed but didn't respond. He shot up from the table and tossed his plate into the sink with a crash. He shook his head, his hair falling disheveled again, matching his attitude. Nothing was going to change. He'd keep killing himself every day until there would be nothing left. My throat swelled as I imagined how this would all end. How horribly. A strange feeling built up inside me.

"I'm going now." Dad glared at me from the end of the kitchen.

The darkness surged.

"Where?" An icky, dirty feeling pumped through me. Thick and black like motor oil pulsing through my veins. Coating everything in darkness. My tongue moved on its own. The words coming without thought. "To get another drink."

His face exploded into a kaleidoscope of purples and reds. He tossed the chair to the side and raised his pointed index finger. "Don't you ever talk to me like that again!"

"Or what?" I stood up at the table and wiped my face as tears broke through my lash line.

He shook his finger and opened his mouth, but no words came out. Instead, he snatched his coat off the back of his chair and stomped out the front door, then slammed it hard enough to make the pictures on the walls shake.

I collapsed in my chair and let the tears fall. Let them drip into my breakfast and pool on the plate like a lake of sadness, growing bigger and bigger by the second. The thickness in my blood receded, and my hands shook.

My phone vibrated on the table. Lane. I let out a few more huge sobs then wiped my eyes and opened my phone.

> **Lane:** *Are you planning on answering my texts today?*
> **Me:** *Yeah. Sorry.*
> **Lane:** *You okay?*
> **Me:** *No. But that's not new.*
> **Lane:** *Meet me before class?*
> **Me:** *Of course. See you soon.*

I dropped the phone on the table top and watched the screen light blink off. I forced a few controlled breaths until the tears stopped threatening to fall. Not like they'd do any good. Maybe once I returned to normal, I could deal with getting my dad back to normal too. The sun blazed through the patio window and burned against the back of my skull. Teasing with its cheerfulness. I shut the blinds and marched back to my room.

TWENTY-SIX

"There you are. Cutting it close to the bell, aren't you?" Lane stalked across the courtyard and met me near our regular table.

"Sorry. I know I said I'd meet you, but I went to grab you a present first." I held out the foam Smoothie Station cup toward her. "I should've called last night, and I shouldn't have ditched you at Divina Tea. It's not much, but—"

"It's perfect." She snatched the cup from my hand and drew me into a hug. I melted into her embrace, letting myself relax for just a second, until she pulled away. "It is strawberry cookie dough, though, right?"

"Of course."

"I so needed one of these this morning." She took a huge sip from her straw and gulped. Her eyes lit up as the flavors hit her tastebuds. "So what happened in the back room with Glinda the Good Witch? I've never seen you run so fast in my life. And I've seen you run almost as fast as me."

She smirked and clamped her teeth on the end of her smoothie straw.

I closed my eyes and let the scene flood back to me. The same uncertain dread I'd felt standing in the back of the café pushed down on my ribcage. "She made the lights flicker and a spoon spin across a table."

"Shut up." Lane slapped me on the shoulder. "She can't really do stuff like that. Can she?"

"I don't know." I shrugged and sat on top of the picnic table, watching my warm breath puff into clouds on the early morning air. "It looked pretty real, but I'm sure it was some sort of trick. Magnets or something like that. I just ... I don't know. Nothing about yesterday makes any sense, but it's also the only explanation I've found so far that might actually fit. Do you know what I mean?"

Lane hopped up beside me and sipped her drink in silence. Her head wobbled back and forth as if her thoughts were arguing inside her brain and she needed to hear each side. Eventually, she slapped her cup down on the wooden table top.

"This is some pretty heavy stuff. So you get a pass for not texting me back last night, just this once." She booped me on the nose and scowled. "But maybe you need to consider other possibilities? Maybe it wasn't a trick at all. Maybe there are things that textbooks can't explain."

I swung my feet back and forth under the table and watched the perfect bows of my shoelaces disappear, then reappear, over and over again. But did believing in witches and magic mean that everything they said about what was happening to me was true? I shook my head. Nope. Still too early to process that kind of revelation.

Lane slipped her hand into mine, the wool of her fingerless gloves itching my naked palm. "Or maybe we just haven't found the answer yet. Totally possible."

"Right?" I forced a smile and squeezed her hand tighter. "Let's just hope we figure it out soon."

"Okay, enough for now." She tugged me off the picnic table then let go of my hand and started walking backward toward the school. "Let's get to class, and we'll meet up at lunchtime to make a plan. Sleep studies, therapists, special doctors, whatever you need, we'll work it out."

With a reassuring wink, she spun back to face the school and adjusted her backpack on her shoulder before bobbing her way toward the doors. I followed close behind, trying my best to keep the dark cloud hanging over my brain back at the table—at least for a little while.

However, as we rounded the corner near my locker, all that gloom crashed back over me like a murky wave pushing me down into the dangerous undertow. A trio of familiar and snarky shadows loomed in our way.

Dabria leaned against the locker bank like a gleaming pillar of obsidian. Dressed, as per usual, in all black, but completely smooth and shiny. Not one detail out of place, from her poker-straight ebony locks to her heeled black booties and pleated leather mini skirt. If it weren't for her less-than-polished crew, I would've thought she'd just stepped off the cover of a high-end fashion magazine—goth edition. She appeared to be the lookout, her eyes widening to the size of clenched fists as she locked stares with us.

Orianna and Kassia closed in from either side of the hall. Circling like vultures in colorless graphic tees to pick the bones of their prey. *Not today, witches.* Between my lousy sleep last night, if I'd slept at all, and the brawl with my dad at the breakfast table, I just didn't have the energy for whatever they wanted.

Lane glanced back over her shoulder and shrugged.

I pushed past her and took the lead, heading us right into their poorly executed trap. "Haven't you given me enough trouble already? What do you want now?"

Kassia crossed her arms and stepped up into my personal space. "Wow. Someone's cranky this morning."

"Really?" I closed the gap between us and straightened my spine to maximize the half-inch of height I had over her and her frizzy ponytail. "I wonder why that might be. Could be that I wasted an entire night dealing with your horror stories, and big surprise, I'm not any better. Thanks for that."

"You're really going to tell me you don't believe your own eyes? Sage told us what she showed you." Dabria peeled off the locker bank and straightened her stance.

The temperature in the hall spiked about ten thousand degrees hotter—mostly in my burning cheeks. Of course she would've told them. Except did that mean they could do the same sort of magic? I shook my head. But it wasn't real anyway. I hadn't figured out the trick yet, and everyone was determined to not let me get a moment to think.

"I believe in facts. Not horror stories told by strangers who know nothing about me." I cringed as the words spewed over my lips. I didn't need to be so harsh, but controlling my emotions hadn't been one of my strengths lately. The controlled and calm Berkley had disappeared and left this broken girl made of ice water and nerve endings. "If you only knew what I'd been going through, you wouldn't be jerking me around like this."

Orianna sighed as she twisted her fingers together at her waist. "We're really sorr—"

Dabria put her index finger across her lips and shook her head at Orianna. "Things happened. We didn't plan them, and yes, they sucked and you're bitter. But we're here to help. If we had anything to do with your unfortunate accident, then we will do what we can to make it right. We talked to Sage and—"

"My accident?" My hands shot to my hips.

Dabria assessed my reaction and rolled her eyes. "Yes, your accident. No one is out to get you. Fate just does messed-up things sometimes."

"Fate? Right." I chuckled and looked over at Lane, but she didn't seem to be in on the joke. *C'mon, Lane, don't abandon me now.* "There's no such thing as fate. There are only carefully calculated plans that you three seem intent on screwing up for me."

Kassia stepped to me again, her permascowl deepening across her dark painted lips. "Well, sometimes plans change."

The bell rang, and the hall emptied as doors around us slammed shut.

"And now you've made me late for class too. Perfect." I tugged the strap of my bag and attempted to sidestep away from the group. I'd rather have no textbook and have to make things up than listen to them any longer. Besides, what if they could do things like their mentor? I had zero interest in finding out.

"You are going to have bigger problems than being late for class if you don't listen to us. Sage wasn't kidding. There is something wrong with you. Something no doctor or anyone else is going to be able to fix." Orianna tapped me on the shoulder, but I refused to turn around. "But she thinks she's found someone who can get rid of the spirit. Can you meet us at Divina Tea again tonight at eight?"

The words stung. A spirit. A ghost. Could that insane theory really be true? My arms twitched at my sides, my body unsure whether to stop and listen or start swinging. Nothing I'd done so far had made a difference. But the only other option meant the one thing I feared most—there was something wrong with *me*. Truly clinical. Neurological? Possibly psychological? Maybe something in my head had finally cracked, and that was the reason everything kept spiraling out of control.

"I'll think about it." I tried again to maneuver out of the conversation, but Kassia stood in my way.

"She said she'd think about it, now can you all just get on your broomsticks and fly away or something." Lane linked her arm in mine and pulled me to the side.

Orianna nodded at Kassia.

Kassia snatched my wrist and smeared my skin with a sticky brown sludge. Bits of hard rocks, or glass, or something scratched my flesh.

"Ouch." I yanked my hand away and glowered at her.

She raised her open palm. "Somnia."

Heat blasted through my skin, and I jerked away from Lane's grip. I cradled my arm against my chest as my wrist seared under the strange paste. The stink of melting plastic stung my nostrils, and I gagged. "What the hell?"

Orianna peeked in front of me, her eyes soft and sad. "You need to understand how much trouble you're in."

"That's not your—" I lurched forward as a darkness descended over my vision, then an invisible force punched me in the gut. My knees wavered as pain burrowed through my stomach. I slammed my hand against the nearest locker to hold myself steady, but it didn't help, my sweaty palm squealing as it slipped down the metal doors.

"What are you doing to her?" Lane shouted from somewhere far away.

Footsteps scuttled in the distance. Muffled voices rumbled, but I couldn't make out the words. My head hung heavy to my chest as the darkness grabbed hold and pinned me down. Colors and light flickered through my brain. Images rolled like a film reel. Memories, maybe illusions. Familiar, yet not. The woods near the park under moonlight, the sound of leaves crunching beneath my feet. Running through a dark downtown alley as angry screams followed close behind. My own hand dripping blood as a pile of smashed liquor bottles littered a tiled floor. The same tile as my kitchen.

No. Stop. I tried to scream out, but my tongue stayed glued to the roof of my mouth. My legs wobbled, and a sharp sting pierced through my knees as I fell to the floor.

The images came faster, swirling in circles as I tried to keep my head straight and avoid vomiting. Smashing the broken furniture in my living room. Candles burning in the dark as I stared up from a pile of dead leaves. A blinding green light growing brighter and brighter.

"Berkley," a voice hissed through the chaos.

The light kept building, and I tried to turn my head, but it wouldn't respond. Nothing responded. My arms. My eyes. Nothing.

"You're mine," the raspy voice echoed again.

My pulse rang in my ears, pounding harder and harder. My chest tightened as I stopped breathing.

"Berkley," it called.

Tears soaked my cheeks. *Go away. Just leave me alone. Please.*

"Berkley."

The burning beneath my ribs deepened as my lungs struggled for oxygen.

A hard smack against my jaw knocked my head to the side.

"Berkley." My name rang again, but the voice had changed.

Fingers dug into my shoulders and shook my unresponsive body. The numbness drained from my limbs, and I whipped my eyes open.

Lane's face hovered inches above mine. Her forehead blazed red as her watery eyes threatened to rain floods any second. "Berkley, wake up."

"Lane," I croaked, and pulled my head up. A woozy sensation swept over me, and I laid my head back on the cold hallway tile.

"You're alive." She wrapped her arms around my aching body and squeezed until I gasped from lack of breath. She let go, and her relief faded into a death glare directed above my head at the three figures that loomed over us.

"We told you," Orianna said. "She needs help."

Lane grabbed my hand and rubbed her thumb against my knuckles. The crimson color in her face glowed brighter, like a bomb about to detonate. But instead, she glanced down at me and heaved a heavy sigh. "Eight o'clock, you said? We'll be there."

Twenty-Seven

A pretty teal sign with fancy calligraphic lettering sat in the window of Divina Tea's door.

Closed today for a special event.

Special event? I guess so. What else would you call a meeting with an angry ghost without having your customers running to the cops or every news station in the state?

I tilted my head toward the night sky, inhaling deeply and letting it all the way out until I had nothing left to purge. A chill shot through my limbs, and I flinched. The same ominous feeling I'd felt on and off all day since Lane scraped me from the school hallway floor and escorted me home. A day I wished I could start over and change everything about it.

"Are you sure you want to do this?" Lane rubbed my shoulder, the rest of her words hanging unsaid between us.

Did I really want to trust a bunch of amateur witches? No. Did I want to be standing outside a random café, trying to gather the courage to walk into whatever weird magical trap they had set out for me? Double no. But there I stood with my hand hovering over the door handle.

I shrugged, and Lane's hand slipped away. "What other choice do I have?"

"Maybe get a second opinion?"

"From who? How many witches do you know that we can talk to? Especially hanging out in the Midwest?"

I snickered to myself. Even though I'd said the words, they sounded ridiculous. A week ago I probably would've laughed out loud at the thought of witches in our little town, let alone existing at all.

"Besides, I need to get my life back. I've already missed the volleyball finals, I still have that scholarship interview this weekend, and I really got into it with my dad this morning. I can't keep going on like this," I added.

"Your dad's a grown man. I'm sure he can handle it."

"Maybe. But what if it makes him worse?"

My throat tightened, the air around us thickening and becoming hard to swallow. I glanced back at Lane, and she looked away, refusing to meet my eyes.

"You know that's not your responsibility, right?" Her lips held a tight line until I nodded in agreement, even though my heart didn't quite feel the same.

"However, this could be a problem for college. Would you need to apply for only yourself, or does the ghost need to get accepted too?"

I dropped my forehead and glared at her. "Not funny."

Lane reached around me and pulled open the door. "I thought it was."

The tiny bell jingled as we threw open the door and walked in. Orianna and the rest of the trouble triplets glanced up from pushing café tables to the edges of the shop. They looked at each other, their lips tightly closed as if searching for the right words, yet finding none. There wasn't much to say anyway. Even Kassia's smirk had disappeared from her smug face. I guess writhing on the floor, tripping on memories you didn't remember having, was as frightening to watch from the outside as it was in my head.

Orianna stepped forward and dropped her head to her chest. "You came."

"Yeah," I responded, my feet still rooted to the spot near door.

"Are you ..." Dabria raised her index finger and swished it around, not daring to come any closer.

Lane opened her mouth, but closed it again and looked at me for guidance.

"I'm fine." Except I wasn't, and from the looks of pity circulating through the room, everyone else knew it too.

The door to the back room swung open, piercing the awkward vibe. Sage rushed across the scuffed hardwood floor and forced a beaming smile.

"Berkley. You made it." She shuffled on the high heels of her black lace booties to greet me, her arms open wide for a hug. "Blessed be, lovely. I'm glad you came."

I held rigid as she wrapped her arms around me, but quickly relaxed in her embrace. A calmness diffused around her. Not just the intoxicating scent of jasmine flower wafting off her skin, but something deeper. Spiritual. Like her soul reaching out to hug mine and tell it things would be okay. I closed my eyes and took it in, even though the small pleasure seemed wrong.

"I received your invitation loud and clear." I glanced over her shoulder at Sage's mentees, but they all busied themselves shuffling chairs and avoiding my accusatory stare.

Sage released me and I straightened my stance, then crossed my arms, putting my armor back into place.

"The Shadow Sisters said you can fix her. Is that true?" Lane added, sidling closer to me.

"Hello, Lane. I didn't realize Berkley would be bringing a guest. But yes, I believe I've found a solution." Sage cast her the same welcoming smile. "Except she isn't a toy to be mended. She's a soul in need of rescue. No one is ever truly broken."

Lane scoffed but quickly choked it down.

The silver bell above the door jingled again.

"Hello." A middle-aged woman slunk through the door and rapped her knuckle against the window glass. Her dark hair snaked up the back of her head in a tight French twist, complementing her gray power pantsuit.

Lane twirled around. "Sorry. We're closed."

"Tamara. You made it." Sage sashayed around us and flung her arms around the woman at the door. She kissed the newcomer on each cheek.

"Of course, I said I'd be here. I'd hoped to be here sooner, but the traffic getting out of the city was absurd." She sighed and shook her head. Her welcoming smile faded as she studied me, then pointed at Lane. "Let me guess, this is the troubled one."

"Yes, but the other is the one with the ghost problem." The woman and Sage laughed while Lane cast them her best death glare.

"You don't look like much of a witch," Lane said. "More like an accountant."

"Lane," I scolded.

"It's okay." Tamara fluttered her hand, dismissing the insult as she slipped out of her jacket and flung it over the back of a nearby armchair. "Being a witch doesn't require a uniform. It's a system of belief, a faith. It's not like you'd walk down the street and go, 'Hey, that girl looks totally Protestant' or 'Check out that guy's Catholic outfit.' And I'm not an accountant, I'm a hedge fund manager."

"But what about them?" Lane pointed at Orianna, Dabria, and Kassia.

Sage sighed. "Some prefer to identify themselves with the practice by dressing in dark clothes and wearing the pentacle and other symbols, but it doesn't make someone any more or less a witch."

Tamara chuckled and nudged Sage with her elbow. "I remember when you used to dress like that too. Three layers of kohl eyeliner never did suit you."

"Don't get me started on your poor fashion choices." Sage stuck her hands on her hips and scowled but couldn't quite keep her lips from curling up. "Tamara and I grew up together, but she's far more experienced in these kinds of dark matters than I am. I thought it best to bring in a professional."

"Ha. You're sweet, but I'm sure you would do fine without me.

You'll just find any excuse to get me to come up here." Tamara slipped her hands into her hair and started pulling out bobby pins, letting her curly locks free. "But yes, living in Chicago has allowed me to see a lot of things I wish I hadn't."

A blank, faraway look fell over Tamara's sable eyes. I recognized it immediately. I'd seen it in my own reflection too many times over the last week.

I cleared my throat and shook my head, the strange chill pulsing through me again. "Have you ever seen a whatever I have?"

Tamara blinked, casting the devils that haunted her back into the recesses of her mind. "A couple of times. It's actually more common than you think and usually goes pretty smoothly. Ghosts don't particularly like to hang around humans. Even if they don't want to pass on yet, they aren't too comfortable walking around in someone else's skin either. It's disorienting. You have to convince them to let go."

"And how do I do that?" I asked.

I scanned each of their faces. Lane shrugged.

"We'll do most of the work." Tamara and I locked eyes, then she wrapped her long, elegant fingers around my bicep and squeezed gently. "You have to focus on letting go yourself. Don't give the spirit anything to hold on to."

"Let go. Got it." I nodded and tried to process exactly what that meant. "Now let's send this ghost packing."

"Relax, Berkley, there's still some prep work we need to take care of, and I'd like to go over things with Tamara before we begin. Why don't you get started draping the windows with those black sheets over there?" Sage pointed to a pile of cloth in the far corner near the front of the shop. "Once you're done and your friends finish moving the tables out of the way, we should be ready to go."

Lane wrinkled her nose. "They are not our friends."

Sage shook her head. "I'm actually surprised you have any."

"She's sorry." I linked my arm with Lane's and dragged her toward the window.

After scooping up the sheets, I slid a delicate white chair near the glass then climbed up to tuck the corner of the cloth around the curtain rod. It slipped easily into place, and I worked along the rod, stuffing more fabric down the edge.

"Let me help." Lane lifted the end of the sheet so it didn't pull against the curtain rod and fed it to me as I leaned closer to the center of the window.

My face reflected back at me, but all distorted and murky. I shuddered, and my balance faltered. As I lurched forward, I caught the back of the chair and managed to keep from falling. My pulse pounded in my temples as I gazed out over the café from my perch.

"Maybe you should go, Lane."

"What?" She pushed more fabric up to me, but I just bunched it in my fists.

"What happens if something goes wrong? Maybe it would be better if you left."

Her head jerked to the side. "No way. I'm never going to get a chance to see something like this again. Besides, it's just like the time you came to the hospital when I had my tonsils removed."

"Um, not really." The image of eleven-year-old Lane doped up on pain meds flashed in my brain. That pain seemed unbearable, and she had been so brave. I never thought I could be as tough as her, but I'd have to be even stronger tonight. "At least your doctor had a degree. I have no idea what qualifies someone to perform this kind of thing."

"I'll be fine. No worries." She rocked up on her tiptoes and leaned closer to the window, pressing her nose against the glass before dropping back down to the floor. "Plus, if I'm here I can keep Ethan company."

"Ethan?"

The bell jingled as the door slowly opened. Ethan peeked his head through the opening until his stare fell on Lane and me. He nodded in our direction then let himself the rest of the way in.

My face flushed, and I nearly fell off the chair again.

"You invited Ethan?" I hissed at Lane.

"He texted when neither of us were in class today, so I told him what was happening. He wanted to be here."

"You could've at least told me."

"Too late now. You should probably go say hello." Lane held out her hand to help me down from the chair, but I ignored it and jumped to the floor.

I rushed toward the door and cut in front of him before he could venture too far in.

"Ethan. Hey, how's it going?" *How's it going? Seriously?*

"Berkley, how are you feeling? I heard you passed out in the hall today." He gazed down at me, his dark eyes wide and questioning.

"I'm okay. I'll be happy when this is all over." I took a deep breath and broke his stare, looking over his thick shoulder at the door. "But are you sure it's a good idea to be here? Maybe you should go."

He dropped his head. "Sorry. I didn't mean to ... but I wanted to ... never mind. I'll go."

My head clouded. I didn't want him there. I didn't want anyone to see whatever might happen to me, but with him standing before me, I didn't want him to leave either.

"Wait," I called.

Ethan stopped, his hand already on the door handle.

"It's not ... It's ..." My tongue tripped over all the thoughts zooming through my head, trying to force them to make sense, but they wouldn't. Just fuzzy clouds. Like my memories. Like my entire world.

He let go of the door and stepped in front of me. He crooked his finger beneath my chin and pulled my face up to meet his. "Don't worry about it."

Then he smiled. A warm, genuine smile that echoed hopefully in his stare. My breathing slowed and for a moment, all the chaos in my head silenced.

I wrapped my arms around him and rested my head against his chest. "Thanks for coming."

"No problem." His breath rustled the hairs on the top of my head as he hugged me back.

"You invited your boyfriend too. You know this isn't exactly a party, right?" Sage's voice cut through the calm, and I pulled away.

Ethan dropped his arms to his sides. "I'm not—"

"He's not—"

Lane giggled in the corner, and I shot her a nasty glare. She straightened up and bit her lip.

Sage looked around the room, her stare resting on each of our faces as if trying to find the punchline. When nothing surfaced, she shook her head. "Whatever. Doesn't matter. Let's get started."

Twenty-Eight

"Now you go here." Sage took my hand and led me to the cushy green armchair in the middle of the room. "The main attraction."

"Great," I muttered as I sat down and tried to get comfortable, but no way I positioned myself seemed right.

Lane rushed over and gave me a quick hug. She sat down on the side of the chair and held my hand in her lap. "It's going to be okay."

"I hope so."

I rested my head on her hip and tried to slow my breathing. Every movement in the circle stirred up my blood and started my palms sweating. Couldn't this just be over already?

Dabria and Kassia swept the floor in preparation and eyed me carefully as they passed.

Lane leaned over and whispered, "I still don't get why they use a broom, wouldn't a shop vac or something be more effective?"

I swatted her arm. "It's symbolic. They aren't actually sweeping anything."

"I know. It just looks stupid."

"Please don't mess this up for me, Lane."

She patted my head like a puppy. "Do you really think that I would do that to you? Come on, Berk."

"I know." I closed my eyes and breathed in deep. Cinnamon and chamomile. Except they didn't provide any calm. "I'm just nervous about this whole thing."

"As you should be. This stuff is messed up."

"Thanks for the support." I rubbed my sweaty palms on my legs and inhaled again. Instead of slowing, my heart pounded faster.

"It's true. It's kinda bananas." Lane flung her arm over my shoulders. "But I do have your back. Don't worry about that."

I gazed around the circle. No one looked overly secure about this whole thing. Sage gave me her biggest smile, but the fakeness of it cracked in her anxious stare. Orianna, Dabria, and Kassia just looked cranky, as always, except in a more antsy kind of way. And poor Ethan, standing there with his arms hanging by his sides, looking lost and useless. He caught me watching him and turned his head to the floor.

Sighing, I leaned back in the chair.

Lane looked down at me, then glanced at Ethan and back again. "It'll be okay. Let's just get your little ghostly friend out of your head, and we can worry about what's going on with you two later."

"Okay, everyone, we need to get this going." Sage stood beside my chair and spun around to grab everyone's attention, then positioned them in a circle around me.

"Been a while since I've had a guy in one of my rituals," she said as she held Ethan by the forearms and guided him backward to stand between Kassia and Orianna.

"Well, I can say I've never done this with anyone else." His eyes widened as his jaw dropped open.

She giggled. "Good to know. I'll take it easy on you."

His face burned redder, which I didn't even think was possible. "Thanks."

She beckoned Lane with a crooked index finger. Lane patted my head again then followed to the left next to Dabria as Sage lit a circle of white candles around my chair.

Sage nodded at Tamara, and she nodded back before standing directly across from me at the top of the circle.

"Okay, now nobody move from where you are." Sage walked

around the outside of the circle three times. "Thrice around the circle's bound, sink all evil to the ground. So mote it be. Thrice around the circle's bound, sink all evil to the ground. So mote it be. Thrice around the circle's bound, sink all evil to the ground. So mote it be."

She rejoined the group standing behind me. "Okay, I've set the circle. No one can leave unless I cut them a door out, or it reopens the circle. So, just to be on the safe side, just don't break the circle. Got it, newbies?"

Ethan and Lane both looked at each other warily then nodded.

Sage bowed her head. "Okay, let's begin."

I sat in my chair, watching them assemble around me like a badly choreographed dance routine. Sage and her disciples positioned themselves across from one another at each of the four direction points of a compass rose. Sage nodded to Dabria at her right.

"Guardians of the east, bring your mighty winds to blow away the evil and keep us safe," Dabria said.

"Guardians of the south, bring your fire and purify this place and keep us safe," Orianna said next at what must be the bottom of the circle.

Then Kassia spoke. "Guardians of the west, bring your water and cleanse this place and keep us safe."

"Guardians of the north, bring the earth to keep us grounded," said Sage, finally completing the rotation. "So mote it be."

Tamara raised her arms in the air and stepped toward me. She'd changed into a flowy white blouse that almost glowed against her mahogany skin, and she'd let her hair fall wild around her face. Her rigid posture radiated strength. Power. Like the same feeling I had when Sage hugged me, but instead of calm came vibrancy. Raw untapped energy.

I shifted in the chair and tried to slow my breath. I had to let go. Relax. Except I'd never really been good at that. At least not lately.

"Visitor," Tamara began, her voice quiet but firm. "You have come to a safe place. We grant you solace to reflect and pass on to the other side."

A light tingle rippled through my skin. I glanced down, but saw nothing. Maybe just nerves.

"We wish you no harm. Please release this child of the earth, and we shall help you to rest in peace for all eternity."

Again, nothing happened.

Tamara's face contorted into a scowl. This must not have been how this was supposed to go down. Tamara glanced over at Sage, but she shook her head in response. The candles flickered in the silence. A ring of orbs lit the ceiling around my chair like bright miniature moons, each one fading and reappearing as Tamara paced around me, whispering to herself.

I slid to the edge of the chair and gripped my hands on my thighs. A heaviness pushed on my ribcage as my breath came in short, shallow gasps. *You have to let go, Berkley. Just let go.*

Tamara knelt in front of my chair and grasped both arms with her perfectly manicured hands. She gave me a sympathetic smile as she scanned my face, then her expression hardened to stone. She stood and leaned over me. "Spirit, leave this place. I compel you."

As she finished her sentence, the doors to the back room blew open and a blast of cold air blanketed the space. I shivered in my seat. The candle flames fluttered.

Ethan shifted toward the door, but Sage shouted after him, "Don't break the circle!"

He froze, shifting back to his assigned spot.

Tamara's eyes widened as her determined glare dissolved into something else. Something fearful. The air in the circle thickened. I breathed deep, trying to force more air into my aching lungs. Black smoke rose over the sides of the chair. It swirled around us. Tamara jumped back, and the smoke expanded. It ran around the outside of the circle, following the same imaginary line Sage and the others had drawn. The smoke sped up. Faster and faster. A strange feeling bled through me. My heart rate plummeted as my blood oozed slow and thick through my veins. The flames of the candles flickered while the smoke continued to circle.

My limbs shook. The muscles burned, searing off my bones.

My eyes closed. Nothingness.

They flashed open again. The flames of the candles shot up two feet in the air. Dabria screamed.

Then dark again.

Then light. My lips moved, my tongue twisting over words that echoed through the room, but not in my voice. I couldn't understand them. Latin. Greek. Something foreign. Ancient maybe. My mouth tasted sour, like turpentine or battery acid eating away at my face. My body didn't respond to me anymore.

Dark.

Light. Everything blurred in and out of focus. Orianna's terrified look. Kassia with her hand clasped over her mouth. Tears glistening on Lane's cheeks as they streamed down her face. Dark.

Light. My arms ached, trembling at my sides. Fresh streaks of blood smeared across the floor around the circle. More screams. My head dropped to my chest. A sticky red substance dripped off my shaking fingers.

Dark. Light. Dark. Light. The raspy voice I'd heard as I lay on the school hallway floor boomed in my head. *You are mine.* I shouted for it to stop, but no sound escaped my lips, only the cackle of the voice ringing through my brain. My head lolled heavily on my neck. The screams came again.

Then finally only dark.

I AWOKE. Pain pounded the back of my skull and ran around behind my eyes. My body hung limp in the chair, drained of every ounce of energy I had left. My head flopped and rolled side to side, as I couldn't bring myself to hold it up. *What happened?*

Everything existed in a haze. Watery tears dripped down my face, but soon figures came into focus. Sage stood before me, light dancing in her wide eyes from the lone candle in her hands.

"Is it gone?" I asked, my parched lips sore from the movement.

"I'm sorry, Berkley, but it's not a ghost"—she put her warm hand on my face and looked at me, her eyes drooping—"and whatever it is, it's furious."

THE FEELING in my limbs returned slowly. I sipped my steaming cup of tea and rested while everyone else tried to put the shop back together. The display near the window lay on its side, and brightly colored pieces of porcelain spread all the way to the door from the broken teapots. Chairs and tables needed to be righted. Even the pedestals of muffins and gluten-free breads in the farthest corner of the shop sat smashed on the ground. If someone walked in, they would've thought a hurricane came through, but it was only me.

I eased up onto my feet. The room spun, and I grabbed the armchair until everything stopped moving.

"Where's Tamara and Sage?" I asked to the busy room.

Orianna put down her broom, the one she used to clean a real mess, not just a magical one, and stepped over to me. "Tamara left. When you were ... well, whatever you were ... you scratched her face, and Sage brought her to the hospital"

I glanced down at my hand. Blood smeared across my fingertips, and dark, dried goo was caked under my fingernails. I trembled and shook on my shaky legs. My knees bent. I fell. Ethan appeared beside me and held me up. I leaned into his shoulder as he rested his head against mine. Lane came up on my other side and helped guide me back to my chair.

"Still a little woozy." I grabbed my forehead and slid onto the arm of the chair until my breathing slowed again. "Lane, what happened?"

"It was messed up, Berk," she said, quivering beside me. "There was smoke and an awful smell, and you passed out. Or at least we thought you did, but then you woke back up and had that creepy smile on your face and that sinister burning red stare."

She closed her eyes as the ghost of my horror show flitted across her face. "You started talking in some sort of weird language and hissed at everyone, and then just broke out laughing hysterically. Like some sort of maniac psychopath."

I bit down on the side of my tongue as if I could taste the things I'd spewed, but only a bitter metallic taste flowed out against the pain. "Is that it?"

Lane shook her head. "Nope. After that, you walked right up to Tamara and shouted at her in that weird language, but she stood her ground, arguing back at you and trying to cast the spirit out. You grabbed the sides of your head and screamed. Over and over." She shuddered. "Piercing shrieks as you raced around the circle until you collapsed back in your chair, writhing and squirming like whatever had control over you set itself on fire."

"Then what?"

"You just stopped. No more screaming. No movement at all." She shuddered and glanced toward the front of the shop, her eyes wide and distant. Her throat bobbed as she swallowed hard. "I thought you ..."

I clutched her hand, her fingers ice-cold against my touch. "Oh, Lane. I'm so sorry you had to see that."

"Me? It looked like that thing was making you a human shish kabob. I thought you were done for."

The bell tinkled at the front of the shop. Sage rushed in and fell against the door as she clicked the lock home. She glanced at the six sets of eyes watching her and immediately straightened her stance.

She strode across the room, although her steps didn't have the same glide they usually did. She cleared her throat and shook her head, pushing the grim expression from her face. "How are you feeling, Berkley?"

"Better. A little shaky, but better. Now that this thing inside of me is gone, I'll probably feel brand new tomorrow." I took another sip of tea and sat up. The heat of the berry liquid eased my ripped vocal cords but did little to help the tightness growing there. I glanced around at the mess I'd made. The destruction. Even though I didn't remember doing it, I had been responsible. "I'm really sorry, Sage. You know I never meant to wreck your shop. I'll do whatever I can to help clean it up."

I tried to stand again, but the vertigo pulsed, and I wavered.

Sage bent down in front of me, her eyes misty.

"Don't worry about the mess, Berkley. It's all fixable, but"—she glanced around at everyone's stares bearing down on her—"we didn't get it out. The thing inside you. It's still there."

"What?" My cup dropped to the floor. Steaming-hot tea splashed on my leg and burned my skin.

She swallowed and tried to choke back sobs. "I don't know if you remember when I said it wasn't a ghost. I meant that because it wasn't a ghost, we couldn't get rid of it."

The world spun, except this time it wouldn't stop. Like a merry-go-round spinning faster and faster as everything blurred together. I gagged on the warm bile rising in my esophagus. "Are you kidding me? I feel like I've been hit by a school bus, and it's still inside me?"

"I'm so sorry." The tears broke through her lashes and streamed down her face. "Tamara thought for sure she'd be able to help, but after what we saw tonight... The foreign tongues. The smoke. We know for sure it isn't a ghost."

I clenched my hands into fists, digging my fingernails into my flesh. "Then what is it?"

Sage stood to face me. "It's a demon, Berkley. You're possessed by a demon."

Short, haggard gasps escaped my mouth as the spinning continued. I closed my eyes, trying to make it stop, but it just made everything worse.

"Like from hell?" I squeaked as I looked up at her again.

Sage nodded.

I scanned each of the witches' faces. Their stares couldn't reach mine. Shameful frowns on guilty faces. But it didn't matter, did it? All the guilt in the world couldn't help me now.

"I'm really sorry," Sage said again, her voice calming and small.

My pulse pounded in my ears. This couldn't be happening. I'd thought it was over. It had to be over. I pressed my hand over my stomach as the world drifted out of focus and everything went dark. Again.

Twenty-Nine

"**S** top!"
The voice echoes around me. Harsh and sharp.

The shadows swirl as pops of color flash through my brain.

Hot pink.

Neon purple.

Blood red.

My heart hammers harder in my chest as my icy breath burns my lungs. I charge forward, my feet pounding hard against the asphalt.

"Stop," the voice yells again.

A man's voice. Deep and commanding, yet strangely familiar.

The cold sting of a chain link grid bites against my flesh. My pulse spikes to a dangerous speed. My head swivels back into the dark night. The thump of heavy footfalls drums louder.

Closer.

My hands bang against the fence, the chilly metal prickling the skin on my palms.

No way out.

I hold my breath as I smash harder against the fence. Finally, the metal clangs as the side gives way. I clamber through the opening and squeeze into the empty street.

The thundering footsteps fade behind me as I escape into the night.

THIRTY

A demon. Seriously? What am I supposed to do with that?

The thought rolled around in my head like a marble on a track, around and around and around, starting over seamlessly when I thought I'd reached the end. Sage texted all night and said she would try to find a solution, but I had no hope left to keep.

The orderly row of textbooks and notes lined against the back of my locker mocked me. Hours of lessons and subjects that did nothing to prepare me for this horror. But what was I supposed to do now? Continue on like normal? Like nothing had changed, when all my hopes and dreams had evaporated in one moment of wrong place, wrong time? I closed my locker and rested my forehead on the door, letting the cool metal soothe my raw skin. It itched. Everywhere. But I curled my hands into fists and fought the urge to scratch anymore. A delightful new ailment in my supernatural sickness.

I tugged at my sleeves and held onto the cuffs. I'd already ripped the insides of my elbows raw this morning, trails of scratches and blood slithering down my arms like rivers breaching new banks. I bit the side of my cheek. It hurt so bad.

After sliding my textbook into my bag, I started down the hall. A familiar navy-blue jacket rounded the corner and stopped. My feet halted, and I almost fell forward from the momentum. Josh. I'd almost forgotten. I'd spent every day worrying and wondering about him. About us. But only a couple of days in hell and he'd become a distant memory. Except now it all flooded back. The shame. The hurt. The guilt.

I adjusted my backpack on my shoulder. "Hey, Josh."

He scowled, but it didn't last. The longer he stared, wordless, the more his eyes softened, the hard edges of his hate challenging him.

"I know you're still mad at me. But I really am sorry how everything turned out."

"Yeah, me too." He exhaled loudly and craned his neck up toward the ceiling. "I just wish you'd said something sooner. Maybe it would've hurt less."

"Maybe. But—"

"Hey, Berkley," a familiar voice called behind me.

I spun around as Ethan headed toward us from the opposite direction.

"Ethan, I—" My throat ached. Thick regret spread along my vocal cords, swallowing my words, but I didn't need to finish.

Ethan's mouth dropped open as he peered from me to Josh and back again. Any softness left in Josh's expression vanished as his jaw clenched and drew harsh shapes in his cheeks.

Josh tossed his hand in the air and glared at Ethan. "Seriously?"

Ethan glanced over at me. Maybe expecting me to say something. Maybe just trying not to look directly at Josh and spark his fuse.

My head pounded as we stood in silent stalemate.

"Nice shiner," Josh said with a smirk.

Ethan shook his head. "Whatever, man." Then he turned back around and walked away.

"Looks like things are working out for you two." Josh stared after him as he disappeared down the hall. "I can't say I didn't see it. I just figured you wanted to be with me more. That you really meant it when you said you loved me, because I meant it when I said it to you."

"I did mean it, I always did." I reached for his arm but froze and retracted my hand. "Things just changed. I didn't want them to, but they did."

He dropped his head back and huffed. "Good to know."

A flash of blue jackets appeared behind him. Brett. Squire. Downey. A pack of wolves that probably smelled fresh blood. *Just great.*

"Hey, Josh, we're all—" Brett smacked Josh on the shoulder and followed his stare right to me. He frowned, the look extremely unflattering on his grouchy face. "Don't try crawling back now. It's about time you set this boy free."

I stuck my hands on my hips, every movement prickling like needles along my flesh. "It's none of your business, Brett."

Josh glanced back at his teammates, and the last of the humanity he wore slipped away. "And my life is no longer any of your business. Stop trying, Berkley. It's kind of pathetic." He tipped his head up and marched past me without another look.

"Oh, sick." Squire's voice echoed behind me.

Fury raged through my veins. But I was more angry at myself than him. But why was this my fault? Everything fell apart after that one night in the woods. Maybe if I'd just stayed inside, things would be different now. I smashed my fist into my locker, the metal clanging loud and garnering even more stares than my run-in with Josh.

"What?" I tossed my arms open wide and shouted to anyone who dared to keep watching.

The crowd dispersed, and I closed my eyes as I tried to mentally force my limbs to stop shaking. *Get it together, Berkley. Don't let everything fall apart.*

The bell rang. I raced down the hall toward my first class. *Great, late again.* The only reason I even bothered coming today was to avoid scratching all of my flesh off my bones and stressing about the demon poisoning me from the inside. Except now I'd made everything worse.

I slipped through the door into my English class, and all eyes were immediately glued to me. Just what I needed. Attention when I felt like dying.

"Your disturbances are getting to be an unfortunate habit with you, Miss James," Mrs. Franklin said as she positioned herself in front of my desk, making her impossible to avoid. "One more infraction and I think I will need to send you to the principal's office. I doubt you would want that on your impeccable school record."

Right. My impeccable record. But for what? Who knew if I even had a future anymore?

Glaring at her, I dropped my backpack onto the desktop. Ethan glanced up at me, but when I caught his eye, he looked away. Another problem I kept making worse. I flopped down into my desk, regretting the decision to bother coming in.

Mrs. Franklin sneered but walked away. I pulled out my notebook and drew pictures in the margins. Swirly lines. Flowers. Crosses. Skulls. It didn't matter. Nothing mattered anymore.

"Could you at least open your book and pretend you're paying attention?" Mrs. Franklin loomed over me as I scrawled along the page. *Since when was I her favorite plaything?* All these years of studying hard, getting good grades, and essentially being the most perfect me I could, counted for nothing.

An apology formed by reflex. The good Berkley. The perfect little student. But it died in my throat. "Nah. I'm good."

"Well ... well ..." Her mouth fell open, but nothing came out.

She charged back up to the front of the room and flipped through the pages of her planner. "If you're so far ahead on the material, maybe you can give us all a sample of your paper that you will be handing in next week."

The paper. The one I'd started twelve times then shredded, and since then not bothered with again. What was even the thesis? I couldn't remember.

"I'm sure you must be long done by now." She crossed around

to the front of her desk and leaned back against the top. "Why don't you start with the witches in the first act."

Witches. The last thing I wanted to talk about. Or think about. Or anything.

I stood up and gripped my pen, the plastic bending to the point it might snap. "Yes, the witches. It's all their fault. Every single thing that happened to Macbeth is because of the witches. He lost his friends. He lost his wife. He lost his throne. He even lost his mind. And they did nothing to stop it. They just sat back and let their actions destroy him bit by bit until there was nothing left. Is that what you wanted to hear?"

I fell back into my chair as Mrs. Franklin scowled at me. "Your argument sounds a little one-sided, but—"

A breeze rustled the tiny hairs at the back of my neck.

"Yes, Ethan," Mrs. Franklin said.

"I think Berkley has it wrong."

I whirled around in my chair, and for the first time today, he held my stare, except it wasn't the pleasant greeting he'd worn earlier in the hall. This look had hardened. Stone cold.

"It's easy to blame the witches for Macbeth's downfall, but Macbeth was the one who acted on their prophecies. They saw his ambitions. The things he kept bottled up and pushed down because those feelings were inconvenient. Maybe the witches gave him a push, but he was already going down that road. The witches were just the catalyst that triggers the plot. Sure, the ending was tragic, but what if the witches freed him to be who he wanted in the first place?"

Mrs. Franklin nodded. "Interesting perspective, Mr. Rhodes. Does anyone else have—"

I jumped up and straddled my chair to glare back at Ethan. "Ha. That's total crap. If the witches freed him, why didn't he succeed? Why did everything just keep getting worse?"

He rose in his seat and slammed his hands down on the desk.

"Because he didn't want to deal with the reality of his feelings. It was easier just to ignore them."

"Enough, you two," Mrs. Franklin shouted from the front of the room. "I'm glad you're passionate about the material, but this is getting out of hand."

I didn't care. I pushed on the seat back and met Ethan's posturing. "Really? Maybe he never acted on things before because he knew it wouldn't work out. Maybe he knew deep down that he wasn't good enough. Wasn't strong enough to take the throne and would just make a mess of things. Hurt people. Maybe it was easier to be miserable than to act on the truth."

"Or maybe he was just scared of the possibility of happiness. Of losing control for once. Of making the best mistake of his life." Ethan spat out the words then lost his breath, gasping just like me. His dark eyes burned. Fire—fierce and dangerous—threatening to raze my entire world to the ground.

My pulse pounded at my wrists, my temples, everywhere. A full vibration like I might take off from this chair and fly. But did I want to scratch his eyes out or kiss him until I stopped breathing? Both seemed possible. Regardless, it didn't matter. Nothing mattered anymore.

"You could be right, but since he's already dead, I guess we'll never know." I ripped my backpack off the desk and stormed out of the room.

"Berkley James, I'm reporting you to the office," Mrs. Franklin yelled behind me.

I slammed the door and ran through hallway after hallway until the harsh light of day showered in from the main entrance.

Too scared? Of course I was scared. He would be too. Anyone would with a demon living rent-free in their body. I pushed open the front door and raced down the steps to the sidewalk.

"Where are you going?" Ethan called after me.

I spun around and flung my backpack onto the grass. "What do you care? You're clearly angry with me. Besides, with this thing inside me, what does it matter what I do?"

"Of course I care." He let the door close behind him and slowly marched down the concrete steps. His harsh glare softened as he approached, but he kept his distance. "I wasn't trying to upset you. It just happened."

"Really? Calling me out in front of our entire English class was your way of not upsetting me? Excellent execution, Ethan. Well done."

He dared to take a step closer, his hands held up in surrender. "I'm sorry. Okay. I shouldn't have done that."

I relaxed my clenched fists slowly as the rage drained from my bloodstream. Closing my eyes, I let the warm morning sun wash over my face as I released a labored breath. The flurry of the last hour spun in my brain, finally catching up to me. The pain. The hopelessness. And worst of all, the shame.

"But did you mean it?" I looked up at him, the golden light teasing the bronze strands from his chestnut hair. He wouldn't try to hurt me on purpose. Would he? "Do you think I was hiding before all this happened? Before ... you know."

Ethan grabbed the back of his neck and craned his head toward the sky as if processing every word carefully. "I don't know. You finally broke up with Josh even though you've basically been avoiding it since August. You haven't let people push you around as much. I miss you being happier, but you're not holding everything back like you used to." He paused again and let out a deep sigh. "Or I could be seeing something that really isn't there. Maybe I'm just being hopeful."

Red crept up the sides of his neck and shaded the tops of his ears as he stared down at the blades of dying grass peeking through the cracked sidewalk. The kiss. Apparently, the one thing I'd still managed to hide from. The sensation of his lips on mine flooded my mind. His fingertips tickling the back of my neck as he held me tight in his arms. I hadn't forgotten, I'd just pushed it down. Buried it beneath all the other things I had to deal with so I didn't have to figure out what it meant. So I didn't have to admit that I didn't want him to stop, or what that realization said about me and how it could change my entire world.

"Look, I know just because I have feelings for you doesn't mean you need to feel anything for me. I get that. It just ... it hurts." Ethan rubbed the toe of his sneaker across the pavement. "It hurts, and it sucks, and I know there is nothing I can do about it. It's like one second you're at my door and you can't get enough of me, and the next you push me away and won't even talk about it. Then I saw you with Josh again this morning, and I guess I made assumptions."

"You know I wasn't myself when I showed up at your house?" Or was I? If only I could remember the things I'd done. "And Josh and I are definitely over. There's no going back there now."

"I do now. But that night, the things you said. The way you ... That's why I kissed you in the courtyard. I knew it was the wrong time, but I needed to know if it was real. That you thought about me the same way I always think about you." He hung his head for a second, then shuffled to the side and scooped up my backpack from the ground. He held it out toward me, his eyes unable to meet mine. "And, I guess, now I know."

I slipped the bag over my shoulder as he nodded and headed back to the school.

My body shook on the sidewalk as everything crashed over me all at once. What the hell was I doing?

"I can't lose you, Ethan."

He froze on the steps, his hand gripped knuckle-white on the metal railing, but he didn't turn around.

"I don't know what happened that night, but it doesn't mean I didn't want it to happen. I mean, not like it did, I just, I don't not feel the same way about you." I threw my hand over my forehead to make the words stay still long enough to get them out, but everything remained muddled.

Ethan looked back over his shoulder, his face twisted with confusion. "What?"

"Everything used to be so easy. I had it all figured out. My perfect life planned down to the last detail. Then stuff started changing, and I tried to hold on to it, to stay in control, but it seemed the harder I tried, the faster it fell away from me."

A tightness started in my chest, expanding down into my stomach and rippling through my spine. I pulled the backpack strap tighter to my body and dug my fingernails into the canvas.

"Then things between us changed too, and I convinced myself I couldn't feel that way about you because we'd been friends for so long and I was with Josh. Now everything keeps getting worse, and I don't know what to think, except that when you kissed me, it wasn't perfect, but it definitely wasn't a mistake."

The tightness clamped harder around my ribs, pushing all the air out of my lungs. I gasped and closed my eyes as a shadow fell over my face.

Ethan's thick fingers wrapped around mine. "Why didn't you just tell me?"

"Because it'll never work." I opened my eyes and locked right onto his questioning gaze. "I'm so screwed up. Right now, I'm freaking possessed, and if I admit that I might want to be with you, then I'll destroy our friendship too."

He tugged my hand and pulled me to his chest. "You can't destroy that. No matter what happens."

"Thank you." The tightness ceased as he wrapped his lean, muscular arms around my sides. I breathed in the sweet smell of cinnamon toast lingering on his T-shirt. *Why couldn't I let this be simple?* Because nothing with me was ever simple, was it?

I tilted my head back against Ethan's shoulder. His lips curled into a wide grin, and although I wanted to copy, I couldn't. He gripped me tighter as he kissed my forehead. "Of course."

My shoulders relaxed as the tension flowed out of my body,

except something still cut sharp inside me. "So where does that leave us now?"

Ethan sighed, his chest rising and falling slow against mine. "I don't know."

Me neither.

The school bell rang and pierced our awkward silence. I jerked upright as Ethan ripped his arms away and stepped back. The heat of him evaporated, and an empty chill took its place.

He pointed toward the front doors as he shifted his weight to his back leg. "We should probably get back in there."

"Yeah." I shook my head and sighed, knowing I should have said something, but unable to figure out what that was. This conversation wasn't finished, but neither of us seemed to know how to end it.

My phone vibrated in my back pocket. Once. Twice. Three times. I slipped it out as messages kept pinging in.

A stream of photos flooded my phone screen. Images of brick covered in pink, purple, and red graffiti tags. I zoomed in on a picture to see clearer, but I couldn't make out the words spray painted across the wall. I flipped to the next photo. More nonsense words, but this time I recognized the pastel green and blue awning of Divina Tea. My hands trembled as I kept scrolling. Four more photos of damage to the outside of Sage's shop. Ethan looked up from his own phone, his mouth open wide. I scrolled faster until I hit the end of the photos to the single line of text at the bottom.

Lane: *Looks like you got your Picasso on last night.*

THIRTY-ONE

What did the words even mean?

I rearranged the photos on my kitchen table for the twelfth time, but they still didn't seem to make any sense. Even though I had blown up and printed the pictures, they still looked like a bunch of random gibberish. How could I be responsible for something I couldn't even read? However, Lane seemed to think I'd done this, and with my other breaks in reality it wasn't an impossibility.

Ding dong.

I glanced up at the microwave. Six o'clock. Right on time. I rushed down the hall and flipped open the front door.

"Lane, I'm glad you're here."

"Hey, Berkley," she said as she pushed her way through the door.

Except she hadn't come alone.

"Hello, Berkley," Dabria said as she followed Lane in, her arms full of orange lilies and deep-purple chrysanthemums.

"I didn't—"

"I hope you don't mind, but we brought you a few things." Orianna filed through the doorway with a cellophane-covered basket in her hands. Kassia came close behind with two steaming trays of disposable coffee cups. She nodded in greeting as she slipped off her black sneakers.

"Lane, I didn't realize you were bringing company." I forced a smile and did my best to keep my tone positive, but slamming the door in their faces was definitely a possibility at this point.

"We figured you wouldn't be too excited to come visit us today, especially since you didn't answer any of my texts." Sage walked over the threshold and then closed the door behind her. She shuddered, letting the fall cold brush off her before turning to me with a smile. "So we asked Lane to help us come to you."

She opened her arms for a hug ,and although I didn't make a move in her direction, she pulled me in anyway. "Blessed be, Berkley."

The irritation at the unwanted guests numbed a bit as I politely hugged Sage back.

"You're right. I'm not exactly in the best mood today," I said.

"Not unsurprising. That's why we come bearing gifts." Sage snatched the basket from Orianna and thrust it into my hands.

I held it out in front of me, my face hiding behind the large polka-dotted bow holding it together. "Not necessary, but thank you. You've already given me enough for one lifetime."

Kassia sniggered loud enough to snort. Dabria and Orianna glared at her.

"What? She's not wrong."

I shook my head. I never expected Kassia to agree with me on anything.

"I get that you're still angry. This is not an ideal situation for any of us, but you need to know that we never meant to harm you, and it is possible that this could have happened anyway. Magic is all around us, and sometimes it goes awry, but we are doing everything we can to make this right." Sage nodded and placed her hand on my shoulder.

"Besides, even if I didn't tell them where you lived, it would take about ten minutes to figure it out in this town," Lane added as she headed toward the kitchen. The four witches followed close behind as I locked the deadbolt.

I raced behind the group and stopped at the doorway.

I'd never seen so much black in my white-tiled kitchen before. It looked like shadows lurking around the cupboards and chairs. I slid the basket on the floor near the fridge and glared at Lane.

"I don't know," she silently mouthed back.

"I see you've taken a liking to your own handiwork." Sage stood over the table with one of the graffiti photos in her hands. Her nose wrinkled as she examined it closer, then placed it back with the others.

"I'm not sure this is something I could've done. The words don't even make any sense," I said as I maneuvered around her and gathered up all the photos, flipping them facedown on the counter away from her.

"It does if you read Ancient Sumerian, but I doubt they teach that at the high school level these days," she said.

"No, I can't say I know that one."

"You wouldn't." She slid off her peacoat and draped it over her arm. Clearly, she wasn't planning on leaving anytime soon. *Great*.

"It's a dead language," she continued. "So dead, not even witches use it anymore. However, it isn't uncommon with demonic scriptures."

I shuddered. "So, if you're right about this demon possession thing, it's possible I did do that?" I pointed at the stack of photos but refused to pick them up again. I didn't need to. The images were already permanently etched in my brain.

"Oh, I know you did it. But it wasn't the language that tipped me off, it was the security camera I have in the front window that you kept smirking into."

Red rushed to my cheeks, and I gripped the back of a kitchen chair as my knees shook. "I'm really sorry."

"Don't worry about it. I wouldn't think of pressing charges with you in your current condition. And that is why we are here." Sage clapped her hands, and the girls assembled around the table.

I glanced over at Lane, and she shrugged, then took a seat around the table as well. I followed along, still unsure if I was comfortable having these witches in my house. What things would they be capable of now that they were in my personal space? Or worse, what things could they do if I tried to kick them out?

Sage dropped her coat over the head chair at the table and grabbed the trays of paper cups. She moved gracefully between each of us, handing out the drinks, her expertise in food service shining through. "I feel like we got off on the wrong foot. I know you didn't come to us under the best circumstances, but had things been different, we could have shown you a much more positive side to witchcraft. I've lived in this world my entire life. My parents were witches and my grandparents as well; even my great-grandmother was a well-known elder around these parts."

She placed a cup in front of me, my name written in beautiful cursive across the front with a happy face underneath. I pushed the cup away, and Sage stopped, staring at me until I picked it back up. I took a sip, and she continued around the table. A cool blast of peppermint hit my tongue with a hint of something citrusy. Orange? Lemon, maybe? Either way, the combination tasted amazing compared to the dirt-flavored tea she'd given me last time. I took another large gulp, the lukewarm latte sparking happily against my tastebuds.

After placing the empty trays back on the counter, she continued pacing at the front of the kitchen. "We've all lived a peaceful and simple life practicing what we believe and causing harm to no one. But just like anything else in the world, any religion, belief, even political system, bad things can happen."

"But good things can happen too." Orianna propped her elbows on the table and looked over at me. Tonight she'd tossed her dyed locks into a messy bun, and the glittery black polish on her nails had chipped in places. If it weren't for the lack of color in her wardrobe, she didn't look any different than the girls off my volleyball team. Except none of them had accidentally hexed me—at least that I knew of.

"I didn't really believe in anything before I met Sage," Orianna continued. "My dad died when I was little, and my mom's string of boyfriends got progressively worse as the years went on. By the time I was in junior high, I hated everything. The world, the people in it, most of all myself. I wasn't looking for anything to help me because I figured I was beyond saving. Then I learned everything has a balance and all the negative things had positives, I just had to look for them. Plus, I met the two best friends anyone could ask for."

Dabria flashed a glamorous smile and reached across the table to grab Orianna's hand. Even Kassia seemed to perk up, though she'd probably deny it if I'd called her out. Lane, however, looked at me and rolled her eyes with a gagging motion.

"And sometimes people find witchcraft because they have abilities to share. Dabria has the gift of seeing auras, and I was blessed with the powers of an empath."

"So you can feel what everyone else is feeling?" I asked, motioning my hand around the table.

"To an extent. I tend to block a lot of it out as it can be extremely overwhelming, but if I touch someone it's even stronger. Plus, others can sense my emotions too, so I have to be very careful how I project certain feelings."

I looked down at my palms and remembered the soothing calmness I felt every time Sage had hugged me. Had it all just been magic?

"And some of us don't have abilities, but it doesn't stop them from learning the craft and growing into skilled practitioners," Sage added.

Kassia scoffed and stood up from the table to stand behind her chair.

"Or maybe they just haven't come into their powers yet. It's a lifelong commitment, not just a club you join. But magic is all around us. People practice it all the time and don't even know. Anytime you wish upon a star or on those birthday candles on your cake. That's magic. The feeling you get in your gut when something is wrong. Magic. The sense of calm when you close your eyes and block out the world and suddenly everything makes sense. Still magic. And that ache and longing in your chest when love grabs hold of you. Well, that's powerful next-level stuff."

"All right, enough with the sales pitch." Lane pushed away from the table, the chair legs screeching across the tile floor. "I get that magic isn't the enemy, but I took you here because you said there might be a solution to Berk's evil brain roommate problem, not to sell us a time share."

Sage's nose wrinkled, and she crossed her arms at the head of the table. "I was getting to that. But I don't want Berkley making choices lightly. This is a pretty heavy decision."

"Decision about what? If there's a way to help me, I want to know about it." I leaned on the table top as all eyes fell on me, except the levity in the room had drained, and my stomach turned from the collective dread.

"It's an exorcism," Sage said as she glowered at Lane. "To remove a demon, you'll need to exorcise it. I've already made calls to every coven in the state, and no one seems to have a better solution. We'll need help and more force to pull it off, but I have a few contacts that might be willing to make the trip for you."

I swallowed my drink, but it caught in my throat, and I choked. "Exorcism? Like in the movies, that kind of exorcism?"

"Not exactly, but it probably won't be pretty. Expelling a ghost like we tried at the cafe was nothing compared to this kind of ritual. We're talking blood magic, heavy witch energy, big-time firepower." The friendly mask Sage wore slipped and revealed a gloom in her eyes. A paralyzing fear.

I shivered and pulled my arms around myself as the temperature in the kitchen seemed to plummet. "But do you think it'll work?"

Sage sighed and blinked, hiding her true emotions again. "It's the only shot we have. But it needs to be your choice. If you are not 100% committed, then it definitely won't work."

I stood from the chair and paced the length of the table, my hand on my forehead. An exorcism. It sounded like something from one of the ridiculous books we'd read in English class. Magic and demons and witches weren't supposed to be real, but I had all three hanging out in my kitchen, drinking tea.

"Is there anyone else who can do this? The last time she let you into her brain, things didn't go so well, or did you want to ask your friend Tamara about that?" Lane challenged.

Sage cast her eyes to the ground. "I have spoken with Tamara, and she knows as well as I do that this is her only hope. What time did you go to bed last night, Berkley?"

"I don't remember. All of this is just—" I swung my hands in the air, my arms trembling. "Ten o'clock? Nine-thirty maybe?"

"It seems to get earlier and earlier these days, doesn't it?" Sage asked.

"I guess, I don't know. I'm tired all the time."

She tiptoed around the table until she blocked my path. She rested her open palms on my biceps, and a soothing sensation flowed through my body. I scrunched up my face, trying to fight it, to fight her magic, but it didn't help.

"Every day is going to get earlier. You'll lose time to the demon until it eventually consumes you. There will be nothing left. You can try to find another coven, even call a priest if you want, but the answer is still the same. If you don't rid yourself of this creature, it will devour you."

"No." I gripped the sides of my head and twisted out of Sage's hold. The raspy voice echoed in my brain. *You are mine. You are mine. You are mine.*

"How long do I have?" I blurted out as my eyes welled with tears.

"I don't know. I would hope until at least the full moon in a couple of weeks. The more power we can draw the better, but if things escalate, we might not have that choice."

I crossed my arms and gazed out the patio door into the night. The trees above the fence swayed and bowed in the fall wind as if to wave or possibly laugh at me. If I'd just minded my own business, maybe things would be different. Or maybe this thing would have found me anyway. Slipped through my window and crept into my head. Who knew?

"Why don't you girls go upstairs and cleanse Berkley's room? Remember to mark all the windows and doors as well," Sage said as chairs shuffled and voices murmured behind me. "Lane, can you show them the way?"

"I don't want to leave Berkley here," Lane said.

"It'll only be a moment. We're just going to talk and then will be right up to join you."

Lane's voice cracked as if she wanted to argue, but the words never came out. She brushed her fingers along my back as she walked around the table and out of the room. A clomping of three sets of footsteps fell in line behind her.

Sage joined me by the window but kept her hands to herself. The perfumey scent of the gifted lilies clouded my head, making it even harder to think.

"Did you know you're one of the bravest people I've ever met, Berkley James?"

I scoffed, my angry breath painting fog on the patio door. I pulled my hand into my sleeve and wiped it clean.

"It's true. It may not feel like it right now, but so many people in your position would've given up already."

"Well, I don't really have a lot of options, now do I?"

"That's true, but at least you've made it this far to make the choice. Exorcisms aren't very common, and it's not because people don't get possessed. It actually happens more often than we know, it's just that most can't handle the strain. They give themselves over to the darkness and fade too quickly to be saved, or they do something worse." She shuddered and closed her eyes for a moment. "Something they can never come back from. But you've fought hard against this monster inside you. I don't know how you've done it."

"Neither do I, but I wake up every morning, and everything feels like it's crashing down around me. Like one day I'll just be so buried deep that I won't be able to dig myself out." The words burned my lips as they flew out of my mouth. I'd thought them for days, but saying them out loud gave them substance. Gave them power.

"Don't think like that. If you want to fight the darkness, you need to keep your light, no matter how dim it may seem right now. What I'm proposing will not be easy—it might even be harder than what you're already dealing with—but I will do everything in my capacity to help you."

"Thanks," I said. Although the offer didn't really dull the dread eating holes in the pit of my stomach.

Sage turned to me again and swept my hair back over my shoulders, then tapped my chin up to look at her. Her soft crystal eyes shone bright with hopefulness, even if it was difficult for me to see it right now. "Think about it. It's your choice. Taking what's offered will not be easy, but it will be your chance at a real life. Or let go and stop fighting. I wouldn't blame you for that decision, but it is all up to you. I'll keep pushing forward until you say the word, but I won't pressure you into something like this."

She forced a sympathetic smile, then rounded the table and disappeared up the steps. I banged my forehead against the cool window glass. Neither option sounded appealing, but it would be nice to quit fighting. To stop questioning all the time. Strong? Not likely. Everything kept spiraling out of control, and I couldn't slow it down. What she saw as strength looked more like weakness to me.

Knowing I shared a body with a dead person had been a lot, but now the reality of a full-fledged Satan's helper coursing through my veins seemed unbearable. I thought somehow it would go away—like a vicious flu, maybe—but it wouldn't. It never would. It would consume me until there was nothing left to take. Tears flooded my eyes, and I let them fall. One after the other, cleansing the pain from my soul. Wringing out all the hurt and ache for things I'd never know.

"Hey Berkley, are you coming or what?" Lane's voice drifted down the staircase and echoed through the kitchen.

I took a deep breath and wiped my tears away with the back of my hand.

"Coming," I called as I glared into the foreboding woods then slammed the blinds shut.

THIRTY-TWO

The fluorescent lights blurred in and out of focus as I dragged myself down the hall. I closed one eye then alternated to the other, but the haze only thickened.

I hadn't slept last night. Although I hadn't really slept in weeks, last night felt worse. Whether it was the heavy blend of lavender and rosemary the witches had used to cleanse my space or just the weight of the decision Sage left on my shoulders, I woke particularly unrested and a little dizzy.

Even now, the smell of oily smoke still lingered on my clothes. I tucked my nose into the collar of my shirt and breathed in the funky smell. School should've been a break from all the chaos, but trouble just kept following me. At least I'd managed to get the witchcraft crew out of the house before my dad came home last night. I couldn't imagine how I'd explain that one.

I spun my combination into my lock and clicked open the door, each grind of metal on metal piercing into my raw brain. Leaning against the frame, I coughed, my lungs sore, probably from crying, or maybe my body was breaking down from my unwanted, demonic guest. Was this how it would go if I didn't take Sage's offer and just let myself drift? A cough leading to a flu-like state until my organs started shutting down. Would it hurt? Or would the thing inside me take over my mind before that happened? It wasn't like anyone made a guidebook for this sort of thing—because, of course, I'd already checked. Anyone who had survived this wasn't talking about it. And if they didn't, I guess there was no one left to write the story.

Bang!

I jumped, smashing my head on the top of the locker. *Ow!* I rubbed the sore spot of skin and picked up the shiny metal and wood grain object that had flown in beside my books. As I pulled it out into the light, I recognized it instantly. The smooth, sleek lines and the small engraved plate on the back with the name Alex James etched in bold serif font. It was the hunting knife I'd bought for my dad for Father's Day about five years ago. My mom had taken me shopping in Chicago, a girl's trip, but I wanted to grab a present while I had more shopping options. What was it doing here? I traced my finger along the side, and the blade popped open. I startled again, and the knife dropped from my grip, clanging loudly on the bottom of my locker.

"Look familiar?" An angry voice snarled from behind me.

I whirled around, nearly smacking my face into Josh's. Except from his steely, narrow glare, I doubted he'd think it was a happy accident.

"Josh. You scared me." Clasping my hand over my chest, I took a deep breath then pointed into my locker. "Why do you have that?"

He didn't bother to look. His eyes locked on me as if I'd try to steal his wallet or something ludicrous. "I scared you? You really do have some sort of malfunction, don't you?"

I slunk back against the locker bank, but it still wasn't enough space between us. Josh rarely got angry. He'd be upset sometimes or maybe frustrated, but only on rare occasion did his jaw clench with enough pressure to break teeth. He didn't even look this enraged when he'd clocked Ethan in the courtyard. However, based on the almost purple shade bleeding up his face, he might lose a few molars today.

"I found it beside my bed this morning." Josh ran his hand through his hair, more greasy than golden today, and glanced up and down the hallway before leaning closer to me. "It's bad enough that you broke into my house, but don't ever threaten me again. Do you understand?"

"What? I didn't—"

"Waking up to you standing over my bed with that knife scared the hell out of me. If that's what you wanted, you win. You're a total psycho. The only reason you don't have the cops at your door right now is because I still care about you, or at least I did."

A knife? I threatened Josh with a knife? My pulse pounded harder at my temples. What had I done? I could have hurt him—no—I could have killed him. I gasped, over and over, as the anxiety choked around my throat. "I'm so sorry. I ... I'm having some stuff going on right now. I never meant to ..."

"Look, I get that you're mad that I punched out your new boyfriend, and maybe you regret breaking up with me, but there is no way I'm ever going to forgive you for this. If there was ever a chance between us, it's dead. You got that? You need help. Like serious professional help, and I'll keep my mouth shut about this, but if I hear of anything from you again, I'm telling everyone."

Tears broke past my lashes as everything started to swirl. The fluorescent lights dimmed and brightened. Josh's face blurred in and out of focus as heat built in my chest and up my neck.

"And for your sake, I hope you weren't the one who destroyed the football field too. There're cameras all over that stadium, and I can't help you out of that one."

I lurched forward and grabbed my knees. I couldn't breathe. "What happened to the field?"

Josh opened his mouth to explain, then shook his head and stared at the floor. "Figure it out yourself. I'm done. I'm so done, Berkley."

Josh tossed his hands up in front of him and backed away.

I slammed my locker shut to hide the evidence. Everyone in the hall stared. Because of the fight or because they knew what I'd done? I closed my eyes, but images of standing over Josh's bed scalded across my brain. Were they real, or was it just my imagination?

The heat bubbling under my skin kept burning. Hotter and hotter. Warm saliva built in my mouth as the hallway spun in circles. Around and around and around.

What had I done? What was I even capable of? My body reached boiling, and I staggered across the hall. People shouted and stumbled as I knocked them to the side. I gripped the edge of the trash can, and everything I had left inside of me flew out.

THE BLADES of grass beneath my feet finally stopped swaying. I pulled my head from between my knees and tried to focus on the wall-sized ram's head painted near the courtyard doors. However, though the spinning had slowed, a cloudy haze remained blanketed over everything. Even my fingers felt two times wider than they should, but at least they stayed still.

I made a pathetic attempt to stand then decided that sitting might be for the best. At least for now. The school doors creaked open in the distance as Lane and Ethan rushed out and across the lawn toward me.

Lane launched onto the picnic table bench across from me, rattling the entire structure. My empty stomach gurgled in protest.

She leaned forward and slapped her arms across the table top. "What happened?"

I looked around the quiet schoolyard, then pulled the knife from my pocket and chucked it down in front of her.

"What is that?" Lane picked it up and turned the closed knife over in her hands.

Ethan plucked it from her grasp and clicked the button on the side to expose the blade. "A hunting knife. I thought you knew everything, Lane?"

She narrowed her stare and snatched the knife back, lowering the blade back into its casing.

"Did you know I stole that knife from my dad, broke into Josh's house, and probably tried to kill him with it?" I tried to keep my voice calm, as if it might keep my body from exploding all over the place again.

"You what?" Lane dropped the knife on the table then started buffing off her fingerprints with her sweater sleeve. "Wait. You didn't? Josh is fine, right?"

"He's not fine. He's absolutely furious. But at least I didn't hurt him, physically or anything."

"Well, at least you didn't do it." Ethan nudged Lane in the shoulder, but she didn't react. His smirk disappeared, and he clamped his fingers together on the table in front of him.

"Not funny. What happens next time if I do? Maybe I'll end up going on a rampage and taking out the student council with a chainsaw." I cringed as the image popped into my brain and I struggled to push it away. "I almost killed a person. And not just any person. Josh. Do you know what that means? I would be a murderer. A killer."

"You wouldn't have killed him. At least I'm pretty sure you wouldn't have." Lane grabbed my hand and bent down to look me in the eye. "Because no matter what happens, it's still you in there. As creepy as you are, you still know things that only you would know. You call my name when you kick my ass, and you always know to come back home. Why do you think that is?"

I banged my head down on the table. "I don't know."

"It's because it's still you." She shook my arm until I lifted my head again. "If you really wanted to kill Josh, he'd be in a morgue somewhere. That demon thing inside you is way stronger than some mediocre quarterback. You are what saved his life. You are still in control of this."

"So if it were you, you'd do it, wouldn't you?" I tossed my head back toward the sky and let out a massive breath before easing it down again. "The exorcism, I mean."

Lane pulled her hand away and sat back, her arms across her chest. Her shoulders sloped as everything weighed down on her. Even her wild curls drooped around her cheeks. "I don't know what I'd do. But I do know that you don't quit. You never do. You keep fighting longer and harder than anyone I know, and even though you don't always win, you don't give up. The only way you are going to get through this is to fight this thing with everything you've got left."

"You sound like Sage."

"Well, on this, Witch Lady might be right."

I rested my face on the table, the rough wood pricking at my skin. "I think I'm going to go home and think about things for a while. Besides, if Josh changes his mind and starts talking, things are only going to get worse."

Ethan swept my hair back behind my ear. I closed my eyes and savored the sensation of his fingertips tracing against my skin. A little joy combating the pain and guilt every other part of my body ached from.

"I can drive you home," he said. "If you want?"

"Thanks. That would be perfect." I sighed and sat up straight again. The metal bleachers surrounding the football field glimmered in the morning sunshine. My stomach churned, and I hunched forward. "Except I need to find out what happened to the football field. Josh said he thought I'd done something else last night."

"Ooh, yeah. That's not good." Ethan pulled his phone from his pocket and tapped at the screen. He blew up an image and slid the device in front of me.

A panoramic shot of the football field filled the width of his phone, but instead of the typical white lines that marked the distance, thick black letters spelling 'RAMS SUCK' were burnt across the green turf.

"Seriously?" I sighed and slipped the phone back to the opposite side of the table.

Lane popped up to get a better aerial view. "At least you didn't actually kill anyone."

THIRTY-THREE

"Don't take this the wrong way, but tagging the football field was hilarious." Ethan laughed again and pounded his hand against the steering wheel.

I sighed and rested my head against the window. The cool glass soothed the fire that had raged in my cheeks since the second Josh dropped my dad's hunting knife into my locker. I closed my eyes and let the refreshing sensation flow through me. If my skin blazed any hotter I might've been able to roast marshmallows with my face. "I'm glad someone is finding this funny."

"Sorry." He cleared his throat and tucked his giddy smirk away then leaned back in the driver's seat. "But I was in History with Brett when that photo went viral and you should've seen him lose his mind. It was epic."

I pictured Brett stalking around his class as his head threatened to explode, that awkward vein in his neck throbbing. My lips curled into a grin, taking a tiny glimmer of joy out of my depravity, but I forced it down. Unfortunately, a moment too late.

Ethan's stare narrowed. "See, you know he's a total jerk. You can't say that guy doesn't get under your skin."

"He was my least favorite of Josh's friends, but he didn't deserve me destroying his playground. Besides, you're a Ram too, shouldn't you be upset about my message?"

He shook his head. "No, football and baseball don't really mix. We take a lot of crap from them, and I'm kind of enjoying watching those guys freak out for once. Especially when I know you didn't really mean it."

"Well, you're welcome."

"I wouldn't panic too much about it. Besides, writing 'Rams Suck' was probably the smartest thing you could've done. Everybody thinks it's just some morons from the next county trying to trash talk our team. No one would suspect someone from our own school of doing this. It's kind of genius."

The window fogged as I let out an enormous sigh. *At least I did something right.*

The car rolled along the quiet street, sun beaming through the windshield. Everyone in the neighborhood had gone off to school or work, leaving my entire block silent and the piles of leaves scattered across the road undisturbed. Ethan rounded the corner and pulled into my driveway then cut the engine. Outside the passenger window, the world stood still, glistening and wholesome, like the paintings you'd see in a dentist's or lawyer's office. A beautiful day to be carrying around an evil demon.

I opened the car door, and a stream of autumn air filled the car. Placing my hand on Ethan's arm, I nodded and gave him a timid smile. "Thanks for bringing me home. I really appreciate it."

"Of course." He covered my hand with his and rubbed his thumb across my knuckles. The humor in his gaze faded. "If there's anything you need, you know you can always ask me."

My fingers tingled under his touch, and he chuckled to himself as if he could feel it too. His dark hair flopped forward across his brow as he hung his head, watching the slow circles as he drew them. My pulse quickened as the car seemed suddenly smaller. Just me and Ethan and not another soul for blocks. This wasn't new. He'd driven me home a million times before, but this time things were different. Maybe knowing how he felt—really knowing—had changed things. Or maybe I could just blame my lack of sleep. Except I doubted either of those reasons could compete with the memory of kissing him. The actual kiss outside the school, not the twisted demonic version that kept playing in fragmented loops in my mind. His soft lips at perfect pressure against mine. His hands sliding against my skin. The ache in my gut for more.

"Are you planning to head back for your next class?" I asked as I slid my hand away and put a foot outside the car.

He fought a frown then shrugged. "Not sure. I'm already skipping, maybe I'll just head home and try school again tomorrow."

I grabbed the edge of the car door and stared at the front of my house. The overwhelming silence slithered under my skin, and I shuddered. The thought of empty rooms and shadowy corners needled at my spine.

"Would you want to come in?" I blurted before my brain could fully think through the request. "I don't really feel like being alone right now. School is too much chaos to think, but sometimes just me and my thoughts are worse."

He paused, running his eyes over me, either looking for a punchline or permission. I wasn't sure.

"If that's what you want," he said.

I nodded and pushed the car door fully open as the chill morning breeze prickled against my warm skin.

We walked down the sidewalk to the front door without a word, our hands hanging at our sides less than a half-inch apart. The air charged, thick and electric, as uncertainty built between us. But what did it mean? I'd been with Josh for so long I couldn't remember the awkward 'I like you' stage, if this was even it. Ethan knew me too well. Things no boy should ever know. It complicated matters. Being friends made it weird, being possessed made it worse, but not knowing what I was supposed to do now was excruciating. I always had a plan, but I hadn't planned on Ethan. As my friend, he was an open book; as someone I'd kissed—that I might want to kiss again—he was just like Shakespeare. Complicated, frustrating, and something I didn't know what to do with.

At the door, Ethan stepped back to give me space, but it didn't help. I fumbled through my backpack and pulled out my house keys, immediately watching them slip through my fingers and jangle on the concrete step.

I crouched to pick them up, but Ethan's long arm swept much faster, claiming the key before I could.

"Here you go." He looped the key ring on his index finger and held it out for me.

I slid the keys off then pressed them between our palms, wrapping my fingers around his. "Thanks."

His eyes widened, but he didn't pull away. "No problem."

My hand trembled in his as I lowered them down near my waist. "I really mean it though. Thank you. I know all the stuff going on with me is pretty messed up, and all the stuff between us is pretty messed up too. But I couldn't get through all this without you and Lane. You've been way better to me than I deserve."

"Don't say that." He squeezed my hand and tugged me closer. "You're not some burden to carry, Berkley. I care about you, I always will. And even if this" — he pulled our joined hands up to eye level and then let them drop again— "doesn't happen, that won't change. You need to stop being so hard on yourself. I'm not going anywhere unless you tell me to."

"But what if I do? What if I can't fight this thing and I just disappear?"

He swept his free hand around my ear and rested his palm against my cheek. "That's not going to happen. But if it does, then I'll be here until you do."

His wide eyes mirrored the sincerity in his words, and I leaned into his touch, my legs threatening to give out and drop me to the ground.

I shivered, but he just gripped me tighter, and I sank into the rise and fall of his chest as he breathed.

"I don't know what to do," I whispered.

"You're one of the smartest people I know. I'm sure you will make the right decision." He eased my face forward then propped his chin on my forehead, holding me close. "And I'll still be here no matter what you decide."

A flash of red and blue lights danced around us. I glanced over to the street as a police car slowed and rolled past my house. The officer stared at us through the window, probably wondering why we weren't in school. Even through the tinted windows, the officer's sharp angular features twinged something in my brain.

"Let's get inside," I said as I pulled away from Ethan and slipped the key into the lock.

The key turned easily. A little too easily. The tremble in my hands morphed into a full-out shake as I creaked open the door, expecting the worst, and not even sure what that was anymore.

A banging noise sounded in the kitchen, as well as the screech of a chair across the floor.

"Stay here." I held my hand up behind me and headed down the hallway.

Ethan closed the door behind us and stayed put but still leaned forward on his toes as if waiting for the word to strike.

A figure crept across the kitchen floor. I tiptoed farther down the hall. The sharp stink of sweat and alcohol burned my nostrils. I gagged and covered my nose, taking the last few steps onto the tile. Across the room, a disheveled man rooted through our cupboards.

"Dad?"

He shuddered and clasped his hand over his heart, his labored breath thick and putrid in the small space.

"Berkley, what are you doing home?" he asked, pulling a bottle of bourbon from its shelf before grabbing a glass left drying near the sink.

"I should ask you the same thing." Except I didn't need to. The empty whiskey bottle on the table and the vodka label poking out of the trash can answered for him. "Shouldn't you be at work?"

He clinked the bottle and the glass together in one hand and stumbled back toward his seat at the table. He tousled his fingers through his oily hair and sat down.

"Turns out they didn't need me today." He spun the top of the untouched bourbon bottle, and I winced as the crack of it opening shivered down my spine.

He poured the caramel-colored liquid into the glass—enough to drop a linebacker on a good day—then took a heavy swig. He clacked his tongue against the roof of his mouth and set the glass back on the table with a thunk. "Sounds like they won't be needing me at all anymore."

I tilted my head back to fight gravity and keep my tears from falling, but it didn't help. "So you lost your job?"

"Yep," he mumbled and took another drink. "Their loss."

I fell into a chair at the opposite end of the table, my legs no longer interested in holding me up. "No, Dad, it's our loss. How are we going to pay for anything?"

He swiped his hand through the air. "Don't worry about it. I'll just get another job. I wasn't very happy there anyway."

"Except no one's going to hire you like that." I pointed at him, and he scowled.

"For someone who doesn't contribute to the finances, you're getting pretty judgey."

"Is that all you need? For me to get a job and then you'll stop all of this?"

"All of what? Do you have a problem with me? Well, line up, because so does everyone else these days."

My tears fell faster and faster, pooling onto the table then running along the wood grains. "You're the one with the problem. Ever since Mom left—"

"Enough." He shot his arm out and pointed at me. "Never talk about that woman to me again."

"Since Mom left—"

He flinched but didn't argue.

"Drinking is the only thing you do. I thought at first it was just a phase. Eventually, you would get over her and get your life back together. Except you didn't. You haven't even tried—"

"Berkley." Ethan's voice cut through my thoughts. I spun around as he stood in the doorway, his wide-eyed expression telling me how much he'd already heard.

"Can you give me a second?" I asked as I swept my sleeves over my face and looked away.

"I can't." He took a step into the kitchen then shuffled back. Probably unsure of whether to help or hide. "The police just pulled up, and they're coming up the driveway."

I glanced back at the mess of my father, but he didn't move. Scrubbing harder at my face, I rushed into the hallway and whipped open the front door. The uniformed officer on the other side jerked his head back and dropped the fist he had positioned ready to knock.

"Hello there, Officer ..."

"Shipley," he responded. "Officer Shipley."

Right. No wonder he'd looked familiar. He'd been here the morning I'd ransacked my own house.

"What can I do for you?" I slipped out onto the front step and closed the door behind me.

"Is your father here?" He sidestepped and looked around me, peering into the small frosted window at the top of the door.

I cringed then stood up straighter to block his view. "I'm sorry, he's not. Maybe I can get him to call you when he gets home. Do you have a card or something I can give him?"

Officer Shipley squinted as he scanned me over. My cheeks flushed as I avoided eye contact.

"Is everything alright, miss? You seem upset. Is there something going on inside?" He leaned toward the door, but I shuffled in front of him.

I tucked my fingers into my sleeves then crossed my arms. "Not at all. Everything's just fine."

"Are you sure? You look like you've been crying." He glanced toward the front window, and fortunately the curtains were drawn tight. Then he leaned closer and whispered, "If something is going on, you can tell me. Did something happen with the young man who answered the door? You don't have to say anything, just nod."

"Ethan?" I laughed. The only thing in my house that wasn't hurting me was Ethan. My dad was a wreck. I couldn't even trust my own body, but Ethan, no worries there. "Absolutely not. We were just watching a movie, and I got a little emotional. That's all."

Officer Shipley's compassion hardened faster than ice on a December day. "Shouldn't you two be in school right now?"

"No, sir, we've both got free classes right now. But I'm definitely heading back after lunch. Wouldn't want to get a bad reputation or anything."

Shut up, Berkley, shut up. One quick call to the high school and he'd know I'd lied. But would he really care? Skipping school wasn't a crime.

His jaw clenched as he processed my response, but he seemed to buy my story, or maybe he just had an excellent poker face. "Very well. But a word of advice, I'd be sure to lock your doors, even when you're home. There have been several incidents around town lately."

"Really?" It came out more high-pitched than necessary, and Officer Shipley flinched.

I cleared my throat and tried again. "Like what?"

"Vandalism at a little cafe down on Kennedy Street, and we're still looking into another incident that occurred at the high school last night."

I tugged my arms closer into my chest and gripped tighter onto my sweater sleeves to mask my shaking fingers. "That's awful. Hopefully, you catch whoever is responsible."

"Indeed. That's why I'm looking for your father. We think these crimes may be connected to your break-in and wanted to see if he had remembered anything else or found any clues since we last spoke. You haven't come across anything, have you?"

I scrunched up my face and pretended to think. If he actually bought it, maybe I'd consider taking one of those drama classes

Lane always tried to talk me into. "Not that I can think of, but I can tell my dad to call if he thinks of anything."

"All right then. Thank you for your time. But before I go, you haven't heard anything around school about these other cases, have you? We are getting the sense that it might be a group of teenagers based on the eyewitness reports."

Eyewitness reports? Someone had seen me. Or maybe Officer Shipley was just trying to call my bluff? I held my breath. "No, sir. I try to stay away from trouble when I can."

He nodded and started down the steps toward the sidewalk. "That's a smart plan, miss."

I exhaled heavily, letting oxygen swim through my limbs again.

"One more thing." The officer turned around, and I gasped. He paused and scanned me over. "We found your stolen vehicle. It's completely destroyed, but we are running fingerprints on the pieces we found. We're hoping it will help with the investigation."

"Here's hoping." I nodded and smiled, the sentiment coming off fake and plastic like an ornamental lawn flamingo. Of course they'd find fingerprints. All of them mine. But who steals and torches their own car? Hopefully, that detail would throw them off my trail. At least for a little while.

Officer Shipley stared in silence for a few moments too long then finally walked away. I stood stone still on the front step, refusing to let my guard down until his taillights disappeared around the corner.

After the street finally cleared and I reassured myself that Officer Shipley wouldn't be coming back again—at least not right away—I raced back inside and locked the door, collapsing against the wooden panels. I tried to take a deep breath, but my lungs ached, and I coughed. Ethan loomed at the end of the hall, and the thought of my drunk father in the other room hammered down over me like a tsunami.

I slumped down to the floor and held my head in my hands.

"Are you okay, Berkley?" Ethan rushed to my side, but I

couldn't even look up. The overwhelming storm of emotions pushed me down. Pummeling me, over and over and over again. I couldn't cry. I couldn't move. The last bit of my sanity flowed out of me onto the doormat. Darkness fell behind my closed eyelids as my pulse slowed, working through the murkiness in my veins. All the hurt, all the fear, galvanized into solid, shiny determination.

I scrambled to my feet and charged toward the kitchen.

Ethan jumped in front of me and held tight on my biceps. "Hold up. You don't have to deal with this right now. He's not going anywhere, so why don't we just go outside, or for a drive, or something to clear your head."

"I can't." I shrugged him off and zigzagged past.

"Do you know who that was?" I asked as I stormed into the kitchen.

Dad shrugged and gazed out the patio doors into the backyard.

"It was the police. And just like always, I covered for you. I've been covering for you for months, and it's exhausting. Telling the neighbors everything is fine, lying to Aunt Meg in California that you're working overtime when you're passed out in the bathroom, constantly coming up with excuses to feed everyone. But I can't do it anymore."

"Do you think it's easy on me?" He slammed his fist on the table, and his glass jumped, whiskey splashing onto the wooden table top. Closing his eyes, he brought his fist back up to his forehead and inhaled slowly, his breath hitching as his chest rose.

"You have no idea what it's like for your entire world to fall apart. To feel so out of control of your own mind that it's just less painful to let it all go. To give in to the bad things instead of fighting." He took a long, slow gulp of his drink then leaned back and slouched in his chair. "I'm so tired of fighting."

I crossed my arms over my chest, either holding myself back or holding myself together, which I wasn't sure. Sunlight streamed through the windows behind him, bathing his crumpled figure in warm golden light, while he cast dark shapes across the kitchen table. The wrinkles in his forehead and around his eyes carved deep. Etched like words into a tombstone. Granite giving way to a memory. Only half a man—half alive, half dead. Fighting his own demons, except at that moment, the figurative ones seemed just as sinister as the real ones.

"I get it. More than you will ever know." My eyes welled up, and I swiped my arm across my face. "Mom left, and it sucks. I know that. It sucks for you and sucks for me, and everyone around us who has to put up with both of us being broken and messed up every single day. But you can't keep doing this to yourself. You can't keep doing this to me."

He gripped his forehead in his shaky hand. "I don't know what I'm supposed to do anymore."

"Get help. Clean yourself up."

"Right. It's not that simple." He shook his head and scoffed. "But I don't expect you to understand."

"No, it's not simple. It's probably the hardest decision you'll have to make, but if you really care about me, about yourself, you'll keep trying. You won't give up."

He swiped the glass from the table and downed the rest of his drink. "Thanks. I'll think about it."

My stomach twisted and writhed in my gut, the darkness flowing again. Seeping through my limbs. Wrapping itself around my core.

"If you don't get help, I'm leaving. I can't do this anymore. I can't watch you fall apart. And the way you treat me—" The tears streamed uncontrollably, and I didn't try to stop them. Not anymore. It wasn't worth wasting my energy. "I'm done."

His head jerked back, and his eyes narrowed. "You wouldn't."

"I will." I stepped forward and slammed my hands on the table, leaning forward. "Unless you can give me a reason to think things will get better."

A sigh. A defeated shrug. He rolled the glass between his hands and stared at the droplets still left in the bottom, over and over, as his silence dragged on. Or maybe it was the only answer he had in him to give?

My body twitched as the last of the darkness took hold. I pushed down onto the table top and launched back upright then headed for the hallway. At the doorway, I paused and turned back. Dad's head still hung to his chest. He didn't look like my father anymore. Just a shattered man that I didn't recognize. My mouth opened, but no words came out.

Flying down the hall, I whipped open the front door to the glorious autumn day swirling outside. I froze on the threshold. How could a world so tranquil exist while mine was imploding? Shimmering leaves fluttered past my front steps, and my throat tightened. It wasn't fair.

Ethan appeared behind me and placed his hand on my shoulder. I leaned my cheek against his soft skin and closed my eyes.

"Where did you want to go?" he asked.

I straightened up and stepped out into the beautiful day. "To listen to my own advice."

THIRTY-FOUR

"**K**assia just texted, and they're almost here." Sage flicked her French-manicured fingers across her phone screen as she paced back and forth in front of the dilapidated barn, gravel crunching under her heavy footsteps.

Hopefully they knew how to find this place. Lucky for us, Ethan followed close behind Sage's Jetta down the two minor highways and onto the overgrown back road. If we'd just had instructions or a map, I would've been so lost after about the fifth unmarked turn I'd never be able to get here—let alone find my way back out. However, knowing what I knew about witches and magic now, the labyrinth required to get here probably wasn't created by accident. The thick brush and mile-high grasses that surrounded the lone unassuming building likely weren't a coincidence either.

"Relax." Tamara strutted up to Sage and rested her hand on her shoulder, her snakeskin heels gliding over the uneven terrain like she'd always hiked through the woods in stilettos. Well, not quite stilettos, but high enough heels that I would've twisted an ankle by now.

Sage clasped her hand over Tamara's and squeezed. "Thanks, but I really wish we could get started. Being out here too late might not be the best idea." Her narrow stare drifted my direction then slipped off into the distance as my gaze met hers.

A cool breeze swirled between us, and I clenched my arms tighter around my chest. Ethan rubbed his hands up and down my biceps as he tugged me closer, so my back fell against his chest. I closed my eyes and relished the warmth sparking along my arms as the heat of the late-afternoon sun flitted across my face. My knees quivered as I tried to relax, even just a little, but the weight of everything still pinched tight around my lungs. Threatening Josh's life. My dad wasted in the kitchen. Marching into Divina Tea to take Sage up on her offer. All of it piled on top of me, stealing my breath in pieces. Like pounding waves on a lake, crashing against my body and dragging me under the surface. Drowning me.

"How much farther is this place?" An irritated whine pierced through the dense woods. "Ow! Stop pushing. I'm going as fast as I can."

I snapped my eyes open again. A black blob meandered through the trees with a bright fuchsia spot in the middle of it.

"Finally," Sage huffed as she moved closer to the barn door.

"Berkley." Lane waved her pink arm as she and the three witches hurried down the overgrown path toward us. "We would've been here faster, but Kassia drives like my grandmother on the way to church."

Kassia jutted out her hip as she narrowed her eyes to give Lane a death glare. "They're called traffic laws. It's not like I can wave my hand to make red lights disappear."

Lane stared right back, refusing to be put in her place, then bit her lip, likely swallowing the clapback burning on her tongue.

"We came as fast as we could." Orianna crossed between the two of them, breaking their stare-down, and proceeded closer to the barn, giving Sage a polite embrace.

"Well, let's get going. I'd really like to get out of here before dark. We can all meet back at the shop after to chat, but I think it's important that everyone knows what they're getting into." She pulled a gold key from the back pocket of her skinny jeans and slid it into the padlock on the door. The metal clinked open, and the massive wooden door groaned as she eased it open a crack. "Remember, we don't talk about this place. It never existed. Got it?"

Sage pointed her finger at each of us, a stern, hard look upon her face. Our strange crew nodded in turn until she seemed satisfied and flung back the door.

She stepped to the side and swept her arm in front of the gaping black hole that led inside the barn. "Welcome to Illinois' oldest coven house. Touch nothing unless I tell you."

Tamara nodded and marched, head high, into the darkness as Sage followed behind her. Each of us glanced around the cluster of remaining faces, but no one moved. In the silence, the leaves overhead whispered ominous indecipherable messages. But were they beckoning us forward or warning us to run while we still could? I shifted back and forth on my already unsteady legs and locked eyes with Lane. She shrugged, her blank expression doing nothing to soothe my nerves. I swallowed hard and willed my feet to step, but stopped as Kassia's army boots smacked the gravel.

"Seriously?" Kassia huffed as she charged toward the open door. She paused for a second just before the threshold, her fingers curling into fists then flexing out again. "You all aren't afraid, are you?"

Dabria scoffed as her expression soured. "Of course not."

She sashayed up behind Kassia, and they both disappeared into the barn. Orianna shot me a half-smile and proceeded after them. I exhaled, then nodded at Ethan and Lane before following Orianna. No turning back now.

As I neared the entrance, Lane gripped my arm and tugged me back. "Berk, wait. We need to talk."

My shoulders slumped, and I dropped my head back toward the clouds, knowing what she'd say before she said it. Ethan grabbed the back of his neck and looked off into the woods, the color draining from his expression. I shot him a glare, but he didn't notice or just chose to ignore it.

"Of course he texted about what happened with your dad. You two are equally awful at keeping secrets from me." Lane nudged Ethan, and he shuffled back a few paces. "Although it didn't stop you from trying. Are you okay?"

"I'll be fine, Lane." I sighed. "And I wasn't trying to keep it from you. There were just more important things to deal with right now, like saving my soul from being devoured by a hell monster. I would've told you later."

"But your dad? Ethan told me what you said. That you're going to leave. That's pretty heavy."

"I know. But I just"—a few tears broke past my lashes, and I wiped them away—"I can't do it anymore, you know? I can't watch him destroy himself."

Lane whipped her arms around me and squeezed tight, her curls tickling under my nose. "Yeah, I do. It sucks, but if you need anywhere to go, you know you have me, right?" She elbowed Ethan in the side. "You have both of us."

Ethan's arm slipped over my shoulders. "Absolutely."

"Thanks, guys." I pulled myself out of the huddle and turned toward the barn door.

The world blurred in and out of focus, and my foot slipped on the loose gravel.

"Whoa." I grabbed my forehead and reached out to the open air, but grabbed onto nothing as I teetered backward.

"Berkley." Lane clutched my right arm as Ethan grabbed hold of my left. "What's wrong?"

I righted myself and took a deep breath. "Nothing. Just turned around too fast or something."

As I forced my eyes to focus on a large birch tree, the woods stopped spinning, and the uneasy pang in my stomach subsided.

Lane and Ethan stared at each other, a wordless conversation passing between them.

"Seriously. I'm good," I said.

"You've had a rough day," Ethan started.

"Maybe we should hold off on all this," Lane finished and waved her open hand at the barn. "There's been enough life-changing events for you for twenty-four hours. Are you sure you need to do this now?"

"Why not? What else am I supposed to do? Wait around until I go on a killing spree and take out the yearbook committee? If I give up now, what does that make me?"

Lane frowned. "Human."

"Really?" I laughed. "Maybe not for long."

Dabria appeared in the doorway and looked each of us over. "Are you coming or what?"

"We'll be right there." I marched the last few feet to the door, pushing through the last wave of dizziness that tried to knock me down.

All light died inside the barn, except for the fading sun that streamed in from the door. Every wall, every rafter had been painted black. Even the wooden floorboards were colored pitch, except for a giant, perfectly symmetrical pentacle drawn in faded white lines on the floor.

I pulled my hands into my sleeves and held a fist in front of my face to block the thick, earthy smell attacking my nose, and slid along the outside of the room in line with the others.

"What exactly is this place?" Lane asked, her head swiveling around, taking in the atmosphere.

"This is the most mystical place in all of Lethe and probably about the next half dozen counties. Generations of witches have gathered here and performed some of the greatest magical feats that have ever been attempted, and no one in this sleepy town has a clue about it." Sage paced in front of us like a drill sergeant, her hands folded neatly behind her back and her knee-high leather boots complementing the military vibe. "The building and the grounds have been in my family's care for decades, but now that most of the covens have moved away from Illinois it's only used in emergency situations."

"Like exorcisms?" Orianna asked, her hand half-raised.

"Exactly. In fact, I know of at least three that have occurred here, but it's been a very, very long time." Sage nodded at Tamara, and she proceeded to close the barn door, shutting us in the dark. A chill slithered up my spine, and I reached for Lane's hand beside me. She hooked her pinkie finger with mine and held tight.

A noise clicked in front of us. Then a spark. Then another click, until Sage held up a small lighter in front of her face. The eerie light cast shadows on her cheekbones, morphing her typical sweet expression into something somber and twisted. She marched in front of me and thrust her hand toward my head. I shifted to the left, my pulse pounding in my temples, but her hand shot past me and pulled a candle off the shelf along the wall. She lit the wick, and the barn glowed brighter.

I exhaled and slipped my hand out of Lane's so she couldn't feel my fingers tremble.

"Let me help." Kassia stepped forward from the line and raised her right hand in the air. She mumbled something under her breath, low and cryptic, almost like a hiss as a strange smile curled upon her lips. After she finished, she glanced up and snapped her fingers. A half-spent candle across the room set aflame.

"Very good, Kassia. You've been practicing." Sage walked over and placed her hand on Kassia's cheek. She turned away and pulled out of her grip.

"Big deal," Lane whispered beside me.

Kassia glared our direction and raised both hands in the air. She struck them together in three thunderous claps as the surrounding walls sparked alive with flames from several dozen candles on shelves of varying heights. Lane swallowed loud enough for me to hear, and Kassia shot her a devilish smirk.

The bright glow illuminated the room and revealed more secrets the barn kept hidden in the dark. Strange geometric symbols painted in shades of muted red decorated the black walls. Dusty jars of unknown ingredients filled a large cabinet on the far wall, flanked by a pair of chains and shackles to the left and a collection of other sharp, pointy implements on the right. I slid backward until the flames of the candles behind me warmed the back of my neck.

Sage caught my gaze, and her eyes widened. "Trust me, it's not as ominous as it looks in here. But it's always important to take every precaution."

I nodded, my eyes still locked on a hook-shaped blade hanging across the room.

Dabria stepped forward, surveying the space, except with a grin that screamed fascination instead of fear. "How come you've never brought us here before, Sage?"

"This isn't exactly the best place for beginners, and I wanted to make sure you focused on the light side of your practice instead of the dark." Sage shielded her candle's flame as she strolled to the center of the pentacle. She placed the candle on a tall altar and dropped her shoulders, her head falling back toward the roof. "There has been some heavy-duty dark magic performed in this room. Things you can't even imagine."

"But—" Dabria edged toward the pentacle, but Tamara shook her head, and she backed down.

"You need to be really ready before working in a place like this," Tamara said as she moved to stand closer to Sage. The candlelight painted shade around the thick scratches across her cheek.

Scratches I'd put there.

My stomach twisted, and I stared down at the painted floorboards.

"That's why we wanted to bring you out here now. Everyone will need to be at their best for this type of ritual to succeed." Sage sighed and nudged closer to Tamara. "Let go of your fear and replace it with confidence."

"But we won't be alone. At least not entirely," Tamara added.

"Yes. We will need all the help we can get, and I've reached out for assistance to all the covens we"—Sage nodded toward Tamara—"have contacts with, but I'm still unsure who will come. Many witches will not want to touch this, and unfortunately, it's our mess to clean up."

"We'll do whatever we can to help." Lane slid her hand in mine and squeezed, then stepped forward. "Won't we, Ethan?"

Ethan nodded and stood beside Lane. "Yep."

"Guys, you don't—" I tugged Lane's hand back, but she ignored me.

Instead, she pushed her chin up higher with defiance. "Don't argue with me, Berkley. You know you won't win."

Sage laughed, her blond hair falling softly around her shoulders. "Thanks, you two, but this is way too much for civilians. The only reason you're here now is because Berkley insisted you knew what was happening."

"You know I'm not letting you do anything to my friend unless I'm here." Lane walked forward but stopped before her toes touched the edges of the pentacle. "Unless you'd like me to let slip what's going on here to the police?"

Tamara stuck her hands on her hips and stared back at Lane with an icy glare. "You know witchcraft isn't illegal, right?"

"Maybe not, but I'm sure people would love to know about real live witches hiding in the suburbs. A few well-placed social media posts and you'll have people crawling all over you, trying to find out more. You'd never be able to practice in peace again."

"You wouldn't," Tamara replied.

Lane shuffled a fraction forward, still careful to avoid the white lines on the floor. "Why wouldn't I? I'm not asking you to raise the dead or anything, I'm just asking to be present for my friend that you all messed with and make sure she's okay."

"But what if something happens to you, Lane?" I tugged her hand again, but she slipped out of my grip. "Maybe it's safer for you to just stay away."

Lane crossed her arms and turned her head toward me. "Really, Berk? If it were me, would you just turn me over to a bunch of witches and walk away?"

A fire burned in my chest. I wouldn't have wished this torture on anyone, especially not Lane. "No, but—"

"All right, that's settled. We're coming." Lane grabbed onto Ethan's arm and yanked him forward.

Tamara marched forward and lowered her head to meet Lane head on. "Who do you think—"

"Fine. You can come, but you aren't taking part in the ritual. You can act as lookouts and make sure nothing interrupts us." Sage rushed between them and eased Tamara back. "Arguing isn't going to do us any good, and the last thing we need is more unwanted attention. Plus, we can always use additional positive energy."

Lane nodded. "Perfect. Just tell us when and we'll be there."

"The full moon," Sage said as she returned to the altar and resumed pacing in front of all of us. "We'll need as much power as we can get, and that's the strongest time. Besides, there is a lot of work that needs to be done before then—protection spells, putting out calls for additional support, gathering supplies—so it gives us time."

I closed my eyes and pictured the calendar on the refrigerator in our kitchen. The little full circle didn't show up in the daily squares for a while. "But isn't the full moon not for a few more weeks?"

Sage nodded. "Seventeen days, to be exact. Now each of us have a list of tasks to complete ..."

Her voice droned on, but I couldn't make out the words. Seventeen days? It hadn't even been seventeen days since I'd gone from the quarterback's girlfriend to his attempted murderer. Who knew what I could do in another two weeks? I glanced around the room, watching the faces of my friends raptly focused on Sage's speech of instructions, wondering whose life I might try to take next.

"Wait." I lunged forward with two large strides. My knees wobbled beneath me as the flames of the candles blurred together into one continuous glow. I placed my icy palm on my forehead and took a deep breath until everything stopped swaying. "Why can't we do this now? I can't spend another day like this. It's too dangerous."

"Patience." Sage rested her hands on my shoulders and gave me a consoling half-smile. "I know it must be pretty uncomfortable for you right now, but the fact is, I want to do this right. You can't rush these things, or nasty stuff happens. If anyone can understand that it should be you."

A soothing warmth washed over me, but I didn't want it. I didn't want to feel okay. I wanted to *be* okay. I shrugged off her hands and pivoted away. "I tried to kill my ex-boyfriend last night. I stood over his body as he slept and attempted to end him. Please don't tell me you know how uncomfortable I must be."

The candlelight swirled again, and I couldn't feel my fingers at the ends of my hands. I stumbled forward and gripped the side of the altar to keep my body upright. "I'm not uncomfortable, I'm completely wrecked."

"Berkley, are you all right?"

I heard the voice, but couldn't place it. Too far away. Mumbled. As if I'd fallen underwater and someone called after me from the shore. Disappearing under the waves. My arm slipped down the altar, and I dropped to my hands and knees on the wooden floor. My nostrils burned with a sour smell as my tongue twisted over foreign words spewing from my mouth. Hissed threats in an ancient language. I focused on forcing my mouth closed, but my lips wouldn't respond to me. Sharp pain shot through my spine, and I bucked forward. A thousand needles stabbed up my back. A scream ripped up my throat as hands yanked me off the floor under my armpits.

"Open the doors. We need to get her out of here."

Fresh air smacked against my face, and I gulped it down. One gluttonous breath after another. The feeling in my limbs returned slowly, until I could finally sense the gravel grinding underneath my feet. My stomach churned as I rushed forward into the woods and fell to my knees. My hands shook as I held them out in front of me, staring at them as if they weren't mine. I rocked back and forth on the dirty ground, the strange surge of power and pain draining from my body. As I tipped my head toward the sky, gold and cinnamon-colored leaves cascaded down around me through the fading sunbeams. The fall breeze kissed my flaming cheeks as it waved the trees into an enchanting ballet overhead. The world radiated beauty in the last embers of daylight. Except for me—a tainted, monstrous thing.

Leaves rustled behind me as footsteps clomped closer, but I refused to look. Sage dropped down beside me, the relaxing scent of chamomile tickling my nose.

"Are you okay?" Sage asked, rubbing her hand along my back and spreading a relaxing tingle through my aching spine.

I exhaled into the twilight and melted lower to the ground. "No, I am most definitely not okay."

"Come here," she said and gave me a hug. "It's going to be all right."

"No, it's not. I'm turning into pure evil. How is that going to be okay?" Hot tears streamed down my face. "I'm not going to make it to the full moon, am I?"

"No, you won't." Tamara crouched beside us, her arms resting on her bent knees. In the dim light, shadows collected on the three deep scratches alongside her face. Another reminder of what horrors I was capable of. "We're going to have to move this up."

Sage scowled. "But without the full moon, we're going to be at a severe disadvantage."

"But waiting might not leave us anything left to save." Tamara slipped her cell phone out of her pocket and flipped through apps with her thumb. "There's always the new moon on Saturday. Two more days. It's not ideal, but better than just any regular day."

"New moons are for new beginnings, I guess." Sage stood up and brushed the bits of forest debris from her jeans. She smiled at me, but her eyes followed Tamara, a grim unspoken message running between the two of them. "There is a lot to be done before then, though. It's going to be a challenge. We'll need everyone's help."

"Whatever you need," Kassia and Lane said in unison, then glared at each other.

"Great. Orianna, Dabria, Kassia, come with me and Tamara back to the shop. And you two"—Sage pointed at Ethan and Lane —"can you get Berkley home? Make sure she gets rest because the next few days are going to be a lot. Plus, I'll need help from all of you tomorrow if we have a hope of pulling this off. Got it?"

"We'll take care of her." Ethan shoved his hands in his jacket pockets and nodded.

Sage smoothed her hand down the back of my head. "We'll do everything we can. I promise."

I rubbed my sleeve over my face as my view of the world blurred again from a new batch of tears threatening to fall. Blinking them back, I listened for the sound of the witches and their hushed whispers to disappear into the woods. The sun dropped lower. Soon night would come and bring out the darkness inside me. The one I couldn't control.

I pushed up to my feet, my body wavering and raw.

"Easy." Ethan wrapped his arm around my waist and guided my head to his shoulder. An uncertainty fell over his expression as he stared past me to Lane.

"You can do this, Berk." She took my arm and helped weave me down the forest paths toward Ethan's car. "It's only a few more days, and then we can all go back to how things used to be."

I sighed, letting the familiar scent of my two best friends and the beautiful autumn air release some of the pressure in my aching chest. "Thanks, but you know that will never happen. No one will be able to trust me again. I won't be able to trust me again. The old me is gone."

Lane sidled up beside me and rested her head against mine. "Maybe. Or maybe the new you will be so much better."

THIRTY-FIVE

My face smacks the surface of the water. It stings. Cold envelops my body and invades the marrow of my bones, freezing me from both inside and out. A sliver of silver moon laughs above my head as I sink down ... down ... down. My mind pleads with my feet to kick, but again, they are no longer mine. My arms flail, hopeless, reaching out to nothing. To no one. To my own peril.

My mouth opens wide, and my muffled scream pierces the quiet. Bubbles float past my head, encasing my last breaths. Earthy, dirty water rushes down my throat. I choke and swallow more as the pressure builds agonizingly in my ears.

Still, I sink down ... down ... down. The whispers of the moon fade into the emptiness of the water. My lungs burn. They ache as if to rupture. I cough and sputter. More water floods in.

Finally, my feet start kicking together, pushing my body up through the abyss. My arms pull me closer to the surface. I break free. My mouth gorges on the fresh air above the water. I'm going to make it. The light fades. I fall back into darkness.

THIRTY-SIX

I slurped the last giant gulp from my smoothie cup then chucked it into the trash can beside the bus stop. The tangy sweetness of mango and pineapple soothed my dry, scratchy throat, and I hesitated before swallowing to squeeze out as much relief as I could. I'd always wanted to try this flavor, but every visit to Smoothie Station ended with me ordering strawberry. The same kind. Always. Just safe strawberry. Except today when Lane pulled through the drive-thru, my stomach churned at the thought of the same boring thing, so I went for it and ordered the Tropical Tornado. And it was totally worth it.

My vocal cords burned. Hoarse and raw, like I'd been screaming all night. Maybe I had. The sopping wet heap of clothes soaking my bedroom carpet this morning might've been the reason, but I was never really sure what was reality anymore. An image flashed in my brain. Water all around me. My body slowly sinking. Dragging. Drowning. Gasping for air. I clutched at my neck and shuddered.

"Berkley." Lane placed her hand on my shoulder and snapped her fingers in front of my face.

I lunged forward, and the morning sun pierced through my terrifying vision, grounding me back in the real world. The one that seemed as much a nightmare lately as the ones on repeat in my head. I rubbed my hands over my face and exhaled, my breath bursting into a puffy cloud in the early-morning coolness.

"Whoa. Where were you just now?" Lane asked as she tossed

her cup in the trash can, then wiped her mouth with her jacket sleeve.

I shook my head. "I'm not really sure, to be honest. But I'm good now."

"Are you though?" She tipped her head to the side and tapped her index finger across her lips. "Or are you just fantasizing about running away to a remote island off the coast of Panama and selling homemade jewelry and funny slogan T-shirts out of your treehouse mansion?"

I blinked and tried to make sense of her words. Must be way too early or I was way too tired for this. "What?"

"Maybe just me then."

I laughed. "What was in that smoothie?"

"Nothing. Just wanted to lighten the mood a little. It's been a while since I've seen you laugh." She slid her hands in her jacket pockets and shrugged.

"I don't know what I'd do without you, you know that?" I stretched my arm around her shoulders and pulled her next to me.

"Probably have a super boring life." She leaned her head against mine for a moment then spun in a circle and out of my grip. "Now let's get in there so I can go back to being the only one convincing you to do appalling things."

Another pretty teal sign with its fancy black letters adorned the outside of the Divina Tea door. *Closed October 3rd and 4th for a special event.*

My hand hovered over the door handle, but I couldn't bring myself to open it. I read the sign over again. Once. Twice. Three times.

"What's the holdup?" Lane pushed in front of me, her eyes flitting back and forth as she read the sign. "You know you're the special event, right? We can go in."

I stepped back onto the sidewalk and sighed. "I know. It's the date. I hadn't even realized it until now, but my scholarship interview is tomorrow. The one that was going to get me out of this town and into any college I wanted."

Lane's lips rounded into an "o," but she didn't make a sound. She hung her head then raised it again, along with her index finger, her mouth opening for one of her signature pep talks. But I cut her off.

"Yes, I get it. There will be other opportunities. I'm smart and capable, and getting my life together is more important than some scholarship, and I'll figure it all out. But it still sucks, you know? Thinking about how everything I'd planned is running through my fingers and I can't seem to catch it."

Tears pricked in the corners of my eyes, but I forced them back down.

"I was actually going to say that if the exorcism doesn't work, maybe you should major in Latin as you'd totally kill it, but those are all good thoughts too."

Her glassy eyes widened as she forced a smile, but I couldn't return it.

"Oh, Berk," she said, the pity in her voice thick and dripping.

I tossed my open palm out in front of me. "No, it's fine. It clearly wasn't meant to be. Let's get this whole witchy spectacle over with."

Lane moved aside as I lunged toward the door and pushed. *Ow!* My shoulder rammed into the window with a thud, but the door didn't move. As I rubbed my sore arm, I glanced over at Lane and shrugged. She frowned and brushed me out of the way, then pounded on the glass while yanking on the door handle.

The lock clicked inside, and Kassia pulled the door open, her irritated scowl already in place even this early in the morning. "Take it easy. It's just a door."

Lane chased after her as she crossed the entranceway and continued farther into the shop. "You knew we were coming. You didn't need to lock it."

"We did know you were coming. Maybe that's why we chose to

lock it." Kassia spun around on her thick boot heels, nearly knocking Lane over as she struggled to stop. Her black-painted lips curled into a devious half-smile before turning her head toward the cash register. "Sage, Berkley's finally here."

Finally? It was barely eight in the morning. How was I supposed to rise with the sun when I stayed out all night?

But it didn't seem like that mattered. Around us, Divina Tea buzzed like a Saturday morning breakfast rush. Faces I'd never seen were hard at work, moving and sorting things from place to place. Some stopped and whispered, trying not to be caught pointing at me, but their stares weighed heavy on my skull, exposing them. Tamara and a red-haired woman I'd never met folded thick sheets that looked like choir robes near the pastry display. Even Ethan had already arrived and struggled to shuffle excess tables around the shop based on Dabria's directions while she sat twirling strands of her glossy hair around her finger, watching him.

"Great. You're here." Sage emerged from behind the counter, the kitchen door swinging behind her and wafting a hideous smell out into the front of the shop. I covered my nose with my sleeve and tried not to puke up Tropical Tornado all over the floor as Sage shimmied through the piles of boxes and plastic storage bins littering her path.

"What's all this?" I asked her as Kassia sped behind me with another box, almost knocking me over.

She brushed her hands on her apron and took a deep breath. "Supplies. I'm trying to get everything together so we only have to make a few trips out to the coven house. We don't have much time now that we've moved from the full moon to the new moon. It's definitely not the ideal timeline for this size ritual."

"Sage, where do you want the case of salt?" Dabria called behind us.

Sage rushed across the room, and we followed close on her strappy-sandaled heels.

"And who are all these other people? Are they all witches too?" Lane asked.

"You can put the salt near the front with the bucket of ash." She nodded toward the front door. "And yes, Lane. These are all witches from other areas who were willing to help. Most from Missouri, but Reese and Luna over there"—she pointed at a set of twins in boho-style skirts milling around near the tea tumbler display—"came all the way from New Mexico. I'd hoped for more, but I'll take what I can get."

I glanced around the room again. The stares hadn't faded, but I hadn't really expected them to, either. My hands itched to move something and focus my uneasiness into productivity. "What would you like us to do? We can start dragging things out to the coven house, if you want? Lane brought her mom's van, so it should hold a lot."

"Oh, no. Lane can head out there, but you aren't going anywhere near that place until tomorrow's ritual. Do you understand?" Sage's face morphed from flustered to fierce as she pointed at the both of us. "That little demonic spell you had last night has made it very clear that we are no longer in the dominant position. That thing inside of you wanted us to know that it knows what we're planning. If it feels threatened, it'll tighten its grip. It doesn't want to let go of you as long as you're still providing it with what it wants."

"Like a parasite?" I asked.

"Yeah, exactly like that. Demons are just big, evil parasites. They will do anything to keep themselves alive. That's what the exorcism is for. If they think their host is compromised, they'll leave. We try to help convince it."

"That actually kind of makes sense." I scanned through the definition from every biology textbook I'd ever read in my mind. "Would that explain the dreams, then?"

Sage's jaw dropped open, and she leaned in closer. "What dreams? Why are you only telling me this now?"

"I didn't think they were important, or that they were even real, but I've been having flashes. Every couple of nights I get a glimpse outside of myself. I can't control my body, but I can see things. Feel things. Every time I'm in some sort of trouble. Maybe it's the demon letting go of my senses a little in case I died."

I shivered at the thought. The visions I'd had recently. Far too many. I could've been dead several times over by now.

Sage hefted another box of salt and moved it with the rest of the pile closer to the door. She wiped the back of her hand across her forehead. "Maybe. I don't know for sure."

"So, we're basically going to scare it out of her?" Lane asked.

"Not quite that simple. But yes, in a way." Sage reached into her pocket and pulled out a folded piece of paper. "I know what you can do. We need a few more things picked up. Can you grab them and bring them back here?"

Lane snatched the piece of paper from her hand. "Sure. Let's go, Berk."

"No." Sage rested her hand on my shoulder. "You need to stay here. Orianna needs you in the kitchen, and we have a few more things to discuss about the ritual." She swiped her free hand nonchalantly at Lane. "Nothing exciting, just boring details."

"Are you sure?" Lane asked, her eyes glued on me.

I nodded, but she stayed locked on me for a few moments before finally turning away.

"Hey, E, want to come shopping with me?" Lane raised the list in the air and flicked it with her other hand.

"Sure," he called from behind me and sprinted up beside Lane. She linked her arm with his and tugged him toward the front door.

"Is Berkley not coming with us?" he asked.

Lane pushed the door open, letting a gush of sunlight pour into the shop. "Nope. She's got her own work to do."

Ethan glanced back at me and paused.

"C'mon, you. She'll still be here when you get back." Lane

dragged him out onto the sidewalk. The little bell chimed as the door shut behind them again.

"That girl requires so much energy." Sage tossed her head back toward the ceiling with a sigh. "Now go help Orianna in the kitchen. I'll grab my coat and meet you out front."

·· ·★· ☾ ·★· ·.

I PUSHED the swinging door into the kitchen and clamped my hand tight over my nose. A heavy-bodied fragrance of month-old garbage with top notes of rotting fish or possibly straight-up raw sewage attacked my nostrils. Clearly, I'd found the source of the stench.

"What's that?" I pointed at a stainless-steel pot bubbling on the cast-iron stove as I gagged against my palm.

Orianna swirled a large metal spoon through the liquid as she popped up on her tiptoes and peered inside. "Just a warding elixir. A little extra protection to pour around the barn for keeping out any uninvited incorporeal guests."

"Is it supposed to reek that badly?" I eased my hand away from my face and regretted it instantly.

"Well, I've never made one of these before, but if the magic doesn't keep unwanted spirits away, I guess the smell will." She laughed and tapped the spoon on the side of the pot, then laid it on the counter. "But maybe it won't be as harsh once it's finished. Just needs one last ingredient, and that's why you're in here."

Orianna turned down the burner then stepped away from the stove. From under the counter, she pulled a worn leather pouch. Her long slender fingers worked quickly as she untied the knotted strap holding it together then spread it open on the empty counter.

A thin silver dagger lay in the middle of the leather, with rubies and sapphires glinting on the hilt under the harsh kitchen lights. She ran her index finger over the blade as her lips turned up into a shallow, reverent smile. Slowly, she slipped the knife from its home and cradled it in her hand, holding it up in front of her. "We just need your blood."

My blood? I jumped backward and smashed the back of my thigh against a wire rack. Metal bowls rattled off the shelf and clanged onto the tile floor.

Orianna huffed and shook her head, her faux black ponytail whipping back and forth behind her. "Relax. We just need a couple of drops."

"But what's with that?" I pointed at the dagger.

"It's a ritual knife. These get blessed as well as high-heat sanitized, unless you'd rather use a regular kitchen knife and risk getting salmonella or something." She closed the blade in her fist and held the jewel-encrusted handle toward me. "Collect the blood yourself, if it makes you feel better."

I leaned forward, refusing to move my feet even an inch closer, and grabbed hold of the dagger, the cool metal tingling against my skin. I passed it back and forth between my hands, surprised at how light it seemed, considering the amount of bling on the handle.

"Is this your thing?" I waved my open hand toward the stove. "Your special power or whatever."

"Hopefully." Orianna shrugged, but a faint whisper of doubt flickered in her eyes. "I want to become a full-fledged kitchen witch, but I don't know if I've got what it takes yet. I just really love making all sorts of potions and spells like these. Mixing up ingredients to make them more powerful than what you started with."

I nodded. "Kind of like a science experiment?"

"Yeah, kind of. But I still have a lot left to learn."

I pictured the collection of test tubes and beakers in the chemistry lab. The rush when I mixed different substances and the anticipation of their reactions. The things I could make them do. "I get that."

She eyed me carefully then grinned, her shoulders dropping a bit as a flash of light brightened her gloomy exterior. "Cool. Did you know you can make at least nine kinds of poison from a window box herb garden and three common household items?"

"I didn't, but remind me never to take a cupcake from you if you offer it."

She laughed and inspected her nasty elixir again. "You're funny."

"Yeah, that's me. Hilarious." I held my breath and placed the blade against the fleshy part of my hand near my thumb. The fading scar from my bottle-smashing experience peered up at me. Another souvenir from this hellish nightmare. Looking toward the wall, I sliced the blade across gently, a burning line sizzling along my flesh. I peeked with one eye as red bubbled up through the cut and streamed into my palm. "And no offense, but I wouldn't want to be one of your guinea pigs."

The metal spoon clanged against the counter. I jumped.

"Whoa, Berkley. I said a few drops. We want to get rid of a demon, not summon a new one." Orianna ripped a mound of paper towel off the roll hanging by the freezer and rushed to my side. She tore the dagger from my grip then cradled my cut hand over the towel. Walking backward, she guided me over to the stove and held my hand over the stinky concoction until my blood dripped off my palm and pooled in the center of the pot. The surface of the liquid morphed from dark brown to a mossy green but didn't smell any better. I scrunched up my nose and turned my head away. It might've even made the stench worse.

Orianna held tight to my hand until I locked on to her penetrating stare. "And you do know that I would never do anything to hurt you, on purpose anyway. None of us would. That's not who we are, or what we stand for."

"Yeah, I do. It's just a lot to take, you know?" I tugged my hand away and blotted it with the paper towel, holding it near my chest. My stomach clenched and gurgled. "I'm ... I don't know. Scared."

"We're all scared. Nothing ever happens if we don't push ourselves past what we think we are capable of. Fear is a way of telling us that things are changing, but they don't always have to be negative." She dipped the spoon back in and stirred very slowly. Her lips moved in silence, mouthing some sort of spell, or maybe just counting her strokes. After about seven swirls, she popped up on her toes again and inspected the inside of the pot. A broad smile broke across her face.

"Is that all you need?" I asked as the red started leaking through the paper towel and threatening to drip onto the scuffed tile floor.

"Yeah, there's a sink over there"—she pointed to the far corner of the kitchen—"to wash up. Plus, there're bandages in the first aid kit, if you need them."

I maneuvered around the long prep table and headed across the kitchen. The dagger lay on the stainless top, the blade soiled with spots of my tainted blood. Blood I shared with something else now. Something sinister. I shook my head and shuddered. The air warmed, or maybe just my cheeks as the room wavered for a moment. I cranked the tap and let the cool water run over my wrists, bringing my temperature back down again. Bright red splashed against the white porcelain. Streams of crimson ran down the drain, eventually fading to shades of lighter pinks until the water ran clear again. I rubbed my palms together, scrubbing lightly against the cut, but no more blood drained into the sink. All clean, except they still seemed dirty, like I could still feel it sticky on my skin.

"Out, out, damn spot," I muttered to myself, finally understanding the infamous line.

"What was that?" Orianna asked.

I turned off the water and shook my hands in the sink. My knuckles blazed red from the cold. "Nothing, just thinking about Lady Macbeth."

"Really?" She tilted her head to the side and narrowed her stare at me like I'd finally cracked.

Maybe I had.

She crossed the room and opened up the latches on the first aid kit on the wall then pulled out a spool of gauze and some medical tape. "Washing your hands makes you think of Shakespeare?"

"It does now." I held out my hand and she wound the gauze tightly around my skin. "Or maybe slowly going crazy makes me think of Shakespeare."

"Well, that makes more sense. I personally really like Hamlet." Orianna ripped three strips of tape and stuck the ends to the side of the sink as she smoothed out the gauze on my palm. "I think maybe under different circumstances we could've been friends. Or at least ... I don't know. But I guess that's kind of messed up now."

"Maybe. But everything is messed up now. My entire life I had plans. I knew what I was doing and where I was going, but now everything is ..." I sighed and tilted my head back, but no answers hid in the tiny dots on the drop ceiling tiles.

She pulled the tape tight on my hand and ran her thumbnail over the seams to help them stick. "Not what you expected. I get it. Two years ago, my life fell apart. I didn't know who I was anymore. Then Kassia introduced me to Sage and this life, and I've never felt more like myself than I do now. I don't even recognize the girl I was before, and to be honest, I'm not sure how much I liked her."

A murkiness seeped into her gaze. Her mind wandered. Somewhere else. Maybe another time. Something from the past dulling her spark.

Bits of the story she told around my kitchen table fell into place, but big pieces were clearly still missing. I placed my hand on her arm. "Are you okay?"

Her head snapped to the side, and her body trembled under my grip. She backed away and crossed her arms.

"Are you coming, Berkley?" Sage appeared at the kitchen door. She glanced at Orianna and frowned. "Is everything all right in here?"

"Yeah, we're all done." Orianna cast her eyes away from me and returned to her potion.

"Okay, see you out front," Sage said as she walked back into the front room, the door swinging behind her.

I waited a second. Two seconds. Three. But Orianna didn't turn around.

Balling my bandaged hand into a fist, I knocked on the stainless table and headed to the exit. "Thanks for the help. I'll see you later."

"Berkley," she said, as I reached the door. "It might feel like everything is falling apart right now, but sometimes even best laid plans are best laid to rest."

THIRTY-SEVEN

Sunlight shimmered on the surface of the river. Rolling waves tossed golden streaks, pulling them under the black water over and over again. I slipped my hand from my pocket and shielded my eyes, staring farther off into the horizon. The hypnotic rise and fall of the waves lulled my hazy memories closer to my consciousness. My bones ached. The cold of splashing down in the icy water last night chilled in my marrow. Was this the river my personal demon decided to nearly drown me in, or was it somewhere else? Light faded into inky darkness around me. My body sank heavily to the bottom of the river's bed. I shuddered. Was it a memory or just a dream?

"It seemed like you and Orianna were having quite the conversation. I hope I wasn't interrupting." Sage's voice pierced through my trance and pulled me back to shore.

"No, it's fine." I shook my head and slid my hand back in my pocket, the edges of the medical tape catching on the zipper. "She was just telling me more about how she came to be a witch, but I think she was finished."

"Really? She must trust you. That's a time in her life she doesn't like to talk about. Even to me and the other girls."

"She didn't say that much, but it sounds like she's been through a lot. What happened to her?"

Sage sighed and took a sharp right onto the path leading toward the main garden. "That's not for me to say. We all have our own stories to tell; all we can do is strive to create our own happy ending, no matter where we may have started."

I waited for more, but she didn't provide it. Only the crunch of gravel beneath our feet filled her silence. More silence. We'd already completed two loops around the perimeter of the park, and I still didn't have any clue why she'd dragged me out there. I was sure there was something more important on her to-do list that I could've been doing, but instead, we'd just walked.

"Will she get hers? Her happy ending?" I finally asked.

Her lips smiled, but the rest of her expression stayed grave. "I think so. She's trying."

The breeze picked up, and I pulled my arms tight over my chest. Leaves swirled around our feet as the wind nipped at the tops of my ears. Sage swiped away a few blond strands of her hair that had blown across her lips and dropped her head back to stare at the sky. Nutmeg and scarlet leaves fluttered down around her, and she opened her arms wide, taking it all in.

"Fall is such a beautiful time of year, isn't it?" Sage said, finally bringing her head back down to face me. The first time she'd made eye contact since we'd left Divina Tea. "Everything in life has a season. It blooms, it dies, and it's reborn again as something new. The same can be said for all of us. Everyone looped in an endless, glorious circle."

"Um, okay." I gazed at her face, but she gave no clues to what she was thinking. Maybe she'd stood too close to Orianna's rotten potion in the shop kitchen. "Is that why you took me out here? To look at the leaves?"

She thrust her hands into the pockets of her cranberry peacoat. The serenity drained from her cheeks, and her lips pursed tight. "No. I brought you out here to talk."

Taking my arm, she led me to a small park bench that looked out over the empty gardens, soon ready for snow. The fountains had been switched off, full of leaves and debris. An empty place just waiting for the worst.

"It's about the exorcism," she said, sitting down and patting the seat beside her.

My knees shook, and I took the offered seat. "It's going to work, right?"

"I believe it will, but we have to be prepared for all possible scenarios. The potential consequences." She took my hand and sandwiched it between her own. A calming sensation tingled in my arms.

"Consequences?" I yanked my hand out of her grip. If she didn't want me to feel this, it meant I probably should. "Like what? Like I might ..." I couldn't say the word. It stung the tip of my tongue, but my mouth wouldn't set it free. As if saying it somehow made it true.

"I thought we'd have more time. The full moon would be a much better option, but Tamara is right, this needs to happen now or we might not be able to help at all."

My pulse thrummed in my ears. "More time for what?"

"For you to make peace with things. Tie up any loose ends." Sage swallowed and her eyes misted over, but she pushed the tears down. "I'm sure you know there is a possibility that this may not work out how everyone hopes. That you—"

"That I might ..." I tried to say the word again, but it still wouldn't come.

Sage nodded. "It's going to be a tough process. Exhausting and draining. That has its risks, especially in your current state, but the longer the entity has been living in your body the harder it is to get rid of, and for spite, it might try to hurt you before it actually leaves. Kind of a final 'screw you' to the coven."

"What?" My stomach clenched, and warm saliva built in the back of my throat. I shot to my feet and paced in front of the bench. My breathing quickened. Short, rapid bursts. I ripped open the zipper of my jacket and pulled it wide, the collar suddenly too tight around my neck. "Hurt me? You mean kill me, don't you?"

She sat up straight and tucked her hands between her knees. "Not necessarily."

"Then what are you saying?" I threw my hands up. A crow

burst off its perch in a nearby oak tree as my pained voice echoed through the park. "I didn't ask for this. You said if I kept the demon inside it would take over, but now you're telling me if I try to get it out it'll probably kill me anyway."

Sage stood up and marched in front of me, forcing me to look at her.

"Hey, hey. It's not for sure, but it is important that you know all the possibilities." She pulled me into a hug. "The best thing you can do now is to try to not dwell on what could go wrong and look forward to the future. The stronger you are, the harder you fight, the better chance we have of this going smoothly."

She let go and looked at me again. Her eyes shone bright and held mine until my heart stopped racing. She brushed a strand of hair out of my face and tucked it behind my ear.

"How am I supposed to be strong when all my options are death?"

"That's not true, as long as you don't give up. I need you to promise to fight."

Sage's face faded behind my watery gaze. "And if I don't? What if I just let the demon take control?"

"Then no exorcism or spell or anything is going to help you, but you won't be you anymore anyway. But it's your choice. It's your life. I will do everything I can to make sure you pull through this, but I couldn't live with myself if I didn't tell you the risks and let you make any amends you need to."

"At least you'll get to live," I choked out.

Sage backed away, her hands palm up in surrender. "I deserve that. But time only moves forward, not backward. We can stop all this now if you want, but it's up to you. What do you want to do?"

I walked around the empty flower beds as the gravity of my decision weighed on my shoulders. If I didn't do this, I'd die. If I did, I'll probably still die. End game, I'd die. But did I choose to die doing everything I could to save myself, or did I fade away into nothing? My mind raced. My limbs ached. Giving in sounded so much easier. Simple. Just sit back and wait for my world to finish crashing down and let it swallow me up with it.

A strange calm surged through me. The possibility of not having to fight anymore. Not having to struggle to keep myself together. Just letting go. Except it wouldn't happen. Darkness bled into my newfound joy. Giving in meant giving up, and I wouldn't do that. Mom gave up on our family. Dad was giving up on himself. I couldn't give up on myself too. I wouldn't. "I stand by my choice. I can't let this demon win."

She placed her arm over my shoulders, the soothing spicy scent of her dulling the edges of my anger. "I think you're making the right decision."

"Let's hope so. Neither option is a good one." I wanted to rip myself out of her grip, but I also didn't want her to let me go, as my legs might not be able to hold me up.

"Focus on the good things, Berkley. I know this sounds dire, but if you have any chance of beating this demon, you need to hold on to that with all you have left. You have amazing friends. People in your life who love you. These can be your most powerful weapons."

I stared off into the thicket of trees. The fear of everything else in the world fell away. No more heavy stares from the woods. No more anything. Just the singular thought that all this might be gone tomorrow. "Can I just be alone for a while?"

Her arm stiffened around me. "I'm not sure that's a good idea. How about we go back to the shop first? I can grab you a latte and whatever else you want. You can even hang out in my office for some peace and quiet. Then I'll be there—we'll all be there—if you need to talk."

"Thanks, but I really don't want to see anyone right now." I rubbed my hands over my face, tears soaking through the layers of gauze. "Besides, what could I possibly do to make this worse?"

She let me go and shuffled back a few steps, except her stare stayed tight to my side. "I don't feel right leaving you here like this."

"I think the definition of right and wrong blurred a while ago."

She frowned but didn't argue.

I wiped my sleeve across my face and tried to stand up straighter. "I'll be okay. I just need time. I'll text if I need anything."

Sage bit her lip and sighed. The sun disappeared behind a cloud and cast her shadow long and ghostly across the leaf-strewn ground. I shivered and hugged my arms around my chest, the chill sinking deeper into my flesh. Maybe her offer of a hot tea wasn't the worst thing after all. But I couldn't face any of them. Not yet.

"Fine," she huffed, an uneasiness bleeding into her stare. "But I will be checking in. I'd probably want time to process this information if it were me too."

"Thank you."

"If you change your mind and need to talk, let me know. Day or night."

I nodded.

"And in case you're wondering, I haven't told anyone else about this. I'm sure everyone knows how dangerous this type of ritual can be, but I need to keep up their confidence. If they think there's a chance of failure, it might mean the difference between living and dying. Everyone in that room needs to fight for you." She placed her hand under my chin and pulled my face up to meet her soft gaze. "And that means you too."

Wrapping her arms around me, she squeezed so tight I lost my breath.

"When all this is over, I understand that you might not want to see me or the others ever again. But please don't keep living your life in darkness. I can feel all your anger and fear twisting inside you. Let it all go. Don't waste a second chance if you get one," she whispered, then slipped away. She forced an awkward grin and tapped my shoulder before heading down the pathway toward the street.

I flopped down on the bench and held my head in my hands. I

didn't try to stop the tears anymore. There wasn't any point. Sage's hazy figure grew smaller and smaller as I tried to concentrate on her silhouette until she disappeared into the distance.

I was going to die. I knew it. Somewhere inside I'd already realized it, but somehow as I heard someone say the words, they struck all that much harder. All the time I'd spent worried about stupid things that wouldn't even matter. Holding myself back so as not to offend anyone. Striving to be the perfect daughter, the perfect girlfriend, the perfect student, the perfect me ... that never existed. All for nothing.

The sun glowed fiery on the horizon, and I watched it crawl slowly across the sky. My mind reeled so fast I couldn't concentrate on a single thought. Probably best, since I didn't really want to think at all. Didn't want to accept the realities I knew I'd been over-analyzing in my head. Instead, I focused on the amber-colored rays burning across the brilliant blue. My body eventually stopped shaking. No longer cold. No longer anything. Numb. But what were you supposed to do when it might be your last day? I'd never really thought about it before. One thing I definitely didn't plan.

As the light dipped low behind the trees, I still hadn't moved. My eyes stung from staring at the sky all day, but I didn't care. My legs itched to move. Go somewhere. Anywhere. But I kept myself seated on the cold bench. At least for a few extra minutes, as it might be the last sunset I'd ever see.

THIRTY-EIGHT

Night fell, and I walked home in the shadows. The streetlights shone in pretty rings down the sides of the street as dry leaves swirled around my ankles. Any other night I'd probably be wary of the shapes lurking behind the looming trees and in between the perfect little houses, but not now. There wasn't anything left in the world that could wreck me more than I already was. Anything that went bump in the night would probably run if they saw me coming.

My phone vibrated in my pocket. Again. It'd been blowing up all day. Lane. Ethan. Lane. Lane. Ethan. Even Orianna a couple of times. I answered at first. One-word responses or emojis to slow the stream of texts, but when I couldn't get my fingers to type anymore, they flooded in like a tidal wave. I pulled my phone out, the screen lighting up the darkness.

> **Lane:** *Where are you? Haven't heard from you in a bit.*
> **Lane:** *Do you need me to pick you up?*
> **Lane:** *Sage's been back for hours. Where did you go?*
> **Ethan:** *Hey. What's up? Lane's really getting worried.*
> **Lane:** *Seriously, I'm gonna kick your butt if you're out doing something fun without me.*
> **Ethan:** *I'm worried too.*
> **Lane:** *????*

My thumb hovered over the screen as I tried to find the right way to answer. Something that said 'I'm okay, but so not okay'. Did they have an emoji for that? Doubtful. But I couldn't really put words to things either. Sage was right. I'd known since the beginning that things would likely end this way. That I would end. Except I'd pushed it down. Convinced myself that this was just another mess that I could hide from and somehow come out okay on the other side.

> **Me:** *Sorry for not responding. Today got busier than I thought. I'm good.*

I clicked send and inhaled the night air, but my chest still ached like I couldn't breathe. Heavy. Suffocating. I never thought much about what I'd do if it were my last day on Earth, but lying to my best friends via text wasn't it. They deserved better.

My eyes burned, but no new tears fell. I'd cried them all out, and now nothing remained, just a pile of regrets and unfulfilled dreams. Plans that would never be.

I stumbled around the corner onto my street and slid my phone back into my pocket. It vibrated against my hip, but I couldn't look. Not right now. If I did, I might just tell them the truth. I might just—

Honk!

I jumped back and slammed my hand over my heart as my pulse hammered in my veins.

Headlights flashed near the curb as a car door swung open. Laughter pealed through the night sky. Carefree, menacing, and undeniably Lane.

I shielded my eyes with my arm as she leaped out of the passenger seat and rushed toward me. Ethan, thankfully, cut the lights and slid out the driver's side.

"You should've seen your face. It was classic." Lane chuckled and gripped her arm across her stomach.

"Thanks. Glad I didn't disappoint." I straightened my coat and rubbed my hands over my sore, cried-out eyes as I plastered on a half-hearted smile.

"Wow, Berk. You look like you've been hit with a garbage truck," she said, her laughter fading as she placed her hand on my shoulder.

"I'll be okay."

"Yeah, so that's a lie, but I'll spare you the lecture this time. Besides, we've got things to take care of. Right, E?"

Ethan disappeared into the backseat of his car and emerged with two pizza boxes balanced on his right hand. He swung his hip against the door until it clunked shut. "Yep. Carlito's. Double pepperoni. Your favorite."

I imagined the spicy sauce on my tongue, and my stomach growled in approval. "You guys really didn't need to."

"Of course we did. It's your exorcism and all, but we weren't going to let our best friend spend tonight all by herself, so we're inviting ourselves over for a slumber party."

I pointed at each of them. "Both of you? Here?"

"Well, it was just going to be me, but Ethan insisted on being here. I don't know, I think this boy's got a problem or something."

Lane bobbled her head and grinned.

"That's not ..." Ethan's cheeks glowed crimson under the streetlights as his stare flitted between Lane and the sidewalk. "You clearly suggested that *we* come over, and I thought it was a great idea and that we should be supportive and be here for—"

Lane nudged her elbow into his ribs, and he teetered, the pizza boxes swaying in his grip. I jerked forward, but he regained his balance before they toppled.

"Easy, psycho, I was just messing with you. Why are you so jittery lately?" Lane shook her head and snorted as she tried to hold back her laughter.

"It's not ... I'm not ..." He rolled his eyes and dared to look at me. "I'd like to stay, even if I have to put up with Lane all night. But only if that's okay with you?"

The lightness in his awkward smile faded into the intensity of his stare. A question still lingering between us, except now we had run out of time for answers. The air shifted, the breeze suddenly stifling and thick. I sighed, pushing down the heat building in my limbs, and turned away.

Across the lawn, my living room window sat in darkness. Not a speck of light peeked through the gap between the drapes. No blue glow from the television bouncing off the ceiling. But it didn't mean ... "I'm not sure."

Lane leaned closer, and her voice dropped to a whisper. "He's not home. We already checked."

My stomach churned again, but it wasn't the hunger this time. Part of me was glad I wouldn't have to face him, but part of me was still disappointed that I couldn't see his face another time.

"Have you talked to him since the other day?" she asked.

I shook my head. "He must've come in late last night and he was gone before you came to get me this morning. He's probably avoiding me."

"Maybe," she said. "Or he realized you're right and is trying to deal."

Maybe. At least one positive thing would've come out of all this. Unless, after I went missing, his entire world crumbled and he ended up even worse. I shuddered as I pictured him crying at my funeral. Drinking away the rest of his pain at our kitchen table with no one there to find him. My nose twinged as my gaze went watery again. I closed my eyes and exhaled, pushing everything down.

Lane wrapped her arms around me, and I buried my head in her neck, her soft curls tickling my cheek.

"It's going to be fine, Berkley," she said as she stroked her hand down my back.

I squeezed her tighter. *No, it wouldn't.*

"If he comes home and you want to talk, we'll get out of your way. Besides, I can't risk another shiner before graduation photos, so whatever you say, we're going to listen." She chuckled, but her voice cracked, betraying her optimism.

Ethan poked Lane in the arm. "Don't forget to tell her about the chickenpox."

I let go of her and backed away. "What?"

"Yeah, if anyone asks you have chickenpox." She quickly brushed her hand over her eyes and forced a smile. "We called that fancy scholarship foundation to see if they would move your interview, and they didn't seem too interested, but Ethan here came up with the idea of telling them you had chickenpox, and they bought it."

"Contagious for long enough to buy you some time, but not life-threatening or disgusting enough that they would want to eliminate you from the competition." Ethan beamed. "It was that, or we told them you still had rabies."

"I never had rabies."

"Sure, you didn't." Lane winked at Ethan. "Anyway, your interview is now in three weeks. Long enough to get your life back to normal and prepare."

Normal. Even if by some fluke chance I survived, I doubted life would truly be normal ever again. But right now, that didn't matter. At least if I died tomorrow, I would never regret spending my last moments with my best friends.

"I love you guys. You know that, right?" I wrapped one arm around Lane and the other around Ethan. They both crowded in and held me tight. I breathed them in, capturing the smell of them in my brain. Imprinting the feel of their skin in my grasp. Consuming them to carry them with me as long as I could. "You know what? Forget it. Let's just go out tonight."

Lane's head jerked back, and she blinked. "What? I figured you'd want to be home tonight."

"And what about the pizza? I'm starving." Ethan hoisted the boxes higher above his shoulder.

"We can eat first. But then let's go do something. Whatever you both want."

Lane glanced at Ethan and then back at me. She placed her palm across my forehead and frowned. "Whatever we want? Even go-karts?"

"Sure." I shrank away from her and backed up a few steps.

"But you hate go-karts." She crossed her arms and stared after me.

Ethan tossed his open hand in the air. "Who could possibly hate go-karts?"

"Seriously, Lane. Anything you want. You deserve it. Besides, you're always telling me to step outside my comfort zone. I thought you'd be pleased I'm actually listening for once." I linked my arm with hers and pulled her toward my front door.

I reached behind me and slid my hand into Ethan's. His fingers froze at my touch, then slowly thawed and wrapped around mine.

"You both deserve the world."

THIRTY-NINE

Today's the day I'll probably die.

I repeated the words like a mantra, as if saying them out loud would somehow make them less true. New bruises appeared on my forearms this morning, but it didn't even matter where I ended up last night, because today was the day I'd probably die.

The first light of dawn broke through the window and started its daily journey across my carpet. Except today it found new things to illuminate. New faces to bathe in golden light, maybe for the last time in this room. My best friends. My soldiers. Knights sacrificing their honor for an unfit queen with a broken crown.

Lane lay near the door, one leg pulled tight into her chest and the other kicked out as far as it could go. The stuffed purple penguin she won in the go-kart arcade last night lay tucked in the crook of her elbow. As she slumbered, the pinch of worry around her eyes disappeared, leaving her skin flawless, likely forgetting all about her needy friend and the threats of daytime. Memories of the two of us flipped through my brain in a highlight reel, and even though each one stung like a fresh cut, I couldn't stop scrolling. Years of moments between the two of us I'd never forget. Even the worst days with her were still some of my best. I crept over and brushed her curls back off her face. She rustled for a second then settled back against the pillow. I'd miss her the most. Her laugh that always made me laugh too. Her hands that always pulled me back when I'd gone too far, and of course, her heart like the sun, bigger than her body and strong enough to power the entire world.

Near the window, Ethan slept restlessly, his limbs outstretched as if grasping for something in his mind. I clenched my hands into fists as I watched his chest rise and fall with each unconscious breath. If Lane was the sun to my moon, then Ethan was my star. Mysterious and bright, circling in my orbit—but still just out of reach. Because of me. If only I'd followed my heart instead of my head, maybe things would've been different. A lot of things in my life might have been different, except there was no turning back now. Only one more regret to add to the list. I tiptoed around him but accidentally nudged his leg with my toe. Holding my breath, I waited. He turned over onto his right side, his messy hair flopping over his face, but he didn't wake. *Phew*.

I climbed up onto my bed and rested my head on my knees.

Today's the day I'll probably die.

I reached over into my nightstand drawer and pulled out a pad of paper. Dad didn't come home again last night. Not that I really wanted to explain what might happen to me, but the thought of never seeing him again burned in my gut. I'd decided to keep fighting. I just hoped he'd do the same if I wasn't there to help him. I wrote his name at the top of the page and held the pen poised to write, except the words wouldn't come. I pictured him reading this note, and I couldn't do it. Another woman in his life, gone, leaving nothing but stationery. It would break his heart. Tears splashed the paper and blurred the faint blue lines. Sage said I needed to let go of my anger and my fear, but it wasn't that simple. Letting go meant letting all the negative things in. I ripped the note off the pad and crumpled the sheet in my fist. But I had to try.

Reaching back into my nightstand, I pulled out my letter. I thumbed the edges of the envelope as the words inside played on loop in my brain. *Leaving you is the hardest thing I will ever have to do.* Except it had been months and I hadn't let her leave. I closed my eyes and tore the letter in half. The pressure around my chest eased slightly, and I took a deep breath. I gazed down at the fractured pieces and ripped them into quarters. Then eighths. The weight kept lifting as I shredded Mom's goodbye into pieces.

Destroying that old life and building mine back up again. When the scraps became too small to tear, I brushed them onto the carpet and sat back against the headboard. Inhale. The rush of oxygen sparked in my blood as I let my emotions wash over me. Exhale. They still didn't feel good, but they seemed less heavy. One less burden to carry.

"You're up early," Ethan whispered from the floor as he rubbed the sides of his hands against his eye sockets. "Or did you not go to sleep at all?"

I snapped out of my meditation and wiped my face as I sat up straighter. "I don't know. Isn't that sad?"

He rolled up from the floor and sat down in front of me on the bed, his hair sticking out at all ends from what looked like a fitful sleep. "Not sad. More like tragic, really. No one should ever have to go through this. I don't think I would survive it, if it were me."

His knee brushed mine, and I glanced down at the slight connection between the two of us. I placed my hand on his leg, and he covered it with his own, the warmth of his palm easing some of the empty chill coursing through my body.

"It's definitely not fun. That's for sure." I forced a laugh, but a few tears broke free and streamed down my cheeks.

"Don't cry, Berkley." He shook his head and ran the back of his hand across my face, gently wiping them away.

I leaned into his touch and closed my eyes, letting myself enjoy it for just a second.

"Unless you have to, I guess." He shrugged. "I don't know what I'd be doing right now. Probably screaming or throwing things or something."

"Maybe. But I think I'm over that now. For once, everything in my head seems really quiet. Clear."

He nodded as his thumb drew circles on my hand at his knee. Like that day in his car when I'd invited him in. When he held me in his arms on my front step and all I could see were his soft lips so close to mine. Only a few days ago, but it felt like months. Entire lifetimes.

"And what do you see?" he asked.

"Regrets. Things I would've done differently." I hung my head and took a deep breath. "Like telling you I'm sorry."

He tilted his head to meet my gaze and frowned. "For what?"

"For not telling you the truth. After everything came out, I didn't treat you very well. Even before then. When I realized I had feelings for you, or maybe one of the million times Lane implied it, I should've just said something. Instead, I held onto Josh and ended up hurting him too. And neither of you deserved it, but I did it all because I didn't want things to change." The tears came harder and faster, but I couldn't stop them. "Everyone I love leaves or gets broken, and I didn't want to lose you too. You and Lane are all I have. And—"

"Shhh. Neither of us are going anywhere, and after all this is over you can tell us how awesome we are and how lucky you are to have friends like us." He flashed a smile—his sexy, goofy smile—and my hand trembled beneath his.

"If I survive this, I will. Every single day." I twisted my wrist and twined our fingers together. "But are we really just friends anymore, Ethan?"

"*When* you survive this, we'll figure that out. And if you decide that it's really not right, don't think I won't still be your friend. Because there's no way I could stop myself from being around someone as amazing as you. You're worth waiting for, Berkley James. At least you are to me. Don't let some evil body snatcher convince you otherwise."

He took my other hand. Knee to knee, palm to palm, face to face, and nowhere to run. Except this time I didn't want to. This time his touch calmed my anxious soul instead of pushing it closer to the brink. A moment of true clarity as darkness loomed heavy on the horizon.

I ran my pinkie over his long fingers, the spark between us

growing brighter and feeding the regret pooling in my chest. "I'm terrified, Ethan."

He sighed, his shoulders dropping as he held my worried stare. "I know you are. But I'll be right here with you the entire time. I can help be your courage, but the strength you need is already yours. Just getting up every day and dealing with all this takes more guts than you think." He rested his forehead against mine. His warm breath fell on my cheeks as his words seeped through my skin, almost making me believe them.

"But what if strength isn't enough?"

"It will be. Besides, I don't think Lane would let you go."

I chuckled, the tip of my nose crashing against his. "We would've been really great together, wouldn't we?"

"Hopefully, one day we'll get the chance to find out."

Sliding my head to the side, I closed the last inch between us, my lips against his.

He pulled his head back, our lips still almost touching. "Are you sure this time? It can wait."

"No, it can't." I inched forward again.

He kissed me back, slow and sure, and everything I wasn't in that moment. And this time I let him in. I clasped my hands tighter around his, pulling him closer. Wanting more. Knowing I wouldn't get enough.

My mind pieced together the years. Snaps of colors, smells, and emotions flickered past. All those things that led us here. To this. A kiss that should've happened months ago. Except now we'd run out of time. I'd run out of time.

He dropped my left hand and brushed the side of my face as I drifted into the kiss, aching for it to linger on forever as I tried to put together words to explain myself. To say the things I should've said before now. But maybe this was all we had left to say. Simple. Sweet. Goodbye.

"You guys had to do that in front of me?" Lane popped her head over the far side of the bed and laughed.

Ethan pulled away, still twisted in my hands. "Sorry, Lane."

I swallowed against the tightness in my throat as my heart squeezed painfully in my chest. Ethan chuckled along with Lane, a deep blush across his cheeks. The sunlight from the window streamed across the two of them, illuminating them like gods against my rumpled purple sheets. Except they wouldn't be able to save me.

"Yeah, sorry," I squeaked out.

Lane propped up her elbow and rested her head on her hand, a devilish grin breaking across her face. "Oh no, continue. It's about time you two got out of your own way."

"Sicko." Ethan laughed, then reached past me and grabbed the pillow from the top of the bed. He chucked it at Lane's head, and it bounced off, mussing her hair across her face, then landed on the floor.

"Perhaps." She shrugged. "But you can't say I didn't tell you this was going to happen."

FORTY

We stood in a line, the three of us, Ethan's hand in my left and Lane's in my right, watching the sun dip behind the battered barn roof. None of us spoke, not like we had anything else to say. The two of them did their best to keep me busy all day until this moment. Maybe Sage instructed them to occupy me, or maybe they just knew I needed to not think about the upcoming battle of me versus myself. Sensed it, perhaps, with a kind of friend telepathy or something.

Voices carried from the barn and mixed with the fall wind as it whistled through the trees and the squawk of crows that circled overhead. The air crackled around us. Thick and alive with energy. Good? Bad? A hint of dread? Either way, it clung to my skin and weighed down heavy on my lungs. The world around aware of the shift about to come. The big show.

"Last chance to change your mind," I mumbled as I struggled to take a full breath. "I'd understand if you bailed."

Lane squeezed my fingers with hers. "If it were me, would you sit outside and wait?"

I hung my head and bit back all the excuses I had on my tongue. They wouldn't help.

"Exactly. We're coming." She took a giant step forward and tugged on my arm, but my feet remained stuck to the ground.

"And you remember what to tell my dad, right? In case something—"

"Yes, Berkley. If something happens, which it won't." She

leaned back and pulled our twined hands to her chest. "It's the first thing I'll do. Your dad deserves to know."

"And you both need to promise me that if anything does happen, you'll run. If either of you were hurt because of all of this, I'd never forgive myself."

"Enough." Ethan stepped forward with Lane and yanked me behind them. "It's almost nightfall. If you keep overthinking, you're going to get so worked up you'll miss the new moon entirely."

He glanced at Lane and laughed, but it sounded wrong. Broken.

I closed my eyes and took a step, my knees quivering. But he was right. I needed to get moving. Gather my strength and face this thing before I no longer had a choice to fight.

Sage slipped out the barn door as we approached and closed it behind her, shielding us from the chaos inside for a few more moments. Instead of her usual fitted T-shirt and skinny jeans, she wore an all-white robe that billowed down to her ankles, her sandaled feet making her a few inches shorter than in her heeled boots. Her blond locks hung loose around her shoulders, gilded in the shimmer of the setting sun, and she swiped a few strands away from her face that had blown across her cheeks in the evening breeze. Not a dot of makeup sullied her complexion, and she looked the most ethereal that I'd ever seen her. Almost angelic. But whether she was a witch or an angel, would she have enough magic to save me now?

"Blessed be, Berkley," Sage said and opened her arms to hug me, then paused, likely unsure of my reaction after our discussion yesterday. "Lane. Ethan. Welcome."

"Blessed be, Sage." I raised my arms in response and brought her in. Maybe I should still be angry, but I didn't have the energy to show it. I needed every ounce I had.

She released me then smoothed my hair behind my ears. She cast a warm smile, but the corners of her lips edged down with worry. "Are you ready?"

"Will I ever be?" I sighed and pulled away, returning to stand with my friends.

"A sound mind and a positive attitude are your best defenses. As well as, of course"—she glanced at Ethan and Lane—"ones that love you."

Ones to fight for.

"Before we go in here, please know that it will not be easy. You will be tried and tested and—"

I raised my hand to halt Sage's speech. "I just need this to end."

"All right. Let's get going." Sage pulled back the barn door and ushered us in before closing it with a deafening thud.

No turning back now.

The chatter dropped to a murmur as all heads turned toward the door. Nearly two dozen white robes flitted around the room, like a haunted house full of nosy ghosts. I recognized Tamara, Dabria, Kassia, and Orianna, and a few others from the shop, but the group seemed to have doubled in size from yesterday.

"Who are all these people?" I asked.

Sage scanned the room and grinned. "They answered my call. No one wants to see you suffer, and we will do everything we can to make this right. Do no harm."

Orianna approached in her white robe, her dark hair laced in a thick braid down her back. Without her thick eyeliner and all-black wardrobe, she seemed almost lost.

She waved at us and turned quickly to Sage. "The wards are set, and the Louisiana witches are doing some sort of protection charm over the property out back. They should be done any minute, then I think we will be ready to go."

"Marvelous. Thank you for all your hard work on this." Sage gripped Orianna's shoulders and nodded. "Just one more thing left. I'll be right back."

Sage rushed off into the crowd.

Orianna looked down at the floor and knotted her fingers in the sleeves of her gown. "I wanted to say good luck, and after this is all over, if you ever need anything, a spell or a blessing or—"

"A poison?" I added.

"Yeah, right." Orianna laughed and finally dared to look at me. "I mean it, though. Anything at all. Just ask."

"Thanks." I wrapped my arms around her.

She hesitated for a moment then finally hugged me back. "I should probably get back to my spot."

She backed away slowly and made some sign with her left hand before turning around and taking her place on the far side of the barn.

Lane stared after her then looked over at me, her mouth wide open. "What was that about?"

"Nothing. Don't worry about it." I rubbed my fingers along the bandage from the dagger cut and sighed.

"Whatever." She shook her head then nudged me with her shoulder. "How much do you think they had to pay the trouble triplets to wear white? They probably started hyperventilating or something."

"No. They understand the importance of following this ritual to the letter. I hope you bring the same seriousness to the situation." Sage returned with a thick pile of red rope looped over her arm.

Lane's face hardened. "Trust me, not one person in here takes the fate of my best friend more seriously than me."

"Perfect. You know, if you channeled half your energy into something positive, you'd probably be a force of nature. Or maybe a decent witch." Sage removed the coil of rope from her arm and handed it to Lane. "Just not in my coven. Now, come with me. I have a job for you."

Lane toddled after Sage but looked over her shoulder and shot me a satisfied smirk, Sage's backhanded compliment clearly inflating Lane's ego.

I followed after them, but Ethan tugged my hand, pulling me back. "Remember, we're both right here if you need us."

"Thank you for that." Lifting on my tiptoes, I slid my hands behind his neck and let myself gaze into his dark eyes one last time. Except the deep sadness looming in his stare started shredding the last of my confidence, and I turned away. I didn't want Ethan to be sad. He deserved to be happy, and maybe once this was all over, he'd find someone who could give him that if it couldn't be me.

His hands circled my waist and held me tight, his fingers digging into my flesh like he might not let me go. He kissed the top of my head, and I closed my eyes, breathing him in.

"I'm sorry things worked out like this," I whispered.

"I'm not. I'd rather have a few moments with you than none at all. No matter what it took to get there."

I pressed my mouth to his cheek, his lips so close, but I couldn't go there and then just walk away. If I didn't break him, I'd shatter myself into pieces.

His athletic arms closed around me and lifted me off my feet. "You're going to get through this. I know it."

My stomach clenched. *But I probably won't.*

Lane returned and faked a cough until Ethan let me go. He kissed me on the forehead, and Lane rolled her eyes.

"All right, time to go, Berk," she said.

She slipped her hand in mine and led me to the center of the pentacle. The new strangers watched and whispered, their judgment sliding off like rain. I didn't care anymore. What anyone else thought didn't matter.

I settled into the lone chair waiting for me. A much more heavy-duty model than the comfy armchair from the shop. Cold, hard, metal. But that plan hadn't worked out too well, so I guess a change made sense.

"Spread your legs a bit," Lane instructed as she tossed the mound of colored rope to the floor and strung it through her hands to find the end. "It sucks, but Sage says I'm going to need to tie you down for this."

"What?" I bolted upright in the chair, but Lane placed her hand on my arm and guided me back down.

"Hey, I don't like it either, but apparently if you don't manage to keep control of your body and run out of here, this whole thing is going to fail."

"I guess that makes sense." I swallowed, my throat tightening. Plan B had always been to escape. If I couldn't take any more, I could always stop, but this made that choice a lot harder. "Why didn't they use the chains from over on the wall? Be completely medieval."

"Sage said it wouldn't matter. Chains or rope, the demon would break them if it really wanted. It's only to slow you down a bit. Besides, she said something about inner strength holding you to the chair, but I didn't quite follow."

I breathed deeply, feeling my chest rise and fall. I hoped she was right.

Lane set to work, looping the rope around my ankles and twisting it into a series of intricate knots. "So, you and Ethan, huh? I wish someone had seen that coming. Oh, wait, I did."

"Yes, Lane, you were right. Like always." I tried to add an edge to my sarcasm, but instead, a few tears rolled down my cheek. "I just wish I had more time."

"Well, hopefully, this won't take long." Lane yanked on the knot near my left foot, and my leg twitched. She backed up on her knees and admired her work, then glanced at my face, the last of her optimism deflating. "Ah, Berk. You're going to make it through this."

I wiped the tears away, but they kept coming faster and faster. She stood up and leaned over me, drawing me closer.

"I don't get how you can be so hopeful. You really don't have to be here to watch this, you know."

"Of course I do." She wriggled away from my grip and stared into my watery eyes. "Do you remember the day we met?"

I nodded. "Kind of."

"You were the only kid in all of the second grade who would talk to me because everyone thought I was weird."

"You were weird." I chuckled through the sobs.

"But *you* didn't care. You shared your My Little Ponies with me anyway. And remember the time you lied to my mom and said you threw the ball through the front window because you knew she would ground me for forever. And when you started the tongue-piercing petition for me in junior high because you knew I wanted it so badly and it went against the school dress code."

She sat back and grabbed my chin, her eyes welling up too.

"And when my dad died, you sat beside my bed for three whole days and just held my hand because you knew I needed it. You're not my best friend, Berk. We're soul mates, you and me. And now it's my turn to take care of you."

"I love you, Lane." I hugged her again, burying my face into her shoulder. Apples and honeysuckle clouded my senses. That smell. More home to me than anything else. Closing my eyes, I breathed her in one last time, letting her swim through my blood. Merge with my soul, or whatever parts of it the demon had left me. Lane was my family. My heart.

She pressed her head against mine and squeezed harder. "I love you too. And don't worry, we're going to be old ladies together, and I am going to be kicking your ass when we're eighty."

"Promise?" I choked against her sweater.

"Of course. Now dry those tears, you need to keep all your strength for the main event."

I let her go and wiped my face with my sleeve.

"Ready?" she asked once she regained her composure.

"As ready as I can be."

She stretched my arms out and tied them to each side of the chair. She sniffled as she worked, but wouldn't look up, only slid her nimble fingers in and out of each knot until my skin stung under the bindings. Just when I thought she'd finished, she reached around from behind me and hugged me again. "I'd never leave you," she whispered as she pressed her cheek against mine.

Sage hurried toward us. "We really need to get started."

"Okay," Lane said as she got to her feet and walked out of the circle. She rubbed her face, and my own tears flowed again.

Sage knelt before me and checked Lane's knots. "Not too tight?"

I shook my head, my throat closing off too much to allow me to speak.

"Now just remember, you need to fight with all you've got. It may hurt and you might start to see things, but you can't stop fighting. As soon as you stop, the demon wins. Got it?"

"Thank you, Sage," I squeaked.

"Don't thank me yet. Thank me when this is all over." She examined the last knot near my fist and gave the ends a rough tug. "Okay, everyone, please take your places."

The robed figures assembled on the curved lines of the surrounding circle, with someone stationed at each of the pentacle points on the floor. As they closed in, the temperature around me spiked. My skin flushed, but I couldn't tell if it was being in the middle of the crowd or from something already reacting inside of me. Thin trails of smoke danced from the corners of the room as the heavy smell of wet pine needles and mud stained the air. Sage puttered around the altar beside me, lighting thick black candles and throwing handfuls of herbs and leaves into a shiny metal bowl.

A strange sensation pricked through my veins. I wriggled my arms in my ropes, but they wouldn't budge, and my pulse quickened. Kassia walked around the circle and lit the white taper candles in between each of the witches. She cast me a sympathetic half-smile as she passed, but quickly turned away and continued on with her task. The light glowed brighter against their white robes and filled the room with a brilliant glow. I closed my eyes and tried to picture calming thoughts. My home. My dad. My friends. My life.

Sage walked to the center of the pentacle and raised her hands above her head. The room fell silent. She lowered her head back toward the roof, her hair trickling down behind her in waves. She inhaled deeply and let the breath out with a loud whooshing sound. The candles flickered as a breeze teased the small hairs at the back of my neck. Sage stepped back up to the altar and glanced over at me, her eyes stern and focused. "It's time."

FORTY-ONE

A sliver of starlight from the crack in the door cast eerie shadows across the wooden planks beneath my feet. In the silence, my heart pumped faster, each thump percussion to the howl of the wind against the rickety old roof. I gripped tighter onto the arms of the chair and swallowed. My thoughts swirled in my head, stirring up emotions I didn't have time to deal with right now.

Today is the day I'll probably die.

But not if I could help it.

Near the door, Ethan stood stick straight, his hands crossed behind him like an army recruit awaiting orders, his face serious and solemn. Lane smiled an uncertain smile, the glossy glimmer of the tears forming in her eyes reflecting in the candlelight. I breathed deeply. *Be strong, Berkley. For them. For you.*

Sage stepped down from the altar and walked around the inside of the pentacle three times, whispering to her gods and goddesses, or anyone out there in the universe who might actually care. No one dared to move. Rigid white-robed statues watched me with curious, uncertain stares. I scanned their faces, each one stone cold and focused. Except for Orianna. She couldn't hide her expression the way the others could, or she just didn't try. The worry bled through. But when she caught me looking at her, she turned her head away, her bottom lip clamped tight in her teeth.

It's fine. Inhale. Exhale. *Just breathe.*

Sage finished her laps and returned to the altar. She glanced down at me, confined in my chair, and nodded.

I held my breath as she raised her arms to the sky and called the quarters. "Guardians of the east, bring your mighty winds to blow away the evil and protect us."

She turned her head to the side. "Guardians of the south, bring your fire to purify this place and ensure the safety of all those within it."

A faint gust of wind whirled around and brushed against the fine hair on my arms. The witches rustled and looked at each other but didn't budge.

"Guardians of the west, bring your water and cleanse this place. Keep our thoughts pure and strong for the task at hand," Sage continued as she swiveled to look in each direction. "And finally, I ask of you, guardians of the north, bring the earth to keep us grounded."

She bowed her head and whispered, "So mote it be."

"So mote it be," the witches echoed back, their collective voices rumbling against the walls and the hum reverberating through my chest.

The flames of the candles surged a few inches higher then receded. Sage lowered her arms and grabbed a knife off the surface of the altar.

She stepped down and stood before me, holding the knife in her hands. The curved blade glinted with orange and yellow reflections of the flames. It wasn't jeweled like Orianna's dagger, but strange symbols were etched across the metal, each one glowing bright purple. I flinched and turned my head, but Sage simply pricked the end of her finger, and in the dim light red blood pooled against her alabaster skin. She leaned forward and smudged the blood across my forehead then squeezed my hand.

Taking her bleeding finger, she marked her own head in the same fashion. A blob, or a star, or whatever, but hopefully it meant a way out. She placed the knife back on the altar, then moved around the circle, smudging the heads of the other witches. Each nodded and said something indistinguishable, but unlike any language I'd ever heard before. When she finished, she took the last empty point on the pentacle. The top of the star. She clasped onto the hands of the witches at her sides and the rest of the circle followed her lead. I bit down on the inside of my cheek. *Go time.*

"Polo poder das forzas da natureza, eu obrigalos lo. Deixar o neno en paz. Non é benvido aquí," Sage yelled aloud.

I didn't know the words, but I felt them. Each one tingled under my skin, slicing thin like paper cuts. Simple little stings. *Not bad. Could be worse.*

Sage repeated the chant again, and this time everyone else joined in like a somber supernatural choir, mixing both the foreign and the familiar. "By the forces of nature, we compel you. Leave the child alone. You are not welcome here."

The flames of the candles shot higher, and I pushed back against the chair. An icy chill crept up my spine and sat in my stomach like a block of ice.

"By the forces of nature, we compel you. Leave the child alone. You are not welcome here," the group repeated.

The cold spread through my arms and legs like an IV of antifreeze coursing through my bloodstream. I shivered against the pain until it faded into numbness. Too cold to function, but too cold to hurt.

"By the forces of nature, we compel you. Leave the child alone. You are not welcome here," the witches repeated louder. Their voices blended together into a single chord, booming against my eardrums. A steady rhythm beating out in unsettling staccato.

I leaned my head back against the top of the chair and closed my eyes, lulled by the chanting. I focused on my breathing.

Inhale.

Exhale.

It's going to be okay.

The cold seeped deeper into my muscles as I slipped into a haze between dreaming and consciousness. Sleep. If I could just fall asleep, maybe I'd wake up and this would all be over.

My limbs shivered as the cold took a firmer hold on my body, and my breath puffed out in a cloud like on a frosty December morning. I clenched my fists and pictured warm things. A cup of Sage's peppermint citrus latte. The duvet on my bed. Ethan's arms holding me tight against his chest. His lips against mine. Heat rose in my cheeks, and the chill retreated. It drained from my limbs and pooled at my feet.

The candles danced through the haze then dimmed low into near darkness as the chanting faded quieter and farther away.

My head lolled as the icy tingle released its hold. I took a deep breath and let my muscles relax. *That wasn't too bad. Maybe I really could do this. Maybe I—*

Sage's roaring voice pierced through my cloudy brain. "Leave this place, demon. By the power of the old ones. Return to hell. Déixanos demo. Regreso ao inferno."

I jerked upright. Molten lava burned through my core, ripping across my arms and chest. Scorching heat blistered my flesh like someone had doused me in gasoline and lit me on fire. I screamed, my vocal cords shredding against the pain. "Help me!"

Lane's face twisted, and she lurched forward, but stopped and tucked her face into Ethan's shoulder. I struggled against the ropes as the knots dug tight into my wrists and ankles.

The heat blasted again, and I thrashed in my chair. The stench of burning hair and scalding flesh surrounded me. My stomach twisted and churned as I sizzled inside my skin. Pain. Blinding pain pulsed through my body. Over and over. Each wave ached worse than the last. "Make it stop. Please, make it stop."

Sage rushed to my side and clamped my arms down to the chair, her fingers like branding irons searing into my muscles.

"You need to hold on, Berkley. You need to fight back."

The heat pulsed through me again. I screamed louder. My voice detached from my body, no longer under my control.

"No. Please. I can't," I cried. I squirmed against the ropes. Each knot scalded my flesh.

"Yes, you can. You've held this thing inside you for weeks and haven't let it win. Just keep trying." Sage moved her head to hold my stare but couldn't catch it.

I closed my eyes and bit down on my lip, the pain melding with the burn.

Be strong. Don't let it win. You can do this.

My body bucked and writhed against the restraints, but I tried to focus my scattered brain. I needed to survive this. My dad's world would collapse without me. I couldn't leave Lane and Ethan. Not yet. Not tonight. I couldn't let fear run my life anymore. I needed to fight.

I squeezed my hands into fists, and the burning diminished. *That's it, Berkley. Be strong.*

My head flopped down to my chest. My body raw. The weight of my clothes ached against my flesh, plastered to my skin with sweat. Tears flowed down my face and dropped into my lap. But the pools didn't splatter clean. Each droplet spilling into my lap splashed dark and red on my thighs. The taste of dirty pennies lined my lips.

Red and white lights like spiderwebs throbbed in my vision as my heartbeat pounded at my temples. The blood tears flowed faster. *Be strong, Berkley, this is just a test. You rock at tests. Just be strong.*

"That's it. Keep fighting." Sage's voice wavered as she eyed the blood pouring from my face and tried not to let it show. She dropped her forehead and released my arms. "Déixanos demo. Regreso ao inferno."

The blaze inside me raged again. Pushing my body down on my seat, I focused. *Not tonight. Be strong.*

I mined my memories and held on tight. Sleepovers with Lane. Camping with my dad at Birdman Creek. My favorite hot fudge sundae. Sounds and smells and tastes flooded down through the pain. The burning cooled. I gasped for air. *I can do this.* The heat surged, but I focused harder. Baseball games with Ethan. Summers with the three of us hanging by the beach. The beautiful silence of freshly fallen snow. My shoulders drooped as the heat dialed back again. *It's almost over. I will survive this.*

My limbs vibrated against the pain, but I refused to let it win. The scent of sulfur burned my nose as black smoke flowed out of my skull. It whipped around, closing in around the chair. Thick. Dark. Then through the black, two red eyes stared back at me. Sinister orbs boring into my brain and scattering my thoughts.

"Foolish human." A deep, menacing cackle echoed off the walls. "You are mine."

The witches gasped.

The smoke encircled my neck and squeezed. Two hands pressing down on my throat, cutting off my air. Fighting against the grip, I snapped my head back and forth. I called out, trying to keep my airway open, but it pressed tighter and tighter.

Darkness crept in on the corners of my sight. Sage and the witches chanted again, but the sound disappeared into nothingness. All that remained was pain. *Keep fighting.*

But I had no strength left.

The blackness turned to light. I tried to wriggle in the chair, but my body stopped responding to my demands. It gave up and left me to die. Just like Sage predicted. I gasped but couldn't catch my breath. My vision faded. Sound drifted away. I'd failed. I'd never see my dad again. My friends. Everything, just gone. My heart stung in my chest. My entire life—

"Don't break the circle," Sage yelled as her voice cut through the fog of impending death.

The invisible hands slackened, and the world flooded back at me.

Dabria flew forward into the circle, Lane casting her aside and charging through the line.

"Get me out of here," I gasped.

"No." Lane's wet face glistened in the candlelight. She pulled Sage's knife from the altar and held it above her head. The purple symbols shone against the blade as she yanked her arm back and swung.

The trail of the knife seared as it sliced the side of my thigh. Thick red blood oozed out onto the floor.

"What are you doing?" I screamed. "Lane, stop!"

"You can't have her if I kill her first." She brandished the knife in the air and swung again. A crooked red line snaked across my bicep. Blood flowed down my arm and soaked my bound hand. I flexed against the ropes, twisting myself away, but there was no escape.

Hot tears streamed down my face. "Lane, please!"

She cast her eyes away from me and spun around. "Show yourself, coward. Come at me."

"Stop it." Ethan raced to Lane's side and gripped her arm. She swiped the blade at him, and he jumped back. "You're going to kill her."

Lane hastily cut my arm again. The metal burned across my flesh.

Lane slashed my other leg, this time much deeper. The room spun. The lights of the candles multiplied and flickered out of focus. Faces blurred.

"Come and get me," Lane howled, her arms wide, the knife still clenched in her bloody hands.

My body heaved forward. I bawled as my wrists and ankles tore against the ropes. I opened my mouth to scream, but instead, a green light poured out. I choked and gagged as it ripped up my throat. The stench of burning grass and rotting sewage cut through my nostrils. I gasped for breath as my lungs ignited. My eyelids drooped. I couldn't hang on much longer. The world dimmed.

"That's right," Lane screamed, her voice echoing in my head. "Take me."

My mouth slammed shut, and I slumped back into the chair. The light hurtled at Lane. The knife clanged on the wooden floor, followed by the sickening thud of Lane's body as she fell.

FORTY-TWO

The relentless beep of the heart monitor echoed in my ears and stirred me awake. I blinked and let reality come back in pieces. The off-white ceiling tiles. The itchy blankets and strange nauseating smells. Yep, still in the hospital.

Stretching in my chair, I yawned and stared at the streaks of moonlight that decorated the otherwise blank walls. A calm stillness compared to the balmy afternoon sunbeams I remembered before I fell asleep.

"Morning, sleepyhead," a raspy voice whispered in the dim light.

I shook my head. *Lane, awake. Finally.*

I jumped up and gripped her shoulders. "I should say the same thing to you. How are you feeling?"

She flinched under my grasp but squeezed my arms and pulled them closer. "Like hell."

I held her tighter; the stitches stung under my bandages, but I didn't care. Lane could rub salt directly into all my cuts, and I wouldn't stop her. My heart thumped in my chest. *Lane. She's okay. She's going to be okay.*

"Do you need anything? How long have you been awake? I should go tell the nurse."

She chuckled, then sputtered a cough. "Down, girl. I haven't been awake long, just give me a couple of minutes first."

"Sure, anything you want." She wriggled in my embrace, and I let her go, even though I wished I could hold on forever. But breathing was probably necessary if she was going to recover. I'd hugged her so hard I might've broken a rib. "Why didn't you wake me?"

She smiled her crooked, carefree smile. "I kind of enjoyed watching you sleep."

"Well, I hated watching you. Don't ever do that to me again."

Lane rubbed her hand across her forehead and winced for a second as she focused on the ceiling. "How long was I out?"

I slid my phone out of my pocket and powered it on. "Just past the three-day mark."

"Not bad." She flashed me a devious smirk. "Just long enough for everyone to miss me. You know how much I love to bring the drama."

"I'm still pissed at you for getting yourself into this mess. You shouldn't have stepped in. I've been waiting here the whole time, hoping you would wake up so I could kick your butt."

"You would. Control freak." She pushed her hands into the mattress and slid higher on the pillow. Her arms quivered beneath her, but she breathed deep and steadied herself. "I did stay in this bed for three days though, no field trips?"

Fighting the urge to hug her again, I straightened the pillow behind her and smoothed her bedsheets. "Thankfully, no."

"Well, that's a plus."

I tapped my cell phone in the air toward her. "I promised your mom I would call if you woke up. She looked wrecked, so I told her to go home. She's been sleeping here since they admitted you."

"Thanks." She laid her head back and grimaced, her lips in an awkward twist. "What did you tell her about why I'm in here?"

The phone rang. Once. Twice. No answer. Maybe she was asleep or in the shower or something. The message prompt started, but I hung up. "I told her we went out for a run and got mugged. I got sliced up, and you saved me, but the robber knocked you out."

Lane raised an eyebrow and settled back against the pillows. "She bought that?"

"I doubt it, but she was too worried to care. I'm sure she'll ask again, plus the police will need you to file a report, so you should start practicing your alibi."

She chuckled, and the color seemed to return to her skin. Her matted curls stuck to the sides of her face, but right now she'd never looked more perfect. She pulled the neck of her hospital gown up and sniffed. "What's that smell?"

"You probably just need a shower."

"There's that, but something else." She pulled her arms in close to her face and smelled again. "Like black licorice or something."

"Oh, that." I stuck my hand through the neck of my shirt and pulled out a silver diffuser necklace. "It's anise oil. Supposed to keep away evil spirits. I put some on your neck and your wrists while you were still unconscious."

"Interesting. Is my goody-goody bestie looking to become a full-blown witching?" She pulled her wrist close to her face and breathed in. Her face soured, and she yanked her arm away.

"Not quite. But I figured it wouldn't hurt." I tucked the necklace back under my shirt and breathed in the heady scent. "Plus Orianna and the others came by earlier and set up a few wards around the hospital as well as some symbol-looking thing called a sigil on the floor under your bed. I doubt they want to be doing another exorcism anytime soon."

"Yeah, no thanks. That thing practically ripped a hole right through my kidneys." She wrapped her arm around her stomach and winced, her plastic identification tag catching on her cotton hospital gown.

"Well, you're lucky it decided to pass through you instead of moving in. Kassia said it's because you were already evil enough that it didn't want to put up with you."

"She's probably right." She laughed. A little wary, but closer to her old self. My shoulders dropped, allowing it to sink in. Lane would be okay. We were both going to be okay.

"However, they were all kinds of upset that you broke the circle and set the demon free again."

"Did it attack anyone else?"

"No. Sage told me it only has a few hours to find a host before it loses some of its power and its hold on the world. Hopefully it didn't get too far, but she's going to watch for any possible signs over the next few weeks."

"Or we might have one crazy-ass squirrel on our hands." She chuckled then grabbed onto her side again. Pain etched across her face.

I reached over and hugged her. Nothing I wanted to say to her felt quite right. The only thing I could do was hold her close.

Lane brushed her hand over the bandage on my arm. "You're not mad, are you?"

"Of course not. You saved my life. I'll never be able to repay you for that."

She rolled her eyes and shifted away, my arms falling off her. "Don't get all sappy on me. I'm sure there will be a midnight request for bail somewhere in my future."

"I'm not kidding. I owe you everything."

"You're right, you do. But how about, for now, you learn how to relax a bit, and if you ever even think about leaving your house in the middle of the night, call me first?" She narrowed her stare and pointed at me. "You only get one kamikaze mission per friendship. I hope you used this one wisely."

I nodded. "Absolutely."

"Maybe we could try yoga again?" She winked.

"Whatever you want," I groaned, the thought of those awkward poses already making my skin itch. But I'd do it. For her. "Oh, and those flowers are from the volleyball team, these are from your cousin in Tulsa, and these ones"—I pointed to an obnoxiously large bouquet of white lilies—"are from Ethan."

She ran her fingers over the delicate white petals and leaned over the metal bed rail to try to smell them. "How's he doing?"

"He's good. He's shaken up, just like the rest of us." I propped up my bandaged arm. "But at least he didn't have a coma or five rounds of stitches to deal with. He should be here in about an hour or so to check up on you."

"Good. I have to give him heck for trying to stop me." She crossed her arms and glared. "You also know you have no excuses now. You're going to have to deal with what's going on with you two. Especially since you won't accidentally try to seduce him in your sleep."

"Don't worry, I know. But we've decided to take it slow and let things settle a bit before I jump back into a relationship."

She nodded as the frown disappeared from her lips. "Sounds like you've got yourself a pretty smart guy there."

I dialed Lane's house again. Mrs. Mackenzie picked up the phone, and I listened as she praised the Lord and hung up mid-sentence to rush over.

"What time is it anyway?" Lane asked, her face turning serious again.

"A little after seven."

"Do you need to get home, or does your dad not care if you're here?"

"He's not home, actually." I cast my eyes down and concentrated on my fingers as they twisted in the cheap bedsheets. "He's in rehab."

Lane shot up straight. "What? Are you sure I was only out for three days?"

"Yeah. He said the speech I gave him the other day stuck. Plus, then I showed up at the hospital ,and he panicked. Don't know if it'll work, but at least he's trying." I shrugged. So far it sounded like it had been rough, but at least he was sticking it out. I crossed my fingers and made a silent wish that he'd make it through. "But until he's back, I'm going to be staying at your house so I can help you get back to normal."

"At least that's a good thing, right?" Lane groaned and pressed her hand across her stomach. "You can go tell the nurse I'm awake now. And if you can get them to sneak me some food, that would be awesome."

"Sure." I slid off the bed and went off to do her bidding.

When I reached the door, I paused and leaned against the doorframe. "One thing, though. Why did you break the circle? Why didn't you let the witches try to finish the ritual?"

"If the demon was threatened, I knew it would leave. A parasite, just like you told me at the tea shop." She turned and stared out the window. "Besides, there was a good chance the demon was probably just going to kill you anyway if I didn't do something."

"Did Sage tell you that?" I shook my head. "I can't believe she asked me not to say anything and then went and told you."

"Sage didn't tell me. You did."

"What? When?" I raised an eyebrow as I searched my memory. "I swore I told no one."

"In your sleep." Lane winked and rested back against her pillows. "Possessed or not, you still can't keep secrets from me. You always tell me everything."

Thank you so much for reading Sleepless. If you are looking for more witches, magic, and romance, try Keeper of Shadows or Wicked Descent also by Scarlett Kol.

LOOKING FOR EVEN MORE PARANORMAL?

Some secrets should stay buried — especially when the truth might kill you.

I hate Shady Creek. It's the middle-of-nowhere small town my mom dragged me to when my grandmother died. The same one she ran away from seventeen years ago, where vicious rumors about our family descending from witches run wild. And it's the last place anyone saw my father before he disappeared.

After all these years, everyone at Shady Creek High still believes the lies and trying to fit in while everyone whispers behind your back isn't easy. I'd do anything to get back to Detroit and my old life.

Then I met Drew.

Wicked Descent is the perfect read for those who love magic, a bit of mystery, and swoon-worthy romance.

ARE YOU READY FOR KEEPER OF SHADOWS?

When you find something worth fighting for giving up is not an option.

The only thing keeping Abby up at night is the fear of not getting into the right college and disappointing her overbearing parents. That's until she stumbles across the dark secrets her neighbor is hiding in the house next door.

Kellan's bad-boy attitude has everyone fooled. One wrong decision sent his life straight to hell and he's impatiently waiting for everything to fall apart. But when Abby uncovers the real torment behind his strange behavior she insists on helping him—even if he doesn't want her to. As if living with a magical curse isn't bad enough, he has to worry about Abby falling into his dark twisted world too.

To keep her out of harm's way, Kellan will need Abby's help to finally break the curse. But this time Kellan can't fail. This time he won't just lose his life...he'll lose the one girl he's willing to die for.

Perfect for fans of Katie McGarry's gritty dual point-of-view romances but who crave a supernatural twist.

ALSO BY SCARLETT KOL

Never miss a new release from Scarlett Kol by signing up for her newsletter at www.scarlettkol.com.

Dystopian

Mercury Rises

Paranormal

Wicked Descent

Keeper of Shadows

Faraway High Fairytales

Falling

Dreamer

ABOUT THE AUTHOR

Born and raised in Northern Manitoba, Scarlett Kol grew up reading and writing about things that make you want to sleep with the lights on. She believed that the treasures in her mother's jewelry box were magic amulets that would give her immeasurable power and old books could transport her to secret worlds. As an adult, not much has changed. Connect with Scarlett on social media or on her website www.scarlettkol.com.

f facebook.com/scarlettkolauthor

⊙ instagram.com/scarlettkol

BB bookbub.com/profile/scarlett-kol

a amazon.com/stores/Scarlett-Kol/author/B078RZ4PWF